THE EVERYWHERE GIRL

BOOK FOUR IN THE CLEARWATER SERIES

JULIE MAYERSON BROWN

For All My Dogs

<u>*Mutts of my Childhood*</u>
Lassie
Sugar
Teddy

<u>*The Boxers*</u>
CeeCee
Max
Lucy
Bogie
Charlie
Palo
Ringo

Author's Note

Animal lovers are a special breed of humans, generous of spirit, full of empathy, perhaps a little prone to sentimentality, and with hearts as big as a cloudless sky.

John Grogan
Author

Dear Reader,

I hope you enjoy The Everywhere Girl. Each book in the series highlights a new main character, and I just loved giving Rebecca her own story. She's certainly earned it!

CHAPTER 1

*S*ummer 2017

THE DOG HUDDLED in the back of the crate. Clumps of matted fur dotted her boney body, parts of her tail chewed down to the skin. The pads on her paws were raw and worn, like old sandpaper.

Rebecca Sparks choked back tears. "What are we going to do with her?"

Willy, the director of the animal shelter, removed his baseball cap and rubbed his balding head. "Not much, I'm sorry to say. Can't see letting this one suffer any longer."

Rebecca curled her fingers around the cage, wondering how the dog had ended up in such terrible shape. She'd been found wandering down a road miles outside of town.

"She's only been here a few hours," Rebecca said. "Can't we at least give her a little more time and see what happens?"

"If an animal's dying, letting her go peacefully is the compassionate thing to do." Willy was a stick of a man with blue jeans held up by suspenders. His loud, low voice didn't match his thin build. "We'll see what the vet thinks. For now just give her a dish of water. We got other dogs to tend to."

"All right." Rebecca's voice broke into pieces.

"You're not crying, are you?"

"No." She swiped her tears with her sleeve.

"Come on, you know they can't all be saved. I told you that the day you started working here." Willy wandered off, shoulders slumped and head hanging. His posture was slouchy to begin with. A dying dog only made it worse.

It was true. When he hired Rebecca a month ago, he warned her there'd be days like this with crushing disappointment over animals beyond saving. She'd seen plenty of malnourished dogs. But never one this bad off.

She filled a small metal dish with cool water and placed it in the crate. The dog refused to look at it, just scratched at her neck with a weak paw and scooted farther into the box. Over the next few hours, Rebecca checked on her multiple times, but the water appeared undisturbed, and she hadn't moved. It was impossible to tell what breed she was, probably a mix of shepherd, retriever, and something else, meant to be big by the size of her feet. At least that's what Willy had said.

Rebecca tucked her long red braid into the back of her jacket. She folded her gangly legs underneath her and sat beside the open crate. With a tentative hand, she reached in and stroked a tuft of fur on the dog's hind end. No reaction.

"You poor girl. I'll bet you've been on the road a long time." There was a story behind every lost animal. "I'd give you a name, but Willy wouldn't approve."

The dog's eyes shifted, although barely, just the twitch of an eyebrow.

"Tell you what, I'll be back in a little bit. We'll talk about it more then." She pointed at the dog's nose. "Don't die on me now."

The dog closed her eyes and let her head roll to the side, as if she were ready to go to sleep and never wake up.

Rebecca hesitated. If she sat vigil beside the crate, maybe the dog would sense her presence and keep breathing. But a long list of chores awaited her.

For the next few hours she answered the phone, cleaned out kennels, filed paperwork, and swept the concrete floor of the old barn Willy had converted into an animal shelter.

Dr. Klansky, a country vet who treated pets as well as farm animals, arrived in the late afternoon. Rebecca had met him once or twice. She liked him, and he treated her with respect.

"Well, Rebecca, looks like we got ourselves a sick one here, don't we?"

"Yeah. I put the water in there hours ago, but I don't think she's taken a sip."

"I'll just take a quick look." The doctor lowered himself onto the ground and placed his stethoscope in several places. With both hands, he prodded around her belly and neck. When he touched the pads on her back left paw, the dog yelped and twisted. "Aww, sorry about that, girl. I'll leave you be then."

"What do you think?" Willy extended a hand and pulled Dr. Klansky to his feet.

"Not good, I'm afraid. Practically starved, dehydrated, and it looks like she might have mange."

"You want to euthanize her?" Willy asked.

Rebecca ached to voice an objection, but she clamped her mouth closed. The decision belonged to the experts, not the hired help. She wasn't meant to challenge people, only to please them. At least that's what she learned during the tumultuous years of her parents' brief marriage.

Be quiet, be good, and do what you're told. Don't upset your daddy.

"I'm afraid so," the vet said. "Can't do it now, though. Used my last dose earlier today, but I'll have more tomorrow. I don't think she's in too much pain, just lost her will to live. You can offer her a little food, Rebecca. Poor animal deserves a steak after all she's been through."

"Alrighty-then. I'll call you tomorrow. Let you know if," he glanced at Rebecca then turned back to the doctor, "if I need you to come or not."

Rebecca knew the hidden message. They doubted the poor animal would live through the night.

"Good plan." The vet slapped him on the back as if they'd just agreed to something as insignificant as going to lunch. The men strolled out of the barn, leaving Rebecca alone with the nameless dog who had lost all hope.

IT WAS dusk when Rebecca finished her shift. She sped home on her bicycle through the treelined roads of Clearwater.

She and her mother, Alice, lived on the grounds of Lakeview Lodge, a cozy inn at the top of Lake Clearwater surrounded by majestic oaks and sweeping stretches of open land. At twenty-two, Rebecca didn't consider herself too old to live with her mother, at least not yet. They'd only been in Clearwater a couple of months, having moved from Denver when her mother landed the job managing the inn. Rebecca needed time to adjust before going out on her own.

For as long as she could remember, it had been just the two of them. Her parents had separated when she was six, and the attachment between mother and daughter was an unyielding source of comfort.

Due to her mother's wandering nature and frequent job changes, Rebecca had been uprooted every couple of years. She'd attended more schools than she could count, which caused multiple delays in her education. Despite her mother's attempts to tutor her, Rebecca ended up repeating two grades, a situation that fueled her insecurity. Every time she entered a new school, she tried to slip in unnoticed. But a girl with wild red hair, taller and older than her classmates, stuck out like a peacock among pigeons.

Rebecca, a solidly average student, ended up graduating from high school shortly before her twentieth birthday. No prom, no grad night, no graduation ceremony. Just a pizza dinner with her mother and overwhelming relief that her school days had finally ended.

Two years later, they left Denver for Clearwater, a welcoming small town in California wine country that offered them both a fresh start and new opportunities. For the first time in her life, Rebecca sensed she'd found her forever home. As soon as she'd unpacked her bags and helped her mother organize their two-bedroom cottage, she set out to find employment.

With a high school diploma and two years of odd jobs waiting tables and babysitting, Rebecca was qualified to work pretty much nowhere. There were no fast food restaurants or shopping malls within biking distance, and the fancy shops and eateries on Main Street weren't hiring.

She was about to join the housekeeping staff at the inn when she stumbled across Furry Friends Animal Shelter and spotted a sign tacked to a tree:

If you like dogs and hard work, come inside and ask for Willy.

After filling out an application and expressing a life-long love of animals, she was hired on the spot.

REBECCA DROPPED the bicycle by the porch and ran into the cottage. Her mother sat at the square dining table that divided the kitchen from the living area. A computer screen illuminated her face.

"Oh, good, you're home," her mother said. "Could you look at this? I need help with the new website I'm creating."

"I will," Rebecca said. "But I need to go to the market first. Can I borrow the van?"

"What do you need at the market?"

"Something for a dog at the shelter. It's a long story—please can I take the van?"

Alice pointed at her oversized satchel. "Keys are in my bag."

"Thanks, I won't be long." She planted a quick kiss on her mother's cheek.

The vintage orange and white Volkswagen was parked behind their cottage. Rebecca turned the key and pumped the accelerator to shoot gas into the fuel line. The van coughed and spit then rumbled to life. Rebecca kissed the steering wheel. "Good ol' car."

At the supermarket, she studied the steaks and picked out a piece of meat that wasn't too expensive but not the cheapest one either.

Rebecca rushed home, excited about bringing the dog a treat that might give her a reason to hang on a little longer.

Inside the cottage, Alice had moved on from the website and now was immersed in a video on towel folding. She paid no attention to what Rebecca was up to until the steak juices snapped and sizzled in the frying pan.

"Something smells delicious. What is it?"

"It's a steak." Rebecca turned the meat over.

Her mother peered over her shoulder at the slab of beef. "We don't eat meat, except for when we cheat and go to McDonalds."

"It's for a dog at the shelter."

"Nice meal for a shelter dog," Alice said.

"Yeah, well, it might be her last one."

FURRY FRIENDS ANIMAL RESCUE, located on an acre of land at the base of Willy's property, was a five minute drive from the inn—less if Rebecca rolled through the stop signs. She parked by the entrance and slipped inside. A few dogs let out low barks and soft growls at the disturbance, as if practicing their watch dog skills.

"Shh, it's only me." Rebecca hoped Willy's house was far enough away that he wouldn't hear the commotion.

Rebecca made her way past the row of dog runs toward Willy's desk in the corner and turned on the lamp. The dim light threw a haunting glow, just enough for her to see into the crate.

The dog had repositioned herself about a quarter turn and angled her head toward the front. When Rebecca unlatched the door and reached in, the dog pulled her paws underneath her body and pushed her face into the blanket.

"I brought you something." Rebecca held a slice of meat near the dog's nose, but she didn't care. The meat might as well have been a rock.

"Come on, girl, please try a little." Rebecca scooted into the cage with the foil wrapped steak. A bit of juice spilled over her hand.

A warm tongue touched her skin. The dog raised her head, and her sad, tired eyes met Rebecca's for the first time.

"Oh my gosh, you do like it." Rebecca dipped her fingers into the juice, and the dog licked it off her skin. Encouraged, Rebecca tore off a tiny piece.

With mild interest, the dog accepted it. Rebecca continued feeding her bites. When she stopped, the dog nudged and kissed her hand. In that moment, Rebecca knew this dog had not lost her will to live—she just needed a reason to keep trying.

CHAPTER 2

*T*he crate rattled. Rebecca bolted upright and cracked her head on the top of the cage. "Ouch!"

Willy stood over her, eyes wide. "What the hell are you doing in there? You didn't sleep here, did you?"

Rebecca crawled out and tried to stand. Her right foot had fallen asleep, and she lurched to the side. "I didn't mean to. I—I just came back to check on the dog, and I guess—"

"You know I could fire you for this." Willy's sunburned face turned even redder. "What if something happened to you? I barely have enough insurance as it is!"

"I'm so sorry." Rebecca hadn't meant to spend the night curled up like a pretzel, but once she'd gotten the dog to eat from her fingertips, she couldn't leave her. "It was an accident."

"An accident? Really? Didn't I tell you not to get attached?" Willy threw his arms in the air. "The vet's coming later to put this dog down, and now I know just what's gonna happen— you're gonna cry and cajole and beg me to give her another day. You think it's easy for me to decide to put a—"

A ferocious bark made Willy jump as if he'd received an electric shock.

The dog was on her feet and halfway outside the crate. Her nose and upper lip ticked upward, showing a line of straight white teeth. A low growl came from her throat.

Willy backed up, his palms out straight.

Rebecca couldn't believe the feeble dog was using what little strength she had to protect her. "It's okay, girl. Settle down." She stroked her behind the ears.

The dog slipped back into the crate and lowered herself onto her haunches, as if that burst of energy had exhausted her.

"Well, I'll be a monkey's uncle." Willy wagged his head. "Would you look at that? I didn't think she could even stand up."

"It's because I fed her steak."

"You fed her what?" Willy yelled again.

Rebecca shrank, certain she'd get fired for sure. "Steak. I came back last night with one. Dr. Klansky said she deserved one, remember?"

Willy smacked his forehead. "Don't you know when someone's kidding? Man alive, you'd think I'd be used to you by now, but lordy, you are something else."

"Please don't fire me. I love working here."

"For Chrissakes, I'm not gonna fire you. But don't ever pull a stunt like this again." Willy cracked his knuckles, and they popped like firecrackers. "Now just, I don't know, go home and change your clothes or something. We got people coming in around nine wanting to adopt, and I aim to get at least a few of these dogs into homes today."

"Okay, but you won't do anything with this dog, right? At least not while I'm gone."

"Nothing's happening until Klansky gets here later." Willy's expression softened. "Sorry I yelled at you."

"It's okay," Rebecca said, grateful for his apology.

"I can't stand seeing an animal suffer either, Rebecca. And if this one is suffering, it's my job to let her go. Everything we do here is in the dog's best interest. You know that, right?"

Rebecca nodded.

"Alright then, go on. I'll see you when you get back." Willy stomped off, slapping his cap against his leg.

She kneeled beside the crate and latched the door. "You be a good girl, okay? I'll get back as fast as I can."

Rebecca drove the van home. She charged into the cottage just as her mother walked out of her bedroom wearing a pink chenille bathrobe and fuzzy slippers.

"Good morning," she said, seemingly unaware of Rebecca's late night escapade.

"Hi, I'm about to jump in the shower."

"But you're already dressed." Alice furrowed her brow. "Didn't you wear those overalls yesterday?"

"Yeah. I spent the night with one of the dogs."

"They have beds?"

"No, I slept in the crate." Rebecca quickly explained the dog's condition. "That's why I got her a steak. In case it—it really ends up being her last meal. But now I'm in trouble with Willy, kind of, and have to get back there as quick as I can. I feel like it's up to me to save that dog's life."

Alice put her hands on Rebecca's cheeks. "With you on her side, she has a fighting chance. I'm sure of it."

Rebecca nodded, blinking on her tears. She knew what it meant to be the underdog, the one nobody believed in. Her teachers called her slow, her classmates called her names, and her father didn't love her enough to hang around after the divorce. The only person who had always had her back was her mother.

After her shower, she dressed in clean denim overalls, a white shirt, and hiking boots. In the kitchen, her mother handed her an oversized mug of coffee, extra sweet and milky, the way they both liked it.

"Thanks," Rebecca said, slathering a piece of toast with butter.

"You're welcome." Alice set her coffee on the counter. "Braid?"

"Sure."

Rebecca's mother wound her curls into a long braid and fastened it with a thick purple band. She turned her around and tapped the tip of her nose with one finger. "Now, don't forget I need help with the website thing. Technology is not my friend."

"Tonight, I promise." Rebecca stuffed her toast into her mouth, gulped her coffee, and grabbed a banana on her way out the door.

She pedaled like a fiend to get back to the shelter. Upon arrival, she caught sight of Dr. Klanksy's white pick-up truck parked out front.

"Oh no!" Rebecca dropped her bicycle on the ground and ran inside.

The veterinarian and Willy stood by the empty crate.

Rebecca broke into a cold sweat. Hope leached out of her like water through a sieve. "What happened?"

Willy turned. "Let me see your hands."

"It's too soon," Dr. Klansky said. "Won't show up on her for a few days."

Rebecca drew back. "What are you talking about?"

"It's like I told you yesterday," said the vet. "The dog has mange, and it's nasty."

"Has? She's not dead then?"

"She's not dead," said Willy. "But she is shaved down to the skin. Gotta keep her completely isolated, too. Don't want her near any of the other dogs."

Rebecca turned to Dr. Klansky. "Does this mean she gets to live?"

"For today, at least. I heard you gave her steak last night." He laughed with a few snorts. "If I'd known you were going to take me seriously, I'd have said I deserve one for working so hard."

Willy laughed with him. "Me, too. My wife hardly ever lets

me have steak on account of my cholesterol." He pulled on surgical gloves and inspected Rebecca's arms.

"I told you, it's too soon," the vet said. "Did you shower, Rebecca?"

It was kind of a personal question, but he was a medical professional. "I showered and washed my hair as soon as I got home."

"Alright then, we just have to wait and hope you don't develop scabies."

Rebecca made a mental note to look up *mange* and *scabies*. "Can I see the dog now?"

"You can," Willy said. "But keep in mind, she is none too happy."

"And she's not out of the woods," Dr. Klansky said. "Her condition's precarious at best, so don't you go getting your hopes up."

"I won't," Rebecca said, her hopes already soaring.

CHAPTER 3

*A*ngry red spots covered the dog's body like polka-dots. The poor animal had been shaved down to her pink skin. Even her snout was bald. Her ribs were like speed bumps along her sides. Rebecca sat on the ground beside the crate, one finger stroking the dog's leg.

Dr. Klansky leaned over. "We have to watch for infection now."

The hairless dog shivered in the sanitized crate.

"Can I at least try to feed her?" Rebecca asked.

"Sure, you can try. Although I doubt she'll be interested."

The barn door rumbled open, and a gray-haired man in a cowboy hat entered.

"Well, look who's here. My old amigo." Dr. Klansky went to greet his friend, leaving Rebecca alone with the sad, trembling animal.

The dog lifted her nose and let out a soft whine, a human-sounding sigh.

"You must be freezing," Rebecca said. "I'll be right back."

In the laundry room, Rebecca pulled some clean towels out of the dryer. She ran back to the crate and wrapped them around the dog, tucking her in like a baby. The dog sniffed at her fresh bedding, pulled her tail in tight, and closed her eyes.

"Excuse me, senorita."

Rebecca scrambled to her feet. "Hi, sorry, I was just covering the dog. I think she's cold."

The old man finger combed his thick, gray mustache, studying the dog as if admiring a painting in a museum.

"She has mange," Rebecca said.

"I see." He placed his cowboy hat on top of the crate, reached in, and gently pulled back the towels. The dog stirred, half awake. He opened his palm and she rested her chin in his hand. Then he spoke to her in Spanish. The dog licked his hand.

"Pobrecita," he said, putting the towel back in place. "She is weak."

"I know, but I, I hope Dr. Klansky will wait another few days before, you know, deciding she's suffering too much. I really think she might recover. She ate all the steak I brought her last night."

The man stood up straight. His thin lips ticked upward. "Steak?"

Rebecca nodded. "I wasn't supposed to, but I did. I think she deserves a chance." Something about the man made her want to confide in him. "I can't give up on her yet."

"I see," he said again. "Are you new here?"

"Kind of. My mom and I moved to Clearwater a couple months ago. She's the new manager at Lakeview Lodge. Have you ever been there? It's very nice, and we live on the property in a cute little cottage." Rebecca shut her mouth, embarrassed by her rambling.

"What is your name?"

"Rebecca."

"I am Benito." His Spanish accent danced around each word like musical notes. His dark brown eyes held a warmth that spoke of concern and compassion and a little sadness.

Willy appeared and broke her trance. He rested an arm over Benito's shoulders. "I'm sure sorry about Antonia. She was a wonderful woman."

Rebecca took a few steps back, separating herself from the men.

"Si," Benito said. "Everybody loved my Antonia. Please thank your dear wife for organizing the funeral reception. I could not have done it without her help."

Between the poor dog on the verge of death and the old man's recently deceased wife, Rebecca was near tears. "I'm so sorry about your wife, Mr. Benito."

"Gracias, querida."

She had no idea what *querida* meant, but it was the most beautiful word she'd ever heard.

TWO DAYS after Rebecca met Benito Becerra, he returned to the shelter and informed Willy he wanted to adopt the sick dog.

A tingle ran through Rebecca. She'd sensed the connection between dog and man, as if they were meant to find each other.

Willy waved his arms. "You gotta be kidding! If you want a dog, we have at least a dozen others that aren't gonna die on you."

"No. That dog is the one." He looked beyond Willy's shoulder and winked at Rebecca. "I can tell."

Willy smacked his baseball cap against his leg. "Come on Benito, don't you want a healthy young pup? Rebecca, go get that sweet basset hound that came in last week. He'd be perfect."

"William, I want this dog. If you refuse me, I take no dog at all."

Rebecca sucked in some air, waiting for Willy to respond.

"Your wife just died, Benito, and now you want a dying dog?"

"I am fairly certain the dog will not die. At least with me, in a home, she will sense she has a reason to live. A home and a master will give her purpose."

Willy's dark eyebrows tilted toward each other. He pointed at Rebecca. "Wait a minute, did she put you up to this?"

The old cowboy laughed, a deep, resonant sound that surprised Rebecca. She wondered how a grieving man could laugh at all, let alone so heartily.

"You've known me for years, William. And you know I am a man who makes his own decisions. Rebecca did not put me up to this."

THE PICKUP TRUCK bounced along the gravel drive toward Benito Becerra's home. Rebecca sat in the back seat beside the crate. The dog slept, seemingly indifferent to her change in locations or what might lie ahead. A weathered farmhouse with a wide front porch came into view.

They carried the crate into the house and placed it beside a brown recliner in the living room. Rebecca inhaled the scent of cinnamon toast.

"Are you going to name her?" she asked.

"Yes. I need to think of the right name. It will come to me." Mr. Becerra hung his cowboy hat on the coatrack by the door then headed into the kitchen, beckoning Rebecca to follow.

A square dinette table was pushed against the wall under open windows covered by muslin curtains. In the middle of the table, salt and pepper shakers, a jar of hot sauce, and a fresh daisy in a bud vase sat atop a crocheted doily.

Mr. Becerra opened a cabinet and removed ingredients. He mixed together honey and olive oil. "Rebecca, would you see if there's any yogurt in the refrigerator, please?"

"Sure." She opened the refrigerator. It was jammed with foil covered casserole dishes and plastic containers full of who-knew-what. "There's a lot of stuff in here."

"Si, when a man loses his wife, people bring him food. One person cannot eat that much. I'm afraid it will spoil."

Rebecca moved a few dishes to the side. "Here's some yogurt." She checked the date on the side. "But I think it's expired."

"The dog won't mind." Mr. Becerra stirred the yogurt into the honey and oil mixture. "Let's take her outside."

Together they coaxed her out of the crate. Rebecca slipped a leash over her head and guided her to the front door. Head hanging, the dog followed with slow, tentative steps. A warm breeze blew, rifling through the leaves of the giant oak trees in front of the house. The dog lifted her nose and sniffed.

Rebecca held onto the leash, waiting for her new friend to set the bowl on the ground. Instead, he crouched on the grass and motioned for Rebecca to bring the dog closer.

"She might not like it at first," Mr. Becerra said. "So hold the leash."

Rebecca did as he requested, appreciating his politeness and calm, low voice. He dipped his fingers into the mixture and applied it to an angry red area on the hairless dog's back.

"Oh, wow," Rebecca said. "I thought it was for her to eat."

"She may eat a little if she'd like," he said. "But not much. We must reintroduce food with caution."

The dog turned her head to smell the salve. Mr. Becerra allowed her lick a spot off his finger as he spoke to her in Spanish.

Rebecca gravitated to the old cowboy who had just lost his wife, taken with his gentle hands and concentration as he ministered to the dog's sores.

"Mr. Becerra, may I ask you a question?"

"Of course," he said, his eyes fixed on the task at hand.

"Why did you want this dog? Why not one of the others who

—who are healthy and probably would be much easier to care for?"

Mr. Becerra looked up at her with the trace of a smile. "Well, I, like you, believe this dog is meant to live. But for that to happen, she needs tremendous care. I cared for my wife throughout her illness, and now that she is gone, I am in need of a purpose."

Rebecca knelt next to them. She dipped a finger into the yogurt and touched it to a red spot on the dog's flank. "I get that."

"Also, she reminds me of a dog I used to have some twenty years ago." He cupped the dog's chin and studied her face.

"How can you tell? She's so skinny and bald, who knows what she'll end up looking like?"

"It is in the eyes, querida. I see her intelligence through her eyes."

Rebecca took a breath and whispered for fear the dog might hear and understand. "But what if she doesn't make it? So much time and energy and love wasted. Plus, your heart will be broken again so—so soon."

"It is the chance we must take. I learned long ago that fear of failure is a weakness most of us must fight to overcome. All quests, great and small, are possible only when we recognize we may fail many times before we succeed."

"Oh my God, that's so profound."

Mr. Becerra inclined his head toward her. "Not original, I'm afraid. I believe many leaders have uttered similar sentiments. Still, it is the truth."

"But if we fail this dog, I don't know if I could stand that. I love her so much already." All of Willy's admonitions and warnings against getting attached had fallen by the wayside.

She expected the old man to assure her that the dog would live, to tell her what she wanted to hear. Instead, he spoke the hard truth.

"That is the gift we are giving her. If she does not survive, she will have known nothing but kindness and love in the end. She will know that she mattered."

Tears flowed down Rebecca's cheeks and dripped off her chin, awed by her new friend's clarity and capacity to accept, regardless of how difficult it may be.

If anybody could give this hopeless dog a reason to keep trying, it was Benito Becerra.

He named her *Milagro*, little miracle.

CHAPTER 4

*A*s the seasons passed, Mila's fur grew in thick and silky, black and brown with flashes of white. Her muscles strengthened, and her eyes glowed with life and love and devotion to her master.

Mr. Becerra, now known as Mr. B, hired Rebecca to help with Mila and small tasks around the house. Their friendship became an integral part of her life. He joined her and her mother for holidays, picnics by the lake, and summer concerts at the park.

Rebecca thrived in an unchanging environment. She craved stability and a life with modest expectations and few disappointments. She enjoyed her various jobs, working part-time at the shelter and at the inn where she helped manage reservations and front desk duties. But her most favorite work was anything she could do for Mr. B.

Life in Clearwater flowed like a narrow stream. It moved forward slowly, uneventful and calm. Rebecca made friends, tip-toed into a few romances over the years, and hid her insecurities behind a cheerful smile and exuberant nature.

But with Mr. B, she was always honest and true to herself. He encouraged her to have aspirations, both large and small.

"What are your dreams?" he'd ask from time to time.

"I don't know. I just like things the way they are."

REBECCA DROVE her late-model Suburban up the long driveway, humming to herself as the farmhouse came into view. She parked in front of the porch and hopped out of the car.

It was hard to believe it had been five years since she'd met Mr. B, the day a dog's life was saved and a grieving man found a new purpose as well as a new friend.

Mila pushed the screen door open with her nose and trotted outside to greet her.

"Hey beautiful girl." Rebecca cupped the dog's face and kissed her head. "It's our anniversary today!" They walked up the wide steps onto the wooden porch that extended across the front of the house, two rocking chairs on one side of the front door. She tapped on the screen door then turned at the sound of clomping hoofs.

"Good morning, my dear." Mr. B sat atop a chestnut horse wearing the same cowboy hat he always wore. His tall leather boots were covered with dust.

"Good morning!" Rebecca brightened. "Do you want to walk with us today?" She loved it when Mr. B joined them, regaling her with stories about his youth and how he had come from a long line of *vaqueros,* cowboys from Mexico who herded cattle across the Pacific Northwest.

Often times, after Mila's walk, Rebecca would sit with him on the porch and drink horchata, the sweet milky beverage Mr. B made from his mother's recipe.

"Seeing as it's a special day, I think I will." He heaved himself off the horse and guided him into the corral.

With Mila a few steps ahead, they crossed the driveway and cut through the yard into the copse of trees. In the distance, the sky was a blend of pink and orange as the sun rose from behind the rolling hills. The warm air carried the scent of ripe fruit.

Mila trotted to her favorite spots where she sniffed and stopped numerous times before moving through the fields. They crossed into the adjacent farm where grapevines grew in long, winding rows.

Mr. B plucked two small bunches from the vine and handed Rebecca one.

"Mmm," she said, the warm, sweet juice flowing around her tongue.

Kids, fresh out of school for the summer, played by the lake. Their voices and laughter floated on the breeze.

Mila ran ahead, always turning back to keep an eye on her master. Her devotion to him was known around town as a story for the ages—the rugged old cowboy and the dog who worshipped him.

Mr. B was capable of walking Mila himself, but he insisted Rebecca spend as much time with her as possible. "Dogs thrive when their worlds are consistent and predictable," he had said. "When the people they love and depend on are present."

Like I do, Rebecca thought. She always felt she had more in common with dogs than she did with humans.

Mr. B slowed his steps. He removed his cowboy hat and mopped his brow.

"Are you okay?" Rebecca asked.

"Just a little warm," he said. "Let's turn back. I think we need some cold lemonade."

"Great idea."

They headed home, their pace unhurried and relaxed.

"I've been meaning to ask, Rebecca, how is your dog walking business these days?"

"It's good. I've been super busy." She'd started walking dogs a couple of years ago, encouraged by Mr. B. "I've saved a little money, finally. And of course I love being with dogs. But Mila is still my favorite."

"Well, you know how much she—" Mr. B. halted his steps. "Hmm, looks like we have a visitor."

Mila lowered her head and growled.

Rebecca squinted. A man she'd never seen before stood on the porch. "Do you know him?" she asked.

"I don't believe I do."

Mila bolted toward the porch, her bark threatening. The man jumped behind one of the rocking chairs. Mr. B released a high-pitched whistle, and Mila skidded to a stop.

"May I help you, sir?" Mr. B asked with polite suspicion.

The man cowered behind the chair. "Is it safe for me to come out?"

"It is. My dog only attacks if I instruct her to do so."

Rebecca could hardly believe Mila's reaction to the visitor. It was as if she sensed something menacing about him.

"I'll only take a minute of your time." The man set the chair aside. He looked to be in his late thirties and wore a tailored gray suit with a dark blue tie and brown dress shoes. "My name is Troy Dayton. I assume you are Benito Becerra, the owner of this property?"

"I am. And how is it you know this fact?" Mr. B stepped closer to the visitor. They were about the same height, but even at over twice the younger man's age, Mr. B appeared to be equally sturdy and able-bodied.

Mr. Dayton glanced at Rebecca then looked away as if determining her presence was insignificant. "It's public record, Mr. Becerra. And I'm here to present to you an offer."

Mila growled, and Mr. B snapped his fingers. The dog sat beside his heel. "An offer?"

"That's right. I'm a real estate agent, and I have a buyer interested in your property."

Mr. B cocked his head. "My property is not for sale, Mr. Dayton."

"Everything's for sale at the right price. And my client is willing to pay top dollar. They, I mean he—he's been looking for lakefront property for some time now."

"They, you said. Do you represent an individual, Mr. Dayton, a private party?"

Rebecca listened with keen interest. She had never put much thought into Mr. B's land. It was beautiful and obviously big. Although she had no idea exactly how big, a few acres probably, surrounded by vineyards owned by wineries.

Mr. Dayton's lips ticked upwards into a smug grin. "Once we open negotiations, I will introduce you to the interested party, and we can hammer out a deal. A very sweet deal for you, to be sure."

Mr. B wiped his palms against each other, as if brushing away dust. "I am not interested. Now if you'll excuse—"

"We're talking millions, Mr. Becerra." Mr. Dayton reached into a leather messenger bag and withdrew a file folder. "And it would be foolish of you not to at least take a look at the offer."

Mr. B extended a hand, accepting the file and flipping it open. He squinted and read the contents. Rebecca held her breath. Would her friend actually sell his home? Where would he even go? The idea of him moving away made her dizzy.

A moment later, Mr. B hemmed. "Very interesting, I must admit."

Troy Dayton's lips spread out over teeth too large for his mouth. "I thought you'd think so. I'll get in touch with the—"

"However..." Mr. B ripped the papers and the folder in half and handed them back. "I have no intention of selling my property. Please take your client elsewhere."

Mr. Dayton blinked. "But—but this is a generous offer, probably twice the assessed value, and multiple times what you paid forty years ago."

"I see that, yet I don't care."

"But the buyer is—"

"There is no buyer, because there is nothing for sale!"

Rebecca was taken aback by his anger. She'd never heard him speak so harshly.

"I will not allow some developer to flatten my land and build high rise condominiums in the middle of Clearwater." Mr. B pointed at him, his finger practically touching the man's nose. "You are not wanted here, Mr. Dayton. Not on my land and not in my town."

He marched into the house with Mila at his heels.

The man's mouth tightened around the edges, and a drip of perspiration trailed down one side of his smooth cheek. "Dammit."

Rebecca backed away, wondering where she'd seen him before. There was something familiar about his big teeth and fancy shoes.

"What an old pain-in-the-ass." Mr. Dayton picked up his messenger bag and stomped down the wooden steps. When he caught sight of Rebecca, he stopped. "I suppose you heard that conversation."

Rebecca didn't answer.

"He's a tough old geezer. Stubborn as hell. But I'll wear him down."

Rebecca raised one shoulder, as if to show indifference. She wasn't about to contradict him.

"Have we met?" Mr. Dayton asked. "You look familiar, and I never forget a pretty redhead." It might have been a compliment except for his sarcastic tone. "Wait, I know, you work at that high-end wine shop on Main Street, what's it called?"

"Mariano's," she said. In addition to her other part-time jobs, Rebecca worked a few shifts a week at the famous gourmet shop in town.

In that moment, she recalled the encounter. He'd come in to

buy wine and then hung around too long bragging about his extensive collection. Still, he might be an important customer, and Rebecca's allegiance to Tessa Mariano was unwavering.

"Now I remember. You bought a case of Syrah. Tessa said you have fine taste in wine." False flattery didn't come easily to Rebecca, but she managed to sound earnest enough.

"She said that, did she?"

Rebecca nodded, leaving out the part where Tessa had called him an *ostentatious windbag*.

"Cool." He moved off the steps and into her personal space. "So, do people call you *Red?* Or do you have an actual name?"

"It's Rebecca," she said. The annoying nickname irked her to no end.

He handed her a business card with his photo on it. "Hopefully we'll cross paths again one day."

Hopefully not, she thought,

The realtor meandered toward his car, a silver Lexus SUV. "If you don't mind, tell Tessa I'd like to buy a case of that Syrah."

"Okay," Rebecca said. A case of *that Syrah* went for over a thousand dollars. "I will."

"Great." He tossed his bag onto the back seat of his fancy car. "See you around, Red."

Troy Dayton drove away, a trail of dust flying from under the tires.

CHAPTER 5

*M*r. B stood at the kitchen counter ladling gravy over a bowl of kibble. The dog sat at attention, her tail thumping against the hardwood floor.

"Oh, Rebecca, I'm glad you're still here." He set down the dog's dish and pulled some cash out of his wallet. "For the next few weeks—and a little extra."

It was a handful of twenty dollar bills. "That's too much, really, you know that."

"No, no. I like to pay in advance. I want to make sure I'm your favorite client." He forced the money into her hand.

"You'll always be my favorite client." Although reluctant to take such a large sum of money, she did appreciate it. Half her dog walking clients had to be chased for payment. "Okay, but no more money until next month."

"Agreed." Mr. B placed his wallet in a drawer and opened a cupboard beside his stove. A large selection of canned soups lined the shelf. He selected one and dumped the contents into an old metal pot. His lips were set in a tight line, his usual pleasant expression darkened by a deep frown.

Rebecca glanced at the kitchen table. Nothing had changed

since the first time she'd been in his house five years ago. A single placemat, napkin holder, salt and pepper shakers standing side by side, the faded doily, and one fresh daisy.

She imagined her friend sitting by himself eating his meals and staring out the window at the lonely hills.

"Are you eating soup for breakfast?"

"I had my breakfast at six. This is lunch." He swirled a wooden spoon in circles in the pot.

"Is that pea soup?" she asked.

"Yes."

"Mind if I have a little?"

Mr. B smiled. "You do know how to make an old man happy, querida."

Querida—his term of endearment for her.

"I like soup. And I like being with you."

"Very well, I'm delighted to have your company." Mr. B set two places at the table, served the soup, and pulled out the chair across from his.

Rebecca sat and looked at him over her shoulder. "Thank you," she said, doubting there were many men left in the world who were as polite and gracious.

"You're welcome." He put two slices of white bread into the toaster and took his seat.

Rebecca ate slowly, thinking about the realtor who had made her friend so angry.

Mila let out a low whine and rested her chin on Mr. B's leg.

"Rebecca," he said, stroking the dog's head. "I have a favor to ask you."

She looked up from her soup. "You need me to take Mila to the vet again?"

"No, no, nothing like that." He rubbed his scruffy whiskers. "Would you mind typing something for me. I expect it will be a few pages at most."

"No problem," Rebecca said. "When do you need it by?"

"Well, I must do a bit of research and then write it out." Mr. B wiped his lips with a napkin. "I hope you can read my scrawl. My hands are a little shaky, so my penmanship is not what it used to be."

She gave her friend a gentle smile. "I'm sure I'll figure it out."

"Thank you." Mr. B reached across the table and patted her hand. "Can you believe I never learned how to type?"

"Well, I doubt you needed that skill to be a cowboy."

He laughed. "That is true."

They finished their meal. Rebecca carried the dishes to the sink. He washed. She dried. And Mila snoozed on a rag rug under the table.

In another dimension, they might have looked like a family. A loving grandpa with his adoring granddaughter.

Mr. B didn't talk much about his family. Rebecca knew one existed because of the picture on the end table next to his recliner. In the framed photo, Mr. B was a dashing young cowboy straight out of the movies. He stood beside a beautiful woman with gleaming black hair wearing a simple cotton dress, the skirt blowing in the breeze. In her arms she held a baby girl.

His wife had died five years ago, shortly before he and Rebecca met. But what about the daughter? She had to be in her fifties by now. What a lucky woman she was to have a father like Benito Becerra. Even after five years of friendship, he had never mentioned his daughter, and Rebecca was too polite to ask.

"Does the stuff you want me to type have something to do with that realtor guy?" She stacked the bowls and placed them in the cupboard.

"It does." Mr. B squeezed water from the sponge and placed it on a dish beside the faucet. "I must send some new instructions to my lawyer."

"Sounds serious."

"It is quite serious." Mr. B folded a dishtowel in half and smoothed out the wrinkles. "And I must take care of it soon."

"Okay," Rebecca said, unsettled by his urgent tone. "You know there's nothing I wouldn't do for you Mr. B."

"I know that, my dear." His voice carried not only affection for her but a note of confidence she wasn't sure she deserved. "And that is why I ask you. I do not have many people in my life on whom I can count. Not anymore."

BESIDE THE BACK door of a fancy townhouse, Rebecca retrieved the key from underneath a planter and let herself into the kitchen. A black and white Great Dane rose off the floor and sniffed her up and down.

"Hello, Curly." Rebeca picked up the harness his owner had left on the gray marble countertop beside the Italian espresso maker. "You're such a good boy." She slipped the dog into his harness and headed out.

Along the way they picked up four more dogs—two cockapoo sisters, a Golden-doodle, and a ten-pound mutt of unknown origin. With expert precision and control, Rebecca guided her pack up and down the winding streets of the new neighborhood with its flood of modern homes, so different from the ranch houses and old bungalows around Clearwater.

After an hour, Rebecca returned each dog to its home, ending with Curly since he required the most maintenance— snack, a bucket of fresh water, ball time in the backyard, and a cuddle.

As she locked the back door, a BMW roared up the driveway. Curly's owner, Tiffany Pressman, got out. She waved, pointed to the earbud in her ear, and held up one finger.

Rebecca waited. Finally, the call ended.

"I was going to text you," Tiffany said. She wore workout

clothes that probably cost more than Rebecca made in a month. "Curly's had a little tummy trouble lately. He's so sensitive, you know. I just wondered if he did his proper business."

"He certainly did." Rebecca grimaced at the memory. "Twice."

"Were they good and healthy? Because you must make note of that."

"I'd say so." Rebecca didn't mind discussing a dog's digestive issues. It was part of the job. But when it came to Curly, Tiffany was a little obsessed. One time when she was away on business, she made Rebecca take photos.

"Oh, good," Tiffany said. "Gotta jump on a conference call starting in five."

"I'm sorry, but I..." Rebecca's shoulders slumped and she tucked her hands under crossed arms. "I, um, did you get my Venmo request? I sent it last week."

"Hmm, I don't think I did," Tiffany said with exaggerated concern. "Resend it, would you? Sorry but I have to get inside. Don't forget to keep an eye on the poop."

She dashed into the house.

"Okay, sure, will do," Rebecca said to nobody. She hated reminding clients that they owed her money, and Tiffany was the worst.

THE BELLS on the knob jingled as Rebecca opened the door to Mariano's Cheese and Wine. Her supervisor, Patty Sullivan, stood on a ladder that slid along the wall of wine.

"Thank God you're here. I can't reach anything." The tiny but mighty manager climbed down, landing on the floor with a little jump. "If I had one wish, I'd wish to be as tall as you."

"Believe me, you wouldn't." Rebecca started up the ladder. "Tall red-heads always stand out, and not in a good way." She looked down at Patty whose hair was even redder than her own. Lucky for her though, she was cute and petite.

"What am I getting up here?"

"That Malbec from Paso. Can you grab two?"

Rebecca resumed her climb. "Sure."

"And then we're going to change out the displays for Fourth of July. I have some new ideas and a bunch of fun red, white, and blue decorations. I want to have it done before Tessa gets home."

The gourmet shop owner and renowned sommelier, Tessa Mariano, had just gotten married. She and her new husband were honeymooning in Hawaii, but she had refused to be gone more than a week. Summer was a busy time of year in Clearwater, especially for *Mariano's Cheese and Wine*.

"Okay." Rebecca yawned. She'd been going nonstop since six in the morning. "But doesn't she get back tomorrow?"

"Yep. And we've got the tasting tonight."

Rebecca came down the ladder with the two bottles. "What tasting?"

Patty's eyes widened with near panic. "Wait. I forgot to tell you, didn't I?"

"Yeah, you totally forgot."

Patty slapped her forehead. "I'm so disorganized without Liza."

Rebecca almost teared up at the mention of Patty's younger sister. She and Liza were best friends and making plans to become roommates, but a few months ago Liza won a spot at a prestigious culinary school in New York. Although thrilled for her friend, Rebecca felt a twinge of envy. Liza had gone after her dream with focus and commitment.

Rebecca didn't have big plans and dreams like other people her age. She was satisfied with her life as it was, knowing her neighbors, walking dogs, and selling wine to rich people.

And living with her mother. Although she didn't intend to

live with her forever, for the time being she didn't have much choice. After Liza left, Rebecca depleted her savings to buy the used Suburban, a car large enough to hold a pack of dogs. Now, just making the monthly payments and keeping gas in the tank ate up a chunk of her earnings.

On top of that, the guy she'd been dating dumped her. That, too, had been a relief. He was sweet but boring and unmotivated. Most of their dates consisted of watching TV and eating take-out. Rebecca had been thinking about breaking up with him, but she'd never mustered the courage. Staying put and waiting for someone else to decide her next move took the onus off of her. This way, nothing could ever be her fault.

With no boyfriend, her mother as a roommate, and dreams still undiscovered, Rebecca's life was going nowhere, like a bird flying into the wind.

"I'm so sorry I forgot," said Patty. "But I really need you. Can you come back for it?"

Rebecca set the wine on the counter. "What time does it start?"

"Eight o'clock." Patty pressed her hands together as if in prayer. "Please say yes."

Rebecca wished she could go home and collapse, but she couldn't refuse Patty who had kind of replaced Liza as her closest friend. "Sure."

"Great! Thank you. In the meantime, cover up those overalls." Patty tossed a *Mariano's* apron at her. It landed at Rebecca's feet. "Is something wrong? You're not your usual perky self."

"I'm fine." Rebecca leaned down and picked up the apron. "Just tired, but when I get home I'll take a shower and a power nap. By the time I return, I'll be completely regenerated."

"That's my girl." Patty squeezed Rebecca's upper arms. "Now let's get started on those window displays."

CHAPTER 6

*T*he wine tasting was presented by Adam Hawk, Patty's boyfriend and the most celebrated wine maker in Clearwater. Tall, broad shouldered, and quick to flash an irresistible grin, Adam owned Hawk and Winters winery and produced several award winning wines.

While Adam and Patty, the cutest couple in the entire town, tended to the guests, Rebecca kept the charcuterie trays filled. Specialty cheeses, smoked meat, salty cashews, dried fruits, olives, dark chocolate—every item selected to pair with a particular wine.

Rebecca tried to keep her head clear. Despite the shower and ten minute nap, she wasn't as chipper and refreshed as she'd hoped to be. As the tasting wound down, a line formed at the register. She switched gears and went to ring up sales.

A customer set a bottle on the counter and placed four crisp "Benjamins" beside it.

Rebecca glanced at the wine. It was a three-hundred-dollar bottle of Cabernet Sauvignon from a winery in Napa. When she looked up to thank the buyer, her mouth snapped shut.

"Well, *Red*, we meet again."

For the second time in one day, Rebecca came face to face with Troy Dayton's greasy smile.

～

REBECCA SAT with Mr. B on his back porch. They were looking out at the lake and drinking smooth, cool horchata. Mila yawned and stretched before settling down in front of their feet. It was a few days after the wine tasting, and Rebecca was still seething over her encounter with the disagreeable realtor.

"And there he was, smirking at me. He is so obnoxious and full of himself, throws his money around like he's a millionaire. And he called me *Red*. You know I hate that."

"Yes, I know." Mr. B leaned back and rocked gently. "I found him offensive as well."

Rebecca tipped her head toward him. "Sorry, I shouldn't have even mentioned him."

"It's not as if he has not been on my mind. His visit disturbed me. But it also alerted me to something I should have been aware of already. I'm angry with myself for not anticipating it."

"What do you mean?" Rebecca asked.

"In all of Clearwater, my land is the only substantial lake front property still privately owned."

Rebecca ruminated a moment. "Do you own part of the lake?"

"No, querida, only to the edge. The lake is public property, but I own a fair-sized piece of land—plenty for a developer to build on. That is why I must protect it. I should have paid closer attention."

Rebecca had never thought of her friend as rich, but the realtor did say the offer was worth millions. It didn't matter to her, though. All she cared about was him.

"I understand Mr. Dayton's motivation, of course. There is demand for lakefront housing. And who wouldn't want to live here?" Mr. B raised his arms like a preacher, gesturing toward the wide expanse of open land.

"It is a totally great view." Rebecca absorbed the blue surface of sparkling water dotted with boats and kayaks and paddle boards. "I never tire of it."

"And you never will. Antonia loved it so. We used to sit in this very spot and watch—" he stopped and took a deep breath. "Anyway, I don't begrudge the realtor. He is doing his job, but it is my job to stop him. The notes I'm giving you to type up will take care of everything."

Rebecca scaled back her indignation. "Good, because having him pop up like a creepy jack-in-the-box really annoys me. When can I start typing?"

"Soon." Mr. B finished his horchata. "You know, I've spoken English since I was seventeen, but when it comes to writing my brain still struggles. And my research is taking me longer than I had expected."

"Whenever you're ready, I'm ready," Rebecca said, eager to support his cause.

"Gracias, mi querida."

Rebecca smiled. "De nada, mi amigo."

They laughed. Mila released a low whine and coaxed her head under his hand. "You remember what she looked like all those years ago?" Mr. B said. "Shaved to the skin, ribs sticking out, tail tucked under?"

"I remember." Rebecca would never forget how sad and listless Mila had been. "If not for you, she would've died."

"Perhaps." He reached for Rebecca's hand and squeezed it. "And if not for her, I would not know you."

"I think we'd have become friends no matter what." A wave of emotion struck Rebecca. She grasped his strong, sturdy hand, the browned skin warm as if kissed by the sun.

"Our friendship has been one of my greatest blessings, my dear. You are like a daughter to me."

The sentiment touched her soul. The absence of a father had left behind a painful longing she'd buried deep within. Over time, the sharp edge had smoothed, like a river rock polished by rushing water. Rebecca attributed her healing in large part to her relationship with Mr. B. He exemplified what every father should be—steadfast, sensible, and trustworthy. And he filled the void she hardly knew existed until he came into her life.

"Mr. B, can I ask you a question?"

"Of course you may. Never hesitate to ask me anything."

Rebecca shifted, unsure how to frame the question. "You've never told me anything about your daughter. I mean, like, where is she?"

Mr. B shook his head. His wistful smile tore into Rebecca's heart. "I—I cannot talk about her. I am sorry."

"Oh. Okay." Rebecca regretted bringing it up. She and Mr. B had discussed countless subjects—large and small—if there were pieces of his past he wanted to keep private, he was certainly entitled to do so.

"I don't mean to be unkind, querida. It is that I—"

"It's okay." Rebecca kneeled before him and clasped his hands. "I love you so much, and you could never be unkind. You're the best person I've ever known."

He stroked her hair. "I fear you overestimate me." Mr. B pushed himself out of the chair with a deep sigh. He faltered, then righted himself.

Rebecca jumped up. "Are you okay?"

"Yes, just a bit unsteady. It will pass." He clicked his tongue at Mila. "Vamos mi buena perra."

Mr. B leaned on the railing for a moment before heading into the house. Mila trailed after him like a loyal soldier. He crossed through the living room to place his hat on the hook by the front door, but it slipped from his hand. He hesitated and pressed his palm against the wall.

Rebecca snatched the hat off the floor, placing it on the hook. "Are you sure you're okay?"

"Yes, my dear, thank you." Mr. B walked toward his chair, his heavy boots hitting the hardwood in rhythmic steps, and settled himself into the recliner.

"Do you want me to heat you up some soup?" Rebecca offered. "Or how about I run into town and pick up a pizza? We can have dinner together."

"No, no. I'm not hungry." He touched the legal notepad on the end table beside his chair. "I want to finish my work so that it is ready for you tomorrow."

"Can I at least feed Mila before I go?"

"You may." He removed the cap from his pen. "Gracias, querida. What would I do without you?"

"That is one thing you'll never have to worry about." She leaned over and gave him a peck on the cheek, her hand on the arm of his chair.

"Rebecca." He grabbed her wrist and squeezed it, as if to hold her in place. "Promise me you won't give up."

"On what?"

He hesitated, as if not sure of the answer. "On yourself. You are stronger than you know."

"I—I'm not sure what you mean."

The intensity of his gaze struck her. His chest rose and fell. "We are all tested in this life, some of us more than others. My life has been full of wonder and beauty, but tremendous heartbreak, too."

"Because you lost Antonia?" Rebecca asked, her voice cracking.

"Antonia, Josephina…" Mr. B glanced at the photo beside his chair, and he swiped a tear off his cheek. "Christopher."

Rebecca had never seen him so vulnerable. Or mysterious. "Who is—"

Mr. B cut off the question. "Life and circumstances will challenge you, but challenges are not for winning or losing. They are meant to push you toward becoming the person you are meant to be."

He released her wrist, and the room shifted, as if the lights had been dimmed. "Now, I must work." Mr. B set his pen to paper and began writing with surprising speed.

Rebecca backed away, baffled and more than a little freaked out. She'd been handed a bag of pebbles in which there were a few nuggets of gold. How was she supposed to parse through Mr. B's words and find the gold? What did he see in her that she did not see in herself?

"I—I'll go make Mila's dinner, now. Okay?"

"Si, querida." Mr. B continued writing.

In the kitchen, Rebecca heated a kettle of water and put the clean dishes from the rack into the cupboard, mulling over Mr. B's bizarre words of wisdom. They had to be wise, because if they weren't, that meant he might be losing his mind.

The kettle released a high-pitched whistle. Rebecca turned off the stove and removed Mila's homemade stew from the refrigerator. She measured out a serving and mixed it with kibble and hot water.

"Mila, dinner time."

She expected to hear toenails clicking on the rough wood floor. Silence. She tapped the spoon against Mila's dish. "Come on, girl. Where are you?"

A low whimper came from the living room. Rebecca moved toward it.

"There you are," she said. "Why aren't you coming to—"

Mr. B looked as if he'd fallen asleep, but his hand hung over the arm of the chair at an awkward angle, and the pen had fallen onto the floor.

Mila pawed at his leg, tilting her head side to side.

"Mr. B?" Rebecca shook his shoulder gently, then harder. "Mr. B, wake up!"

CHAPTER 7

*F*iretrucks rolled up the driveway with lights flashing. Mila flew into a frenzy, yelping and racing in circles. Rebecca grabbed her collar and locked her in the small corral on the side of the house then ran back inside.

She stared in disbelief as EMT's in yellow suits swarmed Mr. B. They hoisted him onto a stretcher and rushed him out the door.

"Where are you taking him?" She followed the stretcher and watched it disappear into the ambulance.

One of the paramedics spoke. "Valley Hospital. It's the closest. Do you know where it is?"

"Yes, but what happened to him? Is he going to die?"

"They'll do everything they can. Are you a relative?"

You are like a daughter to me.

"Sort of." Rebecca choked on a sob.

The ambulance engine revved, and red lights flashed.

"Meet us there, okay?" the paramedic said.

"Okay." Rebecca hiccupped.

"And drive carefully. We don't want you landing in the

hospital, too." He jumped into the red truck and drove off, following the ambulance down the driveway toward the road.

At the sound of the siren blaring, Mila released a heartrending howl from behind the gate. She stood on her hind legs barking frantically. Then, to Rebecca's horror, the dog ran in wild circles before leaping over the fence and bolting after the truck that had taken her beloved master away.

~

"Mom, listen to me, you've got to find Mila!" She shouted into her cell phone as she drove. "She chased after the ambulance, and now I can't find her."

"I will, I'll go right now. Oh, poor Benito. Did they say what was wrong with him?"

"No, but I'm on my way to the hospital." Rebecca glanced to the side as she blew through a stop sign. "I'll call when I know anything. Just please find Mila." Tears flowed down her cheeks. "That dog is everything to him. He'll need to know she's okay."

"I'm on my way now. Call me as soon as you can."

"I will." Rebecca pressed the accelerator and sped toward the hospital, chanting every prayer she could remember.

The sliding glass doors at the front of the small community hospital parted as she ran up the ramp. Inside, a few people milled around. One woman sat by herself in a waiting area thumbing through a magazine.

Rebecca spotted a man wearing blue scrubs at a desk behind a computer screen.

"Excuse me." She rapped on the desk like drumbeat. "I—I, my, um, my grandfather is here. He just came in by ambulance. I need to see him." She fought back tears.

"Name?" the man asked.

"Rebecca Sparks."

The nurse looked up. "Your grandfather's name."

"Oh, sorry." She pushed wild wisps of hair off her face and leaned over the desk to look at the screen. "Benito Becerra. Can you tell me where he is?"

"Hold on." He clicked his keyboard. "Looks like he's not in the system yet. Have a seat right over there, and I'll let you know when I find out if he's been admitted." He pointed to a row of upholstered chairs.

Rebecca sat. Her legs trembled, knee knocking into knee. A round clock on the wall, like the ones in a grade school class-room, ticked as the minutes passed.

The nurse stood and headed down the hall.

"Wait! Where are you going?" Rebecca ran after him.

"To the bathroom?"

"Oh, sorry."

"I'll be right back," he said, his palms forward. "Don't worry."

Rebecca paced in circles, holding her breath then taking in frantic gulps of air when she realized she'd stopped breathing.

"Rebecca!" Patty sprinted in and threw her arms around her. "Have you heard anything yet?"

"No." Rebecca sniffled and dragged her sleeve under her nose, grateful to have someone to wait with her. "There's some guy that sits over there." She glanced in the direction of the abandoned desk "But nobody's telling me anything."

Patty grasped her hand and led her back to the blue chairs. "Here." She handed her a bottle of organic green juice. "Drink this. It's good for you."

Rebecca twisted off the cap and took a cautious sip. It tasted like freshly mowed lawn, but she guzzled it down. "Thanks."

"You should know, the entire town is out looking for Mila. Your mom called Tessa, and Tessa activated the emergency text tree. "

"The emergency text tree." Rebecca took a tremulous breath. "I love our town."

"Me, too." Patty turned teary. "Everybody really cares."

"And everybody loves Mr. B, don't they?"

Patty wrapped her small but strong hands around one of Rebecca's. "Him and you."

The two friends sat in silence as the clock ticked. Other people waiting for loved ones passed the time by pacing back and forth or flipping through a magazine or scrolling on their phones. But Rebecca just stared at the wall, in a trance, reliving over and over the moment she found her friend slumped in his chair. It was a vision she'd never be able to forget.

Her cell buzzed, and she nearly leaped from her seat.

"Oh, thank God," Rebecca said, reading the text from her mother. "They found Mila. My mom's taking her home."

"That's great news," said Patty.

"It sure is. Mr. B would be devastated if anything happened to her. That dog is his—"

"Are you Rebecca?" A doctor in a white coat with a gentle expression stood in front of her.

She rose involuntarily, as if her body had been lifted by a spiritual force. The words he spoke came at her through an echo chamber, snippets of sentences, broken and unintelligible—*everything we could, heart attack, never in pain, so sorry for...*

Rebecca slapped her hands over her ears. Her head filled with the sound of rushing water, her fingers tingled, her vision blurred. Then everything went dark.

CHAPTER 8

*C*hris Harrington lifted his suitcase and shoved it into the overhead bin. "Here," he said, reaching for his girl-friend's bag. "I can get yours in on this side."

"Thanks." Jessica took the seat by the window. "You don't mind, do you? I hate the middle."

"It's fine." He sat beside her and arranged his long legs. The flight from Seattle to Oakland was only two hours. He could manage that.

His pretty, petite, blonde girlfriend leaned close to him. "Smile for a selfie." She extended her arm with cell phone in hand.

"Seriously? No." He angled himself away. "I've told you before I don't want to be in your Instagram stories."

"What's wrong, sweetie? You're so grumpy, and we're on vacation, aren't we?"

He clicked his seatbelt, wondering if he should have made her stay home. "This isn't a vacation; it's a funeral."

"A funeral for a person you hardly even know." Jessica pouted. "Honestly, I was hoping a few days away would be good for us. You're under so much pressure with the new business, we've hardly had time to, you know, get things back on track."

Back on track. That was the plan when they reunited a few months ago. They'd been together for over two years but broke up when it seemed that all they did was fight. During their time apart, Chris was lonely. And his father, hardly a man to mince his words, berated him for letting go of the perfect girl. They got back together with the assumption they'd move forward and eventually get married. After all, she was twenty-nine and he was thirty-two, the age at which one doesn't stay in a relationship that isn't progressing. The truth was, Chris did believe Jessica was good for him. She was perky, spontaneous, adventurous—a compliment to his serious and cautious nature.

Chris squeezed her hand and forced a smile. "You're right. Maybe we can work in a little time for some fun."

Jessica responded by pulling him close and placing a lingering kiss on his cheek. "I've been researching Clearwater, and it sounds very charming. We can take a sunset cruise on the lake. Doesn't that sound romantic?"

"It does," Chris said, mustering up false enthusiasm. He closed his eyes and pictured the lake where he'd played as a child, where the horizon swallowed the sun in an expanse of miraculous color, and where his grandfather took him fishing, taught him how to skip rocks, and told him he'd always have a home on Clearwater Lake.

BENITO BECERRA WAS LAID to rest in a small cemetery on the outskirts of Clearwater, the town he'd lived in and loved for most of his adult life.

Rebecca stood between her mother and Patty, gripping Mila's leash, her nails digging into her palm. The dog stood at attention, staring at the plain pine coffin like a stoic soldier honoring a fearless leader.

As the minister finished speaking and the coffin was lowered into the ground, Mila let out a cry so plaintive it rose to the sky and bounced off the clouds.

With tears rolling down her cheeks, Rebecca fell to her knees and buried her face in the dog's neck.

The service ended, and the mourners filed past the gravesite with solemn faces and soft whispers.

Alice and Patty helped Rebecca stand up.

"Come on, honey," her mother said. "We should speak to the minister. Tell him how nice the service was."

Rebecca followed like a robot with no mind of her own. The minister stood near the grave engaged in conversation with a young couple Rebecca had never seen before.

Patty rubbed Rebecca's back. "I'm gonna go with Tessa and help set up the reception. We'll see you at the park."

Rebecca nodded. "Okay, thanks."

As people cleared out, many of them complete strangers, Rebecca let Mila sniff the grass. The dog stopped at the headstone marking the grave beside Mr. B's. Inscribed on the stone was a cross, a biblical quote, and the name *Antonia Maria Becerra 1936 ~ 2017.*

A bouquet of daisies drooped in the flower holder.

Mila inhaled the flowers then stretched out on the grass. Rebecca lifted the flowers, and water dripped from the stems. Mr. B had been here recently, perhaps even the day he died.

She sat beside the dog and stroked her. "We'll come back here, Mila, I promise. And we'll bring daisies, too."

Rebecca drew her knees into her chest and breathed in the fresh air and the scent of grapes ripening in the vineyards on the hills around them. A leaf fluttered to the ground and landed in front of the headstone on the other side of Antonia's, the same bouquet of wilted daisies in the vase. Rebecca scooted closer to read the inscription.

Josephina Maria Becerra
Cherished Daughter, Beloved Mother
1960 ~ 2004

~

THE GAZEBO in the middle of Town Square Park held a round buffet table laden with traditional Mexican dishes. Every year on Mr. B's birthday, Rebecca and Alice had made a picnic lunch for him. They ate on a blanket in the shade next to the gazebo, the same spot where Rebecca sat now.

"Why are you all staring at me?" She was perched on a folding chair surrounded by a circle of six women watching her like ladies-in-waiting.

"We're not staring," Tessa said. "We're just—making sure you're okay."

Nonna, Tessa's grandmother, nodded in agreement. "That's right, dear. We know how much Benito meant to you. You loved him like a grandfather."

"And he loved you so much," said Rebecca's mother. "As if you were his very own."

Rebecca sniffled. "I don't know what I'm going to do without him." She reached for Mila who lay in the cool grass next to her. The poor dog had little appetite or interest in doing anything other than sitting in front of Mr. B's house waiting for him to return. It broke Rebecca's heart to know the devoted dog might wait the rest of her life for something that would never happen.

"Um... you look really nice," Patty said. "I've never seen you in a dress. Or real shoes."

"Patty!" Cece, the former prima-ballerina turned dance instructor, smacked her best friend's arm. "Seriously?"

"Well, I haven't," Patty said. "She usually wears overalls and hiking boots."

"Cece's right." Natalie, owner of the ballet school and one of Rebecca's favorite friends, scowled at Patty. "We're here to support Rebecca, not analyze her clothing."

"I'm sorry," Patty said. "I actually meant it is a compliment. It just didn't come out that way."

"It's fine." Rebecca eyed the wrinkled black skirt she'd found in her mother's closet. It hung on her like a sack.

"At least she let me do her hair this morning." Alice toyed with Rebecca's long braid.

Rebecca took a bite of taquito, and a drip of salsa fell on her white shirt. "Food's good," she said, not bothering to wipe off the spill. "Where'd it come from? And who paid for all this? There must be over a hundred people here."

"I ordered it from a caterer in Oakland," Tessa said, dabbing the spot on Rebecca's shirt with bubbly water. "And the town council is splitting the cost with me."

"That was so nice of you, Tessa," said Alice. "And good for you getting the town council to step up. Such a stubborn bunch of cheapskates."

"It's the very least they can do for Benito," Nonna said. "After all he's done for this town over the years."

Rebecca plucked a bit of chicken from her taquito and coaxed Mila into eating it. She knew Mr. B did wonderful things for many people, but for the whole town? "What are you talking about, Nonna?"

"Well, he was just about the most generous man that ever lived. And he loved our town. Many years ago, he built this park. Spearheaded the entire project, ran the fundraisers, and paid for the gazebo, the duck pond, and the community gardens himself."

Rebecca scooted forward. "I didn't know that."

"Hardly anyone does," Nonna said. "Benito never wanted the accolades he deserved."

Rebecca's sadness edged in even deeper, regretting the pieces of Mr. B she knew nothing about. In death, he was becoming greater, more significant. "I wish I'd known more. We talked about so many things, but he never wanted to talk about personal stuff." She pictured the headstone with Josephina's name. "Nonna, did you know anything about his—"

Before Rebecca could finish her question, Mila sprang to life, jumping and barking as if a ring of squirrels were running around a tree trunk.

"Wonder what that's about?" Cece said. "She was half asleep a second ago."

Mila yelped and strained against her leash. It slipped from Rebecca's sweaty hand, and the dog bolted through the crowd.

"Oh geez, not again." Rebecca dropped her plate and ran after her, winding her way around people. "Excuse me, sorry, chasing a dog—"

Finally, Mila skidded to a stop. She crouched and scooted toward a man, tilting her head side to side.

Rebecca waved, continuing her jog. "Can you grab the leash, please? I'm so sorry she charged at you like that."

The man picked up the leash. "No problem."

Rebecca caught up to them. "Thank you, thank you, thank you. You're a complete life saver. I have no idea why she—"

It was his hand that caught her attention, large and sturdy with neatly trimmed nails and smooth skin browned by the sun. Her gaze traveled upwards and landed on his dark brown eyes.

CHAPTER 9

*B*efore Rebecca could squeak out a word, a woman with flowing blonde hair joined them.

"Everything okay, sweetie?"

"Sure. Everything's fine."

The woman, who looked to be a few years older than Rebecca, wore a simple black dress with cap sleeves that showed off slim, toned arms. "I'm Jessica," she said, extending a slender hand with manicured nails.

"Hi." Rebecca shook her fingertips as if she were a delicate doll.

The man and his girlfriend—at least Rebecca assumed she was his girlfriend—eyed Rebecca with mild curiosity.

"Well, thanks again for capturing Mila." She slipped the leash onto her wrist and folded her arms over her shirt, attempting to hide the pink spot the salsa drip had left behind. Her skin tingled as the inevitable red blotches broke out—the curse of pale redheads.

"You're welcome," he said. "I like dogs."

The similarities were subtle but unmistakable, most visible

in the shape of his eyes and the square jaw line. Not to mention those Hollywood good looks Rebecca had seen in the old photo.

She brushed back a clump of unruly hair that had escaped her braid. "This might be a weird question, but are you related to Mr. B, I mean Mr. Becerra? You kind of look like him."

"I'm his grandson, Chris."

Chris? *Christopher?*

How was it possible Rebecca didn't even know a grandson existed until this moment? A pang of regret struck. If only Mr. B had told her more about his family.

"Oh, well, that makes sense then," Rebecca said.

"What makes sense?" Chris asked.

"That, that you look like him, I guess."

"Honey, come on." Jessica's strong voice didn't match her tiny stature. "We need to go."

Rebecca tried to get Mila to back up, but the dog resisted, sniffing around Chris's feet and up his legs.

"Your dog seems interested in me," he said.

Rebecca tugged harder. "That's probably because she can tell you're—Mila, stop it!"

The dog was determined to push her nose against every part of him, getting precariously close to creating an embarrassing situation.

Chris knelt on the ground and cupped Mila's face. "She reminds me of a dog I used to—to know."

She reminds me of a dog I used to own...

Rebecca sucked in a breath. It was a scene from the past—only Mr. B had been replaced by his grandson. And as much as Rebecca wanted to extricate herself from the awkward encounter, she couldn't manage to let the big question go. "I hope this doesn't sound rude, but your grandfather, he—he and I were close. Really close." She lowered her voice. "And he never said anything about you."

Jessica expanded like a perturbed puffer fish. "That is rude. And rather insensitive."

"It's okay, Jess." Chris made a slight move in front of her. "My grandfather and I—we hadn't spoken in a long time."

The information circled around Rebecca's head before it started to coalesce. She was good at puzzles, but there were too many missing pieces.

The mysterious grandson let Mila sniff and lick his palm. "Anyway, I'm—we're—here to take care of his house and, you know, wrap things up."

Rebecca blinked. Is that what one does after somebody dies? Wrap things up? Just one more of life's practicalities. The ramifications of a person's death were endless. In her grief, Rebecca hadn't considered any of them.

"I'm sorry you didn't know your grandfather better. He was the most amazing man in the whole world, and if only he'd—"

"Excuse me." Jessica cut her off. "Now you're crossing the line."

"I'm sorry." Rebecca shut her mouth and yanked on Mila's leash. "Okay, um, hope you like Clearwater. Bye."

"Wait," Chris said. "One more thing."

Rebecca shoulders rolled forward. "Yeah?"

"Sounds like my grandfather was important to you, so I'm sorry for the loss of your friend."

The tears she'd kept at bay sprang to life. "Oh, that's nice, thanks," she said, her voice small.

"This is ridiculous," Jessica said. "Chris, we have to get to the house. I don't want to keep Mr. Dayton waiting."

Rebecca's tears ceased. "You mean Troy Dayton?"

"You know him?" Chris asked.

"No, not really. Just ran into him once or twice." Rebecca flashed a fake smile. "See ya." She turned and strolled toward her friends, but after a few steps, she broke into a run.

CHAPTER 10

From the bottom of the long driveway, Rebecca spotted Troy Dayton's flashy silver Lexus parked in front of Mr. B's house.

"Crap!" Rebecca pounded the steering wheel and pushed the accelerator. In the chaos of the last week, she'd forgotten about the notes Mr. B had been intent on finishing. It was possible they no longer mattered, but she needed to retrieve them just in case.

Mila raced across the car, barking and licking the windows as if she believed she were going home to her master. Rebecca half thought so herself, unable to wrap her brain around the idea of being in Mr. B's house without him.

The moment Rebecca opened her door, Mila scrambled across her lap and took off toward the back of the house. Within seconds, Troy Dayton came running from the other direction. He jumped into his car and slammed the door.

Mila's front paws landed on the window. Her claws peppered the glass as she bared her teeth and growled.

"Oh no!" Rebecca bolted toward the ruckus. She clipped the

leash to Mila's harness and dragged her into the corral, securing the gate.

Troy Dayton opened his door an inch. "That dog won't jump the fence, will it?"

Rebecca remembered the way Mila had flown over the rails when the ambulance took Mr. B away. "I don't think so."

He exited the car, keeping a close eye on Mila. "I'm surprised to see you here. Isn't Mr. Becerra's funeral this afternoon?" He showed his toothy smile, an inappropriate expression when referencing a man's funeral.

"Yes. But it's about over." Rebecca felt like a trespasser. "So, um, what are you doing here?"

"I'm meeting the new owner. What a lucky guy he is."

"What do you mean?"

He waved at the house. "This property is his inheritance. Worth a lot of money."

"Oh, right." More puzzle pieces landed. Rebecca didn't want to talk to Troy anymore. She just wanted to find the notes and get out of there. "I need to go inside for some—some things for Mila."

"Go right ahead." He gestured toward the front door with both hands as if he were entitled to give her permission to enter.

She started up the steps, but the sound of a car coming up the driveway made her turn. A plain white compact stopped behind Troy Dayton's Lexus.

Rebecca had hoped to be in and out before the grandson arrived. Now there was no way to avoid another encounter. The passenger door swung open. Jessica's strappy sandals touched the ground. As she got out, she swept up her hair and twisted it into a ponytail.

Mila stood on her hind legs with her front paws on the top rail barking and whining.

"Hello, Chris." Troy stepped forward with an outstretched hand. "Thanks for agreeing to meet."

"The property's amazing," said Jessica, scanning her surroundings. "But the house, geez, I can't imagine anybody—" her commentary halted at the sight of Rebecca on the step. "What's she doing here?"

"Oh," Troy said. "This is Rebecca. She's taking care of the deceased's dog."

The deceased? How could he be so cold?

"I thought she was your dog," Chris said.

Rebecca came down the steps. "Mila belongs—belonged to your grandfather."

"Guess that means she's yours now." Troy slapped Chris on the back.

Rebecca nearly fell off the step. The idea of losing Mila on top of everything else was unthinkable.

Jessica shook her head, her ponytail swinging. "We are not taking a dog back to Seattle."

Rebecca exhaled. She and the pretty girlfriend could at least agree on that.

"If the dog is my responsibility," said Chris, "I can't just let—"

"Mila's my responsibility," Rebecca said. "She sort of belonged to both of us."

"See?" Jessica said. "Problem solved. Now, can we go inside? All we need to do is take a quick look around, see if there's anything worth taking home. Ready, honey?"

Rebecca chewed her lips. Jessica reminded of her of every *mean girl* she'd known in high school.

"I guess so." Chris climbed the steps one by one, his hand on the railing. At the front door he stopped, hesitated, then turned the knob. "It's locked."

"Don't you have a key?" the realtor asked.

"No," said Chris. "You're the listing agent, don't you have one?"

"Beni—Mr. Becerra," Troy Dayton stammered. "Your grandfather intended to give me a key, but then he, you know, he died."

Rebecca wanted to shout *Liar!* at him, but the only thing that mattered now was getting inside and finding the papers. "I have a key," she said, pleased to have the upper hand, even if only for the moment. "It's to the back door. I'll come around to let you in. Might take an extra minute though, because the lock on that door is a little sticky, and it sometimes—"

"Could you please hurry?" Jessica said. "I need to use the bathroom."

"Sure thing." Rebecca scooted around to the side door and slipped into the kitchen, her first time in the house since the day Mr. B collapsed. It felt like forever, but it had only been five days.

Nothing had changed. The kitchen table was set with the placemat, doily and salt and pepper shakers. The daisy had dried up and drooped to the side. She plucked it out of the vase and tucked it into her skirt pocket.

The empty recliner jolted her. The pen lay on the rug where he'd dropped it. The papers were scattered on the floor, crumpled and dirty from being stepped on when the paramedics had rushed in. She folded them into a small square, tucked them into her pocket beside the daisy, and went to open the door.

Chris stepped across the threshold as if he were entering a haunted house. Jessica followed, nudging him forward.

Troy entered with a jaunty skip. "Well, the house is a disaster I'd say, but the value's in the land, right Chris?"

"That is what you told me," said Chris.

Rebecca resented Troy's presence. Mr. B would not approve of him being there peering into rooms and opening doors.

But she didn't belong in the house anymore either, viewing it through different eyes. The wallpaper she'd once admired had gone dingy and gray. There were scratches on the floor, thin tears in the curtains, chipping paint on the molding. The crystal light fixture above the dining room table was coated with a layer of dust.

Early in their friendship, Rebecca observed Mr. B tending to his house like an old friend. Maybe it had become too much for him. Perhaps he'd been weakened by a heart condition nobody knew about. If only Rebecca had paid closer attention in recent months. If she had, he might still be alive.

Troy opened a closet full of brown boxes stacked up high and teetering to one side. He closed the door as if fearful they'd topple over and crush him. "Well, I don't think there's anything of much value around here. And whoever buys the place will bulldoze it. That'll take care of whatever you leave behind."

Chris drew in a breath, picking up the photograph on the end table, the one of Mr. B and the beautiful Antonia holding the baby girl. A sad smile formed on his lips.

Without thinking, Rebecca inched toward him. "I think that baby is your mom."

"It is," he said. "I used to look at this picture all the time... when my mom and I lived here." He seemed to recall the memory with an element of warmth.

Rebecca's confusion and curiosity grew. Why had he not spoken to his grandfather in so long? Why had Chris and his mother lived in Clearwater? And what caused his mother to die so young?

"What are you looking at, babe?" Jessica sidled up to him.

Rebecca retreated. She'd forgotten the girlfriend was there.

"Just an old photo," Chris said.

Jessica took it from him and set it face down on the table. "Let's not do this."

"Do what?" Chris asked.

"Look at every little thing." Jessica voice was gentle. "We don't have much time, and none of this stuff matters anyway."

How could Jessica know what mattered and what didn't?

Mr. B's house was jammed with stuff that mattered. Being in the same room with people who knew nothing about the man who had lived here for decades was unbearable. Maddening, even.

Rebecca fiddled with the edge of her pocket. She'd accomplished what she had set out to do in the house, so there was no point in lingering. Without a word, she backed away and slipped out the kitchen door. Mila was pacing in circles in the corral. Rebecca retrieved the confused dog, jumped into her car, and sped off. The tears she'd kept at bay sprung as if released from a spigot. Being in Mr. B's house with him gone was worse than watching his coffin sink into the ground.

Never again would she sit on the porch with him, drinking horchata and watching the sun set over the lake. His voice, his smile, his kindness, generosity, insight, and knowledge—everything she loved about him gone, extinguished like a candle burned to the end. All that remained was old furniture, books, dishes, and photos that nobody cared about, nobody except for Rebecca.

CHAPTER 11

*R*ebecca smoothed the wrinkled paper and reread a sentence: *upon my death, distribution of the property will be as follows:*

Then he'd listed bullet points naming sections of land: *twenty acres south, ten acres north...*

A cold kiss on Rebecca's cheek broke her concentration. Her mother, still in her robe and slippers, set a cup of coffee on the table in front of her. "You're up early."

"I know." Rebecca wrapped her hands around the cup.

Pale sunlight filtered through the windows and cast a soothing yellow glow across the floor. Alice doctored their coffees with sugar and milk. "So what's in Benito's notes?"

"I guess he wanted to change his will. I had no idea his property was so big. There's a lot of open land and a bunch of vineyards. I wonder how much of it belonged to him." She recalled how he picked grapes for them to taste. Maybe they were his.

"We could find out," Alice said. "I'm sure there's a way to research the property."

"I guess," Rebecca said. "Doesn't really matter though. I still have no idea what to do with these notes. I mean, all he told me was that they were for his lawyer."

Her mother hemmed. "Do you know who his lawyer is?"

Rebecca shook her head.

"Maybe it's Brad," Alice suggested.

"Huh, maybe." Rebecca pondered the idea. Brad Redmond, Cece's husband, was known as the most ethical lawyer around. And Rebecca knew him well since she babysat their little boy sometimes. "I'm not sure what kind of lawyer he is, but I suppose I could ask, right?"

"Exactly," said Alice. "Even if he's not Benito's lawyer, he probably could steer you in the right direction."

Rebecca chewed a nail. Having somebody steer her in any direction sounded like a good place to start. "I'll call him, but first, I'm going to take Mila on a nice long walk."

REBECCA HEADED down the path to the edge of the lake, letting her mind wander. Dew shimmered on the grass and flower beds burst with color.

It was Mila's first real walk in over a week. Rebecca unlatched her leash and let her enjoy some freedom. Mr. B had always let Mila run untethered.

The dog dashed in and out of the water, chasing ripples and sticks that floated on the surface. Rebecca jogged alongside her, the wind blowing through her hair.

Far in the distance was Mr. B's house. Rebecca could see his dock, his little rowboat rising and falling with the water's rhythmic movement. If they continued another half mile or so, they'd be there.

"Come on, Mila, let's turn around."

The dog shook water from her coat. She barked and leaped back and forth, her paws pounding the sand by the water.

"I'm sorry, but you don't live there anymore."

Mila's tail drooped.

Rebecca wondered if the dog would ever forget her old life. She'd heard stories about dogs who spent the rest of their lives waiting for their masters to come home. Mila might be one of those dogs. Her bouts of anxiety—trembling, pacing in circles, and prolonged episodes of barking—were heart wrenching.

Rebecca clipped Mila to the leash, and together they traipsed along the water's edge back to the cottage.

~

THAT EVENING, after a long day of dog walks and a shift at Mariano's, Rebecca left Mila with her mother and drove to Brad and Cece's house, a large Cape Cod home on a rural road lined with trees and split rail fences.

As Rebecca walked up the steps, Brad opened the door and embraced her in a fatherly hug. "How you doing? I mean really, how are you doing?"

"I've never been this sad in my whole life. Even when my parents split up I wasn't this sad." Rebecca clutched Mr. B's handwritten notes to her chest. "But that was a long time ago, so maybe I don't remember. Anyway, I really appreciate you doing this for me."

"Well, I'm happy to help you make sense of the notes. And I'm giving you the friends and family discount, too."

She halted in the middle of the living room. "Oh, okay, well how does that work? I mean, how much will this cost? Can I pay you in babysitting?"

"I'm kidding." The lawyer winked at her and led her toward the kitchen. "It's pro-bono."

"Pro-bono?"

"It's Latin. It means *for the public good*. And helping you, as well as my friend Benito, is definitely for the public good."

Rebecca's tears embarrassed her. "Thank you. And I'll still babysit anytime. I love Noah."

"And he loves you." Cece came into the kitchen, her arms open wide. "We all do."

Rebecca fell into her friend's hug and remained there.

"How about a cookie?" Cece released her. "I picked some up at Nutmegs."

"What kind?" Rebecca asked. "Although it doesn't matter, I love all their cookies."

"Chocolate chip, peanut butter, and my favorite comfort cookie—oatmeal raisin." Cece set the pink box on the table. "I haven't seen you since the funeral. It was a beautiful service."

"I think so, too." Rebecca sniffled. "I've been so scattered though, and every time I look at Mila, my heart breaks all over again—poor thing just wants to go home." She pressed the heels of her hands against her eyes, but it was no use. "A-a-and now I'm here asking your husband to help me figure out what to do with these notes. A week ago my life was so—so ordinary."

"Listen," Cece said. "Life gets turned upside down in a blink. But we're all here to support you."

"That's right." Brad embraced them both.

"You're a good soul, my friend," said Cece. "No matter where this leads, I know you'll do what's right."

Rebecca appreciated her friend's words, hoping they were accurate. Doing what's right sounded so simple, but her tasks were becoming more difficult by the minute.

"Let's sit," Brad said after his wife headed upstairs. "Why don't you start with how you came to be in possession of Mr. B's notes."

Rebecca broke off a piece of oatmeal cookie and launched into the story, telling him everything from the encounter with the realtor all the way up to yesterday when she dashed into the house to retrieve the notes that had been trampled on.

"That's why the paper's torn and dirty." She passed them to him. "I hope you can read it."

"I'll manage," Brad said, putting on his glasses. "Just give me a few minutes."

While he read Mr. B's shaky handwriting, Rebecca's legs jiggled under the table. She glanced around the familiar kitchen with white cabinets, gray granite countertops, and pendant lights over the island. Cece, who was only five or six years older than Rebecca, had achieved so much. Rebecca couldn't imagine living such a grown-up life—husband, house, baby, and career. She wasn't used to comparing her life to her friends' lives, but it was becoming a regular musing. An unsettled feeling that touched on the edge of envy gripped her. Shameful. Mr. B would have advised her to—to what? What would he say about envy? Right now, all the wisdom he had imparted over the years eluded her.

She wandered into the family room and stood by the open French doors. The setting sun glistened on the water, a view similar to Mr. B's but farther away. She smelled burning wood, perhaps from a nearby barbecue or a campfire down by the lake.

Finally, he cleared his throat. "Well, this is definitely interesting."

"It is?" Rebecca returned to the table and sat, hands clasped together.

Brad removed his glasses. "It's clever. Benito wanted to make sure no developer would buy his land, so he broke it up. Looks like the grandson would still inherit the house and plenty of acreage around it, but there are carved out sections to be donated to the land conservancy."

"Why would he do it that way?"

"To make it undesirable for any kind of a large project. Preserving the lakefront and preventing overdevelopment is becoming a hot topic around here, but only recently. We always thought Clearwater was too small and out of the way to attract developers, but I guess that's changing. And Benito's property is in a prime location."

Rebecca pictured the wide open land, the sprawling green hills, and the magnificent, unobstructed view of the water.

"I think that realtor's visit must have set this plan into motion," said Brad.

Rebecca's mood darkened. "Mr. B was really upset afterwards, and that's when he started these notes. Do you think this is why he had a heart attack? Worrying about his property and rushing to get these notes written might have been too much stress." If she could blame his death on something, or someone, anger could replace the heartbreak. And anger was easier than sadness.

"I suppose it's possible, but I wouldn't focus on that."

"You're right," she said, placing a hand on the paper. "Do you think I could find out who Mr. B's lawyer was and show him the notes? Maybe it's not too late to make the changes Mr. B wanted to make."

"I'm afraid that won't work. What you've got here are just handwritten ideas with no proof that Benito wrote them."

"Well, who else would've written them?" Rebecca argued. "And I know he did, because I saw him writing them myself."

"I understand that, and I believe you. But it's not that simple." Brad rubbed his forehead and furrowed his brow. "I'm sorry to disappoint you. The bottom line is, and it pains me to say this, these notes are probably worthless."

"They can't be. They're Mr. B's last words."

Brad rested his chin on one hand. "Are you certain the grandson wants to sell the property?"

"Oh, yeah, I'm sure about that," Rebecca said. "Millions of dollars just dropped in his lap."

"Why don't you show him the notes? If he knows his grandfather didn't want a developer to buy the property it might sway his decision about whom to sell it to."

Rebecca gulped. "Um, I don't think I can do that."

"Why not? Don't you think he'd want to know his grandfather's wishes?"

Rebecca recalled the way Chris acted when he entered Mr. B's house, like a reluctant visitor. "I don't know that he would. The only thing I know for sure is that the realtor, Mr. Dayton, is going to manage the sale and Chris and his girlfriend are going to be rich."

Brad laughed lightly. He took two cookies from the box and handed one to Rebecca, an oatmeal raisin. "Tell you what. Let me do a little digging. I'll see what I can find out about the realtor. The thing is Rebecca, our small town could be changing. And there might not be anything anyone can do to stop it."

CHAPTER 12

$\mathcal{R}$ebecca went about the next couple days trying to forget about Mr. B's notes. Passing the problem off to Brad Redmond, even for just the time being, relieved some of her anxiety. And until he came back with more information, there was nothing for her do.

The reprieve gave her an opportunity to grieve and adjust to a world without Mr. B in it. She hoped that before long she could regain her footing and return to her simple, uneventful life.

Fourth of July weekend exploded in Clearwater. Tourists and wine lovers roamed Main Street. They gathered in the park picnicking, playing frisbee, feeding the ducks. Nutmegs Bakery had a line out the door, and Mariano's Cheese and Wine was packed with customers.

On Saturday afternoon, one day before the lakefront Independence Day celebration, the bells hanging on Mariano's door jingled all afternoon. Rebecca rang up sales, chatted with shoppers, and helped carry cases of wine to customers' cars. For stretches of time, she managed to set her sadness aside and forget about Mr. B's notes hanging in limbo.

Late in the day, when the shop was empty for the first time in hours, Rebecca sat at the counter and leaned on her elbows, resting her chin in her hands.

"How you doing?" Patty took a seat on the stool next to her.

"I'm good." Rebecca twirled the end of her braid and wished people would stop asking how she was.

"You don't have to pretend around me. I know your heart's broken."

"Kinda."

"And what about Mila?"

"She's not good. I've been leaving her with my mom or Willy while I'm at work. All she wants to do is run home." Rebecca poked a toothpick into a square of smoked gouda and ate it with a smear of hot pepper jam. She wondered if Brad would have any news soon, some guidance as to what her next step should be.

The door opened, bells ringing, and a young woman entered. She wore giant sunglasses, a wide brimmed hat, and a flowered mini-dress.

"Oh my God." Rebecca faced Patty. "I think that's the grandson's girlfriend."

"So what?"

"So I don't want to see her. She's very intimidating."

The woman, presumably Jessica, scanned the enormous wall of wine.

"Go help her," Patty said.

"Won't you do it? Please?"

"Nope." Patty pushed Rebecca off her stool. "You're not in high school anymore, so no shying away from the mean girls. Now go."

"Fine." Rebecca approached the customer as if she had no idea who she was. "May I help you?"

Jessica turned and removed her sunglasses.

"Oh, hi," said Rebecca, grateful her Mariano's apron hid her baggy black pants and boring white shirt. "You're—you're um… we met the other day, didn't we?"

"I think we did," Jessica said, toying with the charm on her chest, a gold *J* hanging on a sparkly chain. "Do you work here?"

"I wouldn't be wearing this apron if I didn't." Rebecca's discomfiture had made her sound flippant, even a little rude. "Sorry, I'm just kidding, but yeah, I work here. Can I help you find something?"

"I hope so." Jessica said, perusing the wines. "My boyfriend and I are taking a sunset cruise on the lake tonight, and Troy suggested I come here for a bottle of wine and nibbles." She picked up a can of caviar, checked the price tag on the bottom, then put it back on the shelf.

"Lots to choose from." Rebecca gestured with open palms.

"What do you recommend?"

"I think we…" Rebecca twirled a curl, her mind drawing a blank. Tessa or Patty or Adam were the ones who made recommendations and did all the food pairings. Although some of their expertise had rubbed off on her, she wasn't adept at throwing things together on demand.

Rebecca shot a pleading look at Patty, but her boss ignored her distress.

"How about…" Rebecca went to the window display and grabbed one of the premade baskets. "This? It's the perfect collection of wine and food. It—it's a bottle of wine, obviously. And some food."

Jessica blinked at her. "Can you be more specific?"

"Well, I'd have to open it."

"Is that a problem?"

"I guess not." Rebecca set the heavy basket on the counter and snipped the red, white, and blue ribbon. The cellophane crackled as she flattened it. She carefully poked through the items so as not to upset the arrangement. "Let's see, we've got a bottle of Hawk and Winters Cabernet, one of the best in the region. And these totally delicious poppy seed crackers, mixed nuts, a fabulous caviar, olive tapenade, brie cheese, dark chocolate, dried apricots. What do you think?" she asked, pleased with herself for finding a suitable choice with an already curated selection of products.

"How much is it?"

Rebecca checked the tiny label on the edge of the cellophane. "One hundred eighty-five, plus tax."

"Seriously? That's super pricy."

Her reaction surprised Rebecca, who assumed money wouldn't matter to a fancy girl like Jessica. But she'd been trained to respect any customer's budget. "It's the caviar. And the wine is expensive, too. I can change out a few things to bring the price down."

"Please do." Jessica checked her phone. "Can you do it quickly? I need to meet Chris at the dock."

"No problem," Rebecca said, put off by her customer's lack of appreciation. She switched the cabernet to a red blend, removed the overpriced caviar, and added some gourmet chips and a small package of quince paste. "Let's see," Rebecca said, doing the math in her head. "That takes it to one hundred dollars even."

Jessica extended her pretty hand with a credit card between two fingers. "Great," she said, her glossy lips forming a tight smile.

Rebecca rang up the sale then gathered the crinkly cellophane around the basket and secured it with a new ribbon. "Here you go."

"Thank you." Jessica wrapped an arm around it and headed to the door. Then she turned back to Rebecca and asked in a sweet voice. "Would you mind snapping a quick photo of me with the basket?"

"Sure," Rebecca said, accepting her cell, which happened to be the latest version of the best phone on the market.

Jessica balanced the basket on her hip. "Should I stand in front of the wine or the cheese case?"

"Um, the wine wall is a good backdrop," Rebecca said. It wasn't the first time she'd been asked to take photos for customers. "And the lighting there is best."

"Sounds good." Jessica posed with the basket like a fashion model, sunglasses holding back her hair, a coy tip of the head. If Jessica were taller, she'd probably be a real model with her all-American girl looks and darling figure.

"I took a bunch." Rebecca handed the phone back. "You're very photogenic."

"You think so?"

Rebecca wanted to say *Duh, you're gorgeous!* How could a woman like Jessica have doubts about herself?

"Yes, you take a great picture. And with the wine behind you, it's pretty perfect." Rebecca almost added *just like you*, but she closed her mouth. There was no need to fawn over her.

"Thanks. Okay, I'd better run."

"Have a good time on the cruise," she said with genuine politeness.

"We will." The dazzling girlfriend of Mr. B's grandson exited the shop with a wiggly finger wave.

"That wasn't so bad now, was it?" Patty gave Rebecca a pat on the back.

"I guess not."

"And props on the way you handled her request to lower the price. Excellent job."

Rebecca appreciated the praise. "Yeah, well, I really hope I never have to see her again."

AFTER LEAVING Mariano's at six, Rebecca drove home, unable to get the fancy Jessica out of her mind. She pictured her and the handsome grandson of Mr. B on their little boat sipping the red wine Rebecca herself had selected.

The sky ahead of her was the color of a freshly cut persimmon. Swaths of pale pink blended with lavender, the perfect tableau for a sunset cruise on the lake.

One should never tire of sunsets, Mr. B had often said.

The moment Rebecca walked into the cottage, Mila flew into a frenzy.

"Mom, did you take Mila out this afternoon?"

"Yes, I did." Alice was seated at her small desk tucked into the corner. "Many times. I tried to take her to the office with me, but she pulled so hard on the leash that it slipped from my hand, and she ran straight toward Benito's place. Thankfully, one of the guests caught her and brought her back."

"Oh, geez," Rebecca said, sorry for both her mom and Mila. "That's terrible."

"I know you don't want to think about this, but it might be time to find her a permanent home."

"I can't do that." Rebecca fell to her knees and hugged the dog's neck. "At least not yet."

What to do with Mila weighed on Rebecca constantly. The dog was close to perfect, having been trained by the best, so finding her a new owner would be easy. But Mila had suffered a loss like Rebecca had. They found comfort in each other.

"We'll talk about the dog another time," Alice said, packing her purse and heading toward the door. "And sorry for the short notice, but I need you to manage the front desk tonight."

"Seriously? Where's Zack?"

"He has to go early for some reason, and I have to meet the plumber who's coming to fix the leak in the laundry room. I'm sorry—I know how tired you are. We have one late check-in, and then you're free to go." Her mother gave her a peck on the cheek and left.

Tired was an understatement. Rebecca could have fallen asleep standing up.

She ate two pieces of pizza, swallowed a diet Coke, and threw on a clean sweatshirt. Mila, forlorn on her cushion by the window, whined.

"Come on, girl. You can go with me."

Mila lumbered to her feet and followed Rebecca outside.

In the distance, the sun descended into the horizon, leaving behind a swirl of pastels. "Lucky Jessica," Rebecca grumbled to herself.

At the reception desk in the main lodge, Zack's fingers were flying across the keyboard on his personal laptop.

"What are you working on?" Rebecca asked.

"My resume," he said.

"You just got hired. Are you looking for a new job already?"

"Not actively, but I've got to be ready in case the recruiter calls. I have a degree in viticulture, you know."

"So?"

"So, working the front desk here is not exactly my dream job. I'm in this town to make moves." He dressed the part of a guy on the move with his untucked dress shirt, high-end sneakers, and molded brown hair. "Don't worry though, I'm not leaving anytime soon. This might not be my dream job, but I still like it. Besides, your mom's a crack-up. She reminds me of my mom, which is a good thing. My mom's cool."

"That's really sweet."

"Yeah, I'm a sweet guy. And my mom is the reason I have to leave early. Family dinner for her birthday." Zack slung his backpack over a shoulder. "See you later."

Rebecca sighed, a twinge of envy twisting inside her stomach over Zack's ambition. It was the same feeling she had when Liza went off to culinary school in pursuit of a dream. Most of the young people in Clearwater were there to land a job at a vineyard or winery, hoping some of the golden dust of success would rub off on them. Rebecca just wasn't one of them. Mr. B had always assured her she had plenty of time. He said that one's *twenties* were for discovery, the age in which one must explore and stretch her wings in search of purpose and passion. Rebecca loved the way he could turn her insecurities around, help her to believe in herself. But time was catching up—already twenty-seven, her *twenties* were running out. What if a decade of exploration and wing-stretching landed her no closer to finding her purpose?

Rebecca perched herself on a stool and scrolled through Instagram, checking all the hashtags that mentioned Clearwater. Hundreds of photos popped up—a wide shot of Main Street lined with American flags, the gazebo in the park wrapped in bunting, and a beautiful shot of Mariano's wine wall. She continued swiping her screen, taking quick glances at random pictures posted by her Instagram *friends*—people she hardly knew but for one reason or another followed.

A girl she'd known in high school posted images of herself eating beautifully prepared plates of food. Rebecca couldn't believe she actually ate all the food, not with that figure. In every picture, she wore a tight dress or skinny jeans to show off her perfect body. Then again, she might be one of the lucky ones who could eat whatever she wanted and never gain an ounce.

Rebecca, at five foot nine, was what her mother called sturdy. She wasn't overweight. In fact, she was in excellent shape thanks to her dog walking business and plenty of heavy lifting at the shelter and Mariano's. Who needed a gym or regular workouts with that schedule? Still, she sometimes felt like an Amazon, especially around petite women like Patty and Tessa. Thank goodness for Cece and Natalie who were even taller than Rebecca was. Although the ballerinas were blessed with fine bone structures and slender, sculpted limbs. Rebecca had the muscles of a lumberjack.

She went to her mother's office, just a desk tucked into a corner of the lobby, and opened the bottom drawer. Some people hid vodka in their desks. Her mother hid candy. Rebecca filled a mug with peanut M&M's. She sat in the swivel chair, put her feet up, and returned to the irresistible lure of other people's perfect meals, perfect vacations, perfect lives.

And there it was—a photo of Jessica in Mariano's standing with her basket in front of the wine wall followed by several shots of the magnificent sunset over Lake Clearwater in all its glory—#sunsetcruise; #romanticdate; #lifeisgreat; #Californiawinecountry; #Clearwater

It even included a story: *If you're one of my besties, you know my sweetie lost his dear grandfather, so we're in Northern California to sort things out. Made a little vacay out of it in a darling town called Clearwater in the heart of Sonoma. Can't wait to spend more time here! XO, Jess*

CHAPTER 13

*R*ebecca gawked at her screen. "Are you kidding me?"

"What's wrong?"

Rebecca swung the chair around, almost tipping it, to find her mother leaning over her shoulder.

"Geez, you scared me."

"Sorry, but I've told you a thousand times to quit looking at that crap." Her mother dug a few M&M's out of the mug. "Did I tell you about my friend's daughter? Her self-esteem dropped to record lows thanks to those *snappychats* and *Instant-grams*. You know, there's a direct correlation between being on social media and depression."

"I'm aware." Rebecca rolled her eyes. At the moment, she was pretty depressed herself. "Please tell me you're taking over the desk."

"I'm afraid not, just came in to get a key to cottage six. The husband texted and asked if it was too late to order the 'night of romance' special, and of course it is too late, but I'm trying to be accommodating." She grabbed a bottle of champagne from the wine refrigerator. "Can you get the silver tray and ice bucket for me?"

"Sure." Rebecca reached the top shelf with ease.

Alice boxed up her supplies, added some dark chocolates from Mariano's, tea lights, and a bag of pink rose petals to scatter on the bed. "I have to hurry. They'll be back from dinner soon. And then I'm going to play Maj with the girls at the library."

"Fine, enjoy your social life," Rebecca said.

Her mother wagged her head, as if disapproving. "You could have a social life, too, my dear. Just because that last guy broke up with you doesn't mean every guy will."

Rebecca shuddered. The break-up hadn't hurt her heart as much as it had crushed her ego. She didn't even like the guy that much.

"I don't want to talk about it. What time is the last check-in? I'm so tired."

"No idea." Alice looked at her watch. "They'll be here when they get here."

As soon as her mother was out the door, Rebecca went back to her phone. Her finger hovered over Jessica's bio in her Instagram account. Against her better judgement, she tapped.

According to social media, Jessica owned a successful event planning business, was an accomplished flower arranger, and had about twenty-five thousand adoring followers. All her posts featured beautiful images of decorated ballrooms, exquisite centerpieces, brides tossing bouquets. Rebecca couldn't help being impressed. And totally jealous.

She continued scrolling, searching for a photo of Jessica and Chris and more evidence of the perfect life they shared. For whatever reason, very few posts featured her handsome boyfriend.

"Why are you even doing this?" Rebecca shut off her phone and put an end to the torture.

Viewing other people's glamorous lives only served as a

bitter reminder of how dull her own life was. Mr. B flashed through her mind. He would never approve of her wallowing.

A light bark sounded. Mila ran to the door as it swung open and the guest entered. Rebecca nearly fell out of her seat.

Jessica, the last person Rebecca expected—or wanted— to see, walked into the lobby. They eyed each other with awkward stares. Rebecca recovered first. "Hello."

"Don't tell me you work here, too." Jessica nudged Mila away with the back of one hand.

"Guilty as charged." Rebecca cringed at her nerdy response.

"You really are everywhere in this town, aren't you?" The observation was more curious than unkind, but Rebecca took it as an insult.

"You could say that," she said, teeth grinding. "So, how was the cruise?"

"Absolutely gorgeous! The colors in the sunset are reminiscent of a Monet painting." Jessica sounded like an event planner selling the activity as part of a package. "I hope our room is ready."

"Wait, you're the late check in?"

Jessica's eyes widened. "It isn't a problem, is it? I told the guy I spoke to this afternoon we'd be late. I think he said his name was Zack."

"No, it's not a problem." Rebecca needed to gather her wits and quit sounding like an uninformed fool. "Not at all."

Mila sniffed Jessica as if she were hiding treats in her pocket.

"Go away, please." She pushed Mila to the side and set her purse on the counter. "Chris is just getting our bags out of the car.

When he entered, Mila spun in circles.

"Hello girl." He put his backpack on the floor and knelt to pet the dog, allowing her to lick his face and hands. "You're sure a friendly one, aren't you?"

"You're going to have to shower off all that dog slobber," his girlfriend said.

Chris ignored Jessica's remark and looked up at Rebecca. "Do you work here?"

"I do." Rebecca chose a more appropriate response this time.

"Can we check into our room now?" Jessica asked.

"Right, of course," Rebecca said, happy to wrap things up. She opened their reservation. "Says you'll be here three nights."

"Correct." Chris removed a credit card from his wallet.

"Let's use mine," Jessica said. "I'll be able to write off our expenses here for sure."

Chris ignored her again. "Use this one." He handed Rebecca his card.

She tried to figure out what was going on between the two of them. They'd just been on a wonderful, romantic outing, and now it seemed they were a little testy with each other.

Swiping his card, she noticed his last name was Harrington, not Becerra. It took her moment before realizing it made sense. His mother's last name had been Becerra, not his father's. The memory of Chris's mother's grave bumped into Rebecca's brain. Why had Mr. B buried his daughter with her maiden name? The disconnects about Mr. B and his family continued to pile up.

"So, Rebecca," Jessica said, tucking her credit card back in her purse. "I seem to be running into you all over Clearwater." Her raised eyebrow suggested she expected an explanation.

Although Rebecca owed none, the words tumbled out of her mouth like pebbles down a mountainside. "I, yeah, I work at Mariano's, which you already know. And I have a dog walking business, which is really my main thing, and I work here, too. My mother manages the inn, and we have a cottage up the hill where—"

"You live with your mother?" Jessica's question sounded more like statement.

Rebecca grew hot, and she felt red blotches break out on her chest. Her nervous rambling was impossible to contain, always telling more than she should and sharing facts about herself that nobody needed to know.

"Yeah," Rebecca said, twisting some wisps of loose hair. "For now."

An awkward silence fell. Between the numerous encounters and the secret she carried regarding the notes Mr. B had left behind, Rebecca couldn't wait to get away from them. "Let me take you to your cottage. You'll be in Blue Meadow, a lovely room with a view of the lake."

A view of the lake, just like at Mr. B's.

With Mila prancing along beside them, Rebecca escorted the couple to their cottage. It was the last one at the end of a path lined with rosebushes.

"This is a beautiful spot," Jessica said. "Don't you think so, babe? Better than the last place, that's for sure."

"Where were you staying before?" It was an obvious next question, but Rebecca feared she sounded nosey.

"It was a drive-up motel about a half hour from here," Chris said. "Too far away considering everything I have to get done in the next few days."

He didn't explain further. Rebecca wondered why they didn't sleep at Mr. B's house—Chris did own it, after all. And it had plenty of room. But she resisted asking any more questions which no doubt would lead her down a rabbit hole of embarrassment. The blotches had subsided, and she wasn't about to invite them back.

The gray shingled cottage had its own brick walkway that led to a pale yellow door with a white wooden bench and flower pots on either side.

Rebecca opened the door and stepped back, letting them go in ahead. She hesitated in the doorway to avoid entering their cozy, intimate space. "Here we go. Is there anything you need?"

Jessica peeked into the bathroom. "Some extra towels would be nice."

The bathroom had plenty of towels, but Rebecca responded like a dutiful concierge. She set the key on the table next to the door. "Towels, sure, be right back."

With only a sliver of sunlight left, she jogged in near darkness to the laundry room with Mila at her heels. She grabbed a stack of fluffy white towels from the shelf and carried them back to the cottage.

Through an open window, the sound of Jessica's shrill voice shot out.

"Why are you so mad? You know it's my job. Do you have any idea how much pressure I'm under to create posts for my followers? Posts that make everything in my life look—look perfect?"

Rebecca froze. Had Jessica just admitted to being a phony?

"I'm mad because I've asked you to leave me out of your posts." Chris's voice was quiet, but thick with anger. "And look at this—*my sweetie lost his dear grandfather*—come on, Jess. He wasn't my 'dear' grandfather. I barely knew him anymore, and your posts make this all sound like some kind of, I don't know, like a joke."

Rebecca scooted closer to the open window.

"But look at the reaction the post is getting." Jessica sounded as if she were crying. "Everybody sending back such nice messages. And thousands of 'likes' from friends."

Chris's laugh was caustic. "These aren't your friends. They don't know you. They don't care about you."

"You're wrong. They do care."

Rebecca wondered if Jessica was right. All those followers, at least some of them had to care.

"Jesus, Jess, whatever. I can't talk about this anymore. I'm gonna take a walk."

Rebecca dropped the towels on the bench between the

flower pots and took off at lightning speed. She scrambled up the hillside and made her way through total darkness into a thick of trees.

A root caught her shoe, and she flew forward, landing hard. She lifted her face and spit out dirt.

The perfect way to end a perfectly awful day.

CHAPTER 14

*R*ebecca sat on the swing on the back porch of their cottage with her legs tucked underneath. Early morning dew on the grass reflected the sun. Even though the Fourth of July festival was at least a mile away, the sounds preparation echoed between the hills—hammers pounding, loudspeakers squawking, the high school band practicing.

Normally, she'd be excited, but not this year. Not without Mr. B. As a naturalized citizen, he loved honoring his country's birthday. Plus, he loved hotdogs and cotton candy, children playing, and fireworks.

A year ago, Rebecca, Alice, and Mr. B had set up chairs on his dock and watched the fireworks exploding over the lake. At the time it was just another fireworks display and a fun night. Now it was a precious memory, bittersweet, one that made her smile and cry at the same time.

Mila jumped on the swing. The dog rested her head on Rebecca's thigh and whined. Rebecca calculated how long it had been since Mr. B died—today was day nine.

"I miss him, too, girl."

The screen door hit the frame as Alice came outside carrying a tray with coffee and sticky buns from Nutmegs. "I thought you might need some cheering up today."

"Thanks, Mom." She took a bite of sticky bun. Mr. B loved sticky buns, too.

"Are you going to the lake this afternoon," her mother asked. "I think it'd be good for you."

"Yeah. Brad Redmond is meeting me there, so I hope he tells me something that'll help me decide what to do with Mr. B's notes."

"I hope so, too. You need to get this behind you. It's making you very nervous and a little nutty. Nuttier than usual."

Rebecca couldn't agree more.

BRAD, sitting on a bench in the shade, waved Rebecca over. "Hello, and happy 4th of July."

"Hi." She wiped her palms on her shorts as she sat beside him.

He gave her crooked smile. "You seem nervous."

"I am," she admitted. "My mom says I'm nuttier than usual, which I totally am. I just hope you're going to tell me something that'll make this whole situation go away, you know, make it not my responsibility."

Brad drank from a water bottle. "That'll be up to you."

Rebecca tensed. She was looking to unload decisions, not take on more. "What do you mean?"

"Let me start with this. I didn't find out who's interested in Benito's property or what somebody might want to do with it. But that part doesn't really matter. What I did confirm is that there are more than a few people in favor of large development."

"You mean destroying lakefront property? That's crazy."

"Depends on how you look at it." Brad folded his hands. "New development brings in a lot of money."

Money, the ultimate pursuit. Everybody loved money, and the more of it the better. But at what cost? "Are you saying some big building project on Mr. B's land is a good thing?"

"It would be for some," Brad said. "Take Tessa for example. The more people coming into Clearwater to live or visit, the more customers she'll have and the more wine she'll sell."

"And the richer she'll get." Rebecca regretted her snippy tone. After all, Tessa was one of her favorite people in the whole world. "I didn't mean to sound nasty about it."

"It's not nasty—it's the way it works. Look at it this way, the busier her shop is the more people she employs. A few years ago, she had one part-time assistant. Now she has a full-time manager and you."

"And Patty's always asking me to work more hours. I get it." Rebecca had never taken an economics class in her life, but most of the concepts were common sense. "Are you saying I should forget the whole thing and just let whatever's supposed to happen, happen?"

"Not necessarily." Brad tightened his lips. "Regardless of what you do at this point, Clearwater might be changing. It's hard to keep small towns small, but that's a different issue. All you want is for Mr. B's wishes to be honored."

"That's true."

"And the best way to do that is by sharing what you know with the grandson. Show him the notes."

Rebecca frowned and chewed her lower lip. "I'm kind of afraid to do that."

"Afraid? Why?"

"I don't know. What if he thinks I'm butting in where I don't belong? And what if he gets mad at me? People are weird about money."

Brad put a fatherly arm around Rebecca's shoulders. "First of all, you're not butting into anything. You have information that might mean something to him. Benito's wishes for how he wanted his property handled speaks to the kind of man he was."

Rebecca nodded, recalling how deeply Mr. B cared about others and about his community.

"And as far as the grandson getting mad at you, who cares?"

"I don't like people being mad at me. Even people I don't know."

Brad gave her shoulders a squeeze. "Then you need to toughen up. Don't be afraid to enter the fight when there's something important at stake. Our friend Benito knew that better than anyone."

Rebecca leaned back. She stared at nothing and picked at a hangnail. "You really think it's the only choice?"

"It's the best choice. He needs to know what his grandfather wanted. Despite the fact they weren't on speaking terms, and we have no idea why, he's entitled to the truth. You owe him that. And then it's up to him. You will have fulfilled your obligation to Benito and that'll be the end of it."

"You're right," she said, forcing confidence into her voice. "And I—I guess I can do it."

"Good for you. Let me know how it goes."

"I will. Thanks for your help."

"Anytime." Brad stood. "I'm going to go track down my family. As always, if you need me, you know where to find me."

"Thank you." Rebecca fell against Brad and gave him one of her exuberant hugs. He was a wonderful man, just like Mr. B.

They parted ways. Rebecca lingered under the tree looking into the crowd, feeling slightly better now that she had a plan. She would give Mr. B's grandson the notes, and then the rest was up to him.

As she wandered into the carnival, Rebecca kept an eye out for Chris and Jessica. After all, the Fourth of July celebration was one of Clearwater's biggest events of the year, and the entire town came out for it.

That was what Rebecca loved about living in a small town. Everyone went to the same gatherings; they ate at the same restaurants where the hostess knew their names and the chef knew how they liked their steaks; they visited each other's homes and looked after each other's kids and brought food when someone was sick. Friends and neighbors showed up whenever somebody died. And there were always people to count on. How could anyone in Clearwater be in favor of changing it? Mr. B didn't just want to protect his land—he wanted to preserve his town.

A balloon artist danced by Rebecca, twisting long skinny balloons into silly hats and animals. A girl with a rainbow snow cone bumped into her, and sticky bits of ice fell on Rebecca's arm. The aroma of sizzling hamburgers filled the air. Kids climbed trees and played soccer on the lawn.

Mr. B would have loved it.

After running into almost all her friends, playing a few games, and greeting many of her doggie clients, Rebecca went home to Mila. The parking lot at the inn was almost empty, most notably Chris's rental car wasn't there. Just as well, Rebecca thought. She wasn't quite ready to present Mr. B's grandson with the notes that might throw a wrench into his plan for becoming a multi-millionaire.

The grounds of Lakeview Lodge were deserted since all the guests were down by the lake or at some other Independence Day party. Rebecca made herself a glass of sweet milk sprinkled with cinnamon and sugar, not exactly horchata but similar enough to conjure the memory. On the back porch of the cottage, she curled up on the swing with Mila.

The moment it turned dark, the fireworks began. In the distance, great bursts of color lit up the sky and explosions shook the ground.

Rebecca snuggled closer to Mila. She pressed her nose into

the dog's neck, inhaled the warm, familiar scent, and imagined Mr. B sitting beside them.

~

First thing in the morning, as Rebecca set up the coffee service in front of the lodge, she spotted Chris dragging the giant suitcase up the path toward the parking lot.

With Mr. B's notes tucked in the front pocket of her overalls, she walked over. The confidence she'd hoped for hadn't materialized, but she plowed forward anyway.

"Good morning!" Rebecca raised a hand and waved.

"Good morning." His face was dark with stubble, his hair disheveled, his shoes untied. Just the right amount of scruffiness.

"I, uh, I thought you were checking out tomorrow." Rebecca shook off the attraction to him as if it were an annoying fly.

"Actually, I'm wondering if I can keep the room a few more days." He glanced back at his cottage. "Jessica has to get home, but I need to stay longer. Figuring out what to do with all the stuff in my grandfather's house is a bigger project than I expected it to be."

Rebecca wondered if his girlfriend's sudden departure had anything to do with their argument the night they arrived. "Oh, yeah, I'm sure it'll be fine. When I get to the office I'll double check the reservations. If somebody's booked the room I can try and move—" she closed her mouth to shut down her nervous over-explaining.

"That'd be great." He continued toward the parking lot, the wheels of the suitcase bump-bumping along the path.

Rebecca fell in step beside him, her stomach churning. "Before you go, there's something I—I need to tell you."

He stopped. "What is it?" His dark eyes fell upon her.

The folded up sheets of paper in her pocket against her chest took on weight, as if to remind her they were there, heavy with words that could change the future of Clearwater. Rebecca pressed a hand against them. "I made coffee."

"Oh, okay."

"Do you drink coffee?" Rebecca asked, veering away from her intended topic. Despite being angry with herself for avoiding the conversation, at least she'd come up with a clever alternative motive for stopping him.

Chris rubbed one eye with the heel of his hand. "I do. And I could use some, thanks."

"It's up by the lodge on the patio. Good coffee, too. Strong. And there's milk—skim milk, two percent, half and half. And— and paper travel cups if you want to take some with you, because it looks like you're—" *Shut-up!* she told herself.

A slight smile formed around his lips. "I'll get some before I leave for the airport." He removed his cell phone from his jeans pocket. "Hey, do you mind giving me your mobile number?"

He wanted her number? Why?

As if he'd heard her inner thoughts, he said, "I'll call it, and then you'll have my number just in case you need to switch me to a different cottage."

"Oh. Sure. No problem." Rebecca recited her phone number as he typed it in. Her phone buzzed. Now she had his number— it gave her a shiver.

"Thanks again," he said. "I'd better go. I'm sure we'll hit traffic."

"Traffic." Rebecca repeated the word for absolutely no reason. She took two steps backwards, her arms swinging. "Lots of traffic going to the airport, okay, well, I'll—I'll text you, you know, about the room if I need to. But like I said I'm sure it's fine. Oh, and don't forget to get coffee, it's the good—"

"Right, the good kind. See you later." Chris grabbed the handle on the suitcase and speed-walked toward his car.

CHAPTER 15

*R*ebecca relived the encounter in her head over and over as she drove. *I made coffee? I'm such an idiot.*

Mila stuck her head over the seat and licked Rebecca's ear. "Sit down, girl. I know you're excited."

They arrived at Tiffany's house just as the busy executive was loading her trunk with her workout bag, sneakers, and the giant leather purse that held her electronics.

Rebecca parked at the curb and got out with Mila. "Hi, Tiffany."

Curly's owner frowned. "What's this?"

"What's what?"

"This dog."

Rebecca tugged Mila's leash to keep her from sticking her snout up Tiffany's short skirt. "This is Mila, Mr. B's dog. You know he died, so I've kind of adopted her."

"That's nice of you, Rebecca, but I've told you I don't want Curly walking with other dogs—he's large, and smaller dogs are intimidated by him, so they get aggressive. And he's too gentle to defend himself. You know how rescued dogs tend to be insecure."

"But I walked them together the other day, and everything was fine."

Tiffany pushed the button to close her trunk. "Doesn't matter. Curly needs your full attention, so you're going to have to figure something out."

Rebecca deflated. "Okay, I will, but today I'm kind of stuck, so…"

"Fine." Tiffany rubbed her temples and blinked rapidly. "I have to get to work, and Curly needs his walk. But don't bring that dog with you again."

Rebecca stood in the driveway, watching the black BMW speed away, now even angrier with herself. She'd forgotten to remind Tiffany about her unpaid bill. If Rebecca didn't love Curly so much, and if she weren't so intimidated by the high-powered female executive, she'd tell her to find herself another dog walker.

THAT AFTERNOON, Rebecca returned to the inn and found Zack in the office arranging bags of homemade granola, fancy mixed nuts, and lemon sugar cookies from Nutmegs on a display shelf.

"Hi, Rebecca, your mom asked me to ask you if you could book a series of wine tastings for a group checking in on Thursday."

"Are you kidding? That's only a few days away." Rebecca groaned. Last minute requests were always problematic.

"I'm just the messenger."

"I know." Rebecca unleashed Mila and gave her a treat. "Hey, so, any nibbles on your resume?"

Zack shrugged. "A few. Nothing to get excited about. Although I might be lining up an interview at a winery in Calistoga."

"Wow, great." Rebecca suppressed the little green monster creeping around her chest. "Good luck."

She left the intrepid college graduate at the desk and went to the laundry to gather towels for Chris Harrington's cottage. Since he was staying a few more nights, he probably needed fresh towels. Besides, it was a good excuse to drop in on him. The notes she'd been carrying around in her pocket all day were growing heavier by the hour. She needed to hand off the information to him and be done with it.

With a stack of fluffy white towels piled in her arms, Rebecca knocked on the cottage door. She shifted her weight side to side waiting for a response, half hoping he didn't answer.

"Just a sec." Chris's voice was loud and quick, as if he didn't welcome any interruption.

Mila whimpered, her tail swinging and ears twitching.

"Be good." Rebecca looked at the dog. "And stay put."

Chris opened the door, and Mila dashed inside then out then inside again. She sat in front of his legs and licked his hands, tail thumping.

"I brought you some more towels." Rebecca patted the one on top. "Obviously."

"Thanks," Chris said, taking them. "I do have plenty though."

"Oh, well, you can never have too many towels. Now you won't run out. And you can use clean ones every day, although that's not very environmental, is it? But, you know, whatever you—"

He leaned on the doorjamb, an amused smile brightening his otherwise serious face. "I can use a towel more than once."

Rebecca sensed he was waiting for her to leave. She could see his laptop open on the table. But she was there with a purpose, and it wasn't to deliver fresh towels.

"I, I have something that…" Rebecca removed the folded up sheets of paper and held them in her hand. "You need to read this."

Chris set the towels on the bench and took the notes from her. "What is it?"

"Something your grandfather wrote," she said, her voice raspy. "About your—your inheritance."

"I'm in the middle of work," he said. "So I'll read this later."

It shocked her that he would be so cavalier about something so important. "No, you have to read it now, and those notes belong to me. I can't leave them with you." Rebecca's response was harsher than intended, but she felt a sudden and unexpected ownership of Mr. B's words. As much as she wanted to rid herself of the responsibility, Rebecca couldn't just hand the problem off without knowing how Chris would deal with it.

"All right, fine. If it's that important."

"It is."

He sat on the bench next to the stack of towels. Mila rested her head on his knee.

Rebecca pulled her braid over her shoulder and twirled it. Showing Chris the notes was the most significant action she'd taken since Mr. B's death.

They were his last request of her—*I must take care of it before it's too late*, he had said. And then it was too late. He died, unaware that he'd left Rebecca with a responsibility she had no idea how to manage.

Chris's expression was impossible to decipher, maybe a hint of mild interest, but nothing more. He read both pages then reread the first.

The hot July sun pounded on her bare arms. Her skin prickled with heat and nerves. Rebecca held her breath, praying Mr. B's words would have an effect on his grandson and convince him to—to do the right thing.

Chris folded the pages. "Where'd you get this?" he asked, raising one eyebrow.

"What do you mean? I got them from your grandfather."

"Really?" He studied Rebecca's face until she squirmed. "He just handed them to you one day, like out of the blue?"

"It wasn't like that at all. Mr. B asked me if—what I mean is, well, I know he wanted me to..." her mind wandered back to the day she retrieved the papers, the precious notes that had fluttered to the floor and been stepped on like trash.

"Listen, Rebecca, you seem like a nice person, and you obviously had some kind of friendship with my grandfather. But those notes mean nothing to me. He and I had no relationship since I was a little kid, and after my mom—" he stopped and rubbed his face with both hands. "It doesn't matter. And what I just read doesn't matter."

"But it does matter. Mr. B was worried about his land."

"How am I even supposed to know he wrote this?" Chris asked, holding the papers up. "You think I remember his handwriting?"

"Do you think I'm lying?" Rebecca backed away. Doubt and uncertainty made her dizzy. The mission she'd set out to accomplish lost clarity.

"I'd be an idiot if I didn't question your motive."

Rebecca steeled herself, offended and disappointed in him. "I have no motive. Other than to finish what Mr. B wanted me to help him do." She snatched the notes from him, hands trembling. He'd not only insulted the memory of a wonderful man, he'd pretty much accused her of having a hidden agenda.

"I'm sorry, really I am." Chris took a deep breath. "But this isn't a good time for—for any of this. I've already been stuck in Clearwater longer than I was supposed to be. So, let's just end the conversation, because I've got work to do."

Rebecca clamped her jaw tight and considered Chris's perspective. Why should he believe her, a total stranger? And what made her think Mr. B's notes would matter to a grandson who hadn't seen him in nearly two decades? Her sense of purpose slipped from her grasp. Any hope of accomplishing what she'd set out to do evaporated like a single drop of water in a hot pan.

"You're right," she said. "I'm sorry I bothered you. I'll let you get back to work." She hooked Mila's leash to her collar and pulled her off the bench. "Let me know if you need anything."

"Maybe a few more towels." His attempt at a joke fell flat.

Rebecca laughed politely anyway, pretending to be the courteous, attentive, helpful guest relations specialist she was meant to be. "We have an endless supply." She turned away and hiked up the path, Mila at her heels.

CHAPTER 16

*C*hris leaned on the doorjamb and watched Rebecca walk away with his grandfather's dog. For a moment, he considered calling her back and asking if the dog could stay with him for a while. Mila reminded him of the gentle mutt he'd loved so desperately the year he lived in Clearwater, the dog his grandfather had tried to give him when his father appeared out of nowhere and reclaimed his family. The memory was seared into Chris's brain. How he'd clung to his grandfather as his father pulled him away.

Papa, don't make me go! I want to stay with you.

You must go, mi hijo. Your mother needs you.

Then he shouted at Chris's father,

At least let the boy take the dog, please let him take the dog.

But his father refused. At the time, Chris resented both his parents and his grandparents, the ones who made him leave and the ones who allowed him to go.

Why then did Rebecca's notes hit a nerve? Although he'd claimed not to recognize the handwriting, he did. It was shakier, less perfect than it used to be, but unmistakable. His grandfather had written countless letters after his father had dragged him back to Seattle. At the time, Chris held out hope of returning to Clearwater, but then his mother died, his father remarried, and his grandfather's letters ceased.

A chirp from his cell phone broke the trance. Chris returned to his make-shift desk set up on a round table in the corner of the cottage. The screen flashed at him, he hesitated, then clicked.

"Hey, Dad."

"Christopher, what the hell are you doing? I thought you would've wrapped up everything by now. And by the way, your girlfriend is not happy with you."

"Why'd you talk to Jessica?"

"She called me on her way home from the airport to tell me you hadn't returned with her."

Chris rubbed his temples. Jessica had left Clearwater in a terrible mood, angry with him for deciding to stay longer. And now she was calling his father? "It's taking more time than I thought it would. That house is loaded with stuff that I—I need to deal with."

"There is nothing of value, I assure you. That realtor, Troy something or other, said to sell it as is with everything in it. All that crap can be the buyer's problem to deal with."

"You talked to the realtor?" Chris had wanted to keep his father out of the transaction. "How did you connect with him?"

"Jessica gave me—you know what, it doesn't matter. The bottom line is you need to get the property listed and get yourself back here. We've got a meeting with the venture capital firm next week, and you have to revise our presentation. With a few million, or more than a few, from the sale of the land, we are a far better prospect now."

Chris could hear the excitement in his father's voice, his entrepreneurial juices pumping. Mitch Harrington was smart, driven, and obsessively opportunistic.

"I understand, but I have responsibilities here that—"

"No, you don't. Nothing there is your responsibility. In case you've forgotten, your grandfather abandoned you."

Chris swallowed hard. It never made sense why his grandfather had stopped writing. Why he never tried to see Chris again, especially after his mother died.

"There is nothing to keep you there, Christopher. You have no connection to that town."

"Don't I?" Chris didn't often argue with his father, but he pressed the point anyway. "Jesus, Dad, my mother is buried here. She died almost eighteen years ago, and I never even saw her grave until the other day."

Being in Clearwater brought every unanswered question back to the forefront of his mind, making him wonder what might have been.

"Listen," his father said. "I understand this is hard for you, and we can discuss it all when you get home. But right now we have a small window of opportunity with these VC guys. So you need to buck up and do your job. And I say this not as your father but as your boss."

Chris clenched his jaw. "Got it." He ended the call without waiting for a response.

CHAPTER 17

*R*ebecca knelt in the cool grass beside Mr. B's grave and arranged fresh daisies in the flower holders on Antonia's and Josephina's headstones. Mila wandered and sniffed before turning in a few circles and settling herself on the ground where her master was buried. Someone, the cemetery caretaker most likely, had placed a wooden cross with Mr. B's name on it where his headstone would eventually go.

Rebecca scattered daisy petals around it.

"I'm sorry I failed you." She wiped her eyes in the crook of her arm. Over the past twenty-four hours, Rebecca had ruminated on her conversation with Chris nonstop, wondering how it all went so wrong. If she'd typed up the notes before presenting them to him, perhaps they would have looked more official. Although she doubted it would've changed his mind.

Rebecca drew her knees into her chest and wrapped her arms around her legs, wondering why Mr. B and his grandson, who seemed to be a pretty good guy, had been estranged. And now it was too late—too late for them to reconcile, too late for Mr. B to change his will, and too late for Rebecca to make a difference.

The property, the vineyards, the beautiful view of lake—everything Mr. B had cherished—would be sold to the highest bidder. Chris and Jessica would walk away with millions, Troy Dayton would earn his big fat commission, and some developer would build a horrible condominium complex that would change Clearwater forever.

Rebecca stood. She kissed her fingertips and touched them to the cross. "I can't find a reason to keep going," she said to him. "I've done everything I could, but I think I have to move on." *Moving on*, she thought. A euphemism for giving up.

That evening, Rebecca curled up on the couch with her head in her mother's lap and released every last bit of pent up emotion and regret.

Alice stroked her hair and uttered vague assurances that everything would be okay.

Finally, Rebecca raised her head. "I'm done crying."

Mila, who had been watching with concern, licked her cheeks and chin.

"Are you sure?" Alice asked. "You know you can cry on my lap as long as you want."

"I know." Rebecca dragged her sleeve under her nose and sniffled. "But I'm hungry."

"Let's have dinner, then. You can always cry more later."

Alice microwaved some leftover spaghetti and meatballs, and Rebecca made a salad. Together they sat at the kitchen table.

"You know," her mother said. "I think Mr. B would've been proud of you for trying."

"Maybe. Either way, there's nothing I can do about it now." Rebecca twirled her spaghetti noodles round and round until she had a golf ball sized bite on her fork. Another round of tears threatened to erupt, but she swallowed them along with the giant bite of spaghetti.

THE CLEARWATER LIBRARY sat adjacent to the old Mayfair hotel, a two-story, southern style house across the street from Town Square Park. The library was a mini version of the hotel, like a little sister, with the same white wood siding, double-hung windows, wide porch across the front.

Rebecca, who had just finished several hours of walking dogs in blistering heat, walked into the air-conditioned building. She lifted her braid to feel the cool air on the back of her neck and dropped her mother's library books in the return bin in the foyer.

"Hi, Mrs. Larson," she said.

The librarian, a stylish older woman with purple glasses and magenta lipstick, smiled broadly. "Rebecca, how nice to see you."

"You, too.

"I don't think I've seen you since Benito's funeral last week."

Rebecca's mind drifted. Only one week since Mr. B was buried, and not even two weeks since he died, but it felt like a lifetime.

"It was a lovely service," Mrs. Larson said. "And that reception at the park afterwards was especially nice."

"It was." Rebecca nodded politely. She didn't have the time or desire to talk about the funeral. "I'm just on my way to—"

"And I'm so grateful Benito came by the library. We had a nice little chat."

Rebecca paused. "When did you see him?"

"A day or two before he died. He was doing some research into the town charter."

"I didn't know we had a town charter," Rebecca said, her curiosity piqued.

"Of course we do. It's sort of like a miniature constitution. Benito was interested in some old ordinances. Small towns have all kinds of rules and regulations, although most of them are never enforced. However when it comes to the library, we have very strict—"

"Sorry to interrupt, but did he find what he was looking for?"

"I'm not sure." The librarian reached for a volume on the shelf behind her desk and hoisted it onto the counter.

The title on the worn cover read: *Clearwater Town Charter—history, laws, codes, ordinances, and rules for a Cohesive Community*

"That's quite a title," Rebecca said. "And it looks ancient."

"Well, the town was established back in the nineteen-thirties." Mrs. Larson removed her glasses and wiped the lenses with a cloth. "Anyway, I photocopied a few pages for him. That was it."

"Do you know which ones you copied?"

"No, dear." Mrs. Larson fanned the delicate pages. "All I remember is that they were in the section on *Land Usage.*"

Rebecca vacillated. Mr. B's notes had been put to rest, thanks to his grandson's lack of interest, but the possibility of new information was impossible to ignore. "Can I check the book out?" Rebecca asked.

"I'm afraid not. We don't lend reference books. One of those annoying rules. But you can sit here and read it." Mrs. Larson pointed to a heavy wooden conference table. "That's what Benito did. And he seemed quite riveted."

Rebecca tapped her fingers on the counter, contemplating. "I don't have time now, but maybe I'll come back later."

"The Charter will be here. It always is." The librarian placed the book back on the shelf. "Do you have any idea why this subject mattered to him?"

Rebecca hesitated. Mrs. Larson, although well-meaning, knew everyone in town and was not known for her discretion.

"Not really, " Rebecca said with a noncommittal shoulder lift. "But I—I did a little work for Mr. B from time to time, some clerical stuff. No big deal, but I still need to help tie up a few loose ends."

Mrs. Larson flashed a knowing glance. "I see. This wouldn't have anything to do with that handsome grandson of his, would it?"

"Excuse me?"

"His grandson, Chris. I saw you talking to him after the funeral." Mrs. Larson pushed her round rimmed glasses up on her prominent nose. "My goodness, I hadn't seen that boy in ages."

"You knew him?"

"Well, sort of. I certainly knew his grandmother. She and I were quite friendly. We used to take needlepoint lessons together. Such a lovely woman. Did you ever meet her?"

Rebecca shook her head. "No, she died around the time my mom and I moved here."

"Too bad." Mrs. Larson tsk-tsked. "Antonia was one of the sweetest people I ever met. And oh, did she love her daughter and grandson. Shame how all that ended up."

Rebecca's eyes widened. The chatty librarian had turned out to be a treasure trove of information. "Mr. B didn't talk about them much," she said, feigning only mild interest. "I did hear that Chris, um, his grandson, lived in Clearwater for a while."

"He did indeed. Had to be almost…" she twisted her mouth to the side. "Maybe twenty years ago, give or take."

Their eyes met, and Rebecca could tell Mrs. Larson wanted to keep going, but she needed a little prodding.

"I've actually gotten to know Chris a little bit."

"Uh-huh," Mrs. Larson said with a sidelong glance. "Is there something romantic budding between—"

"Oh gosh no! Of course not, I hardly know him at all. Besides, he has a gorgeous girlfriend." Rebecca's denial sounded defensive even to her.

Mrs. Larson leaned over the counter. "That doesn't surprise

me. His father had a weakness for beautiful women, too. In fact, that's the reason Antonia's daughter came back to Clearwater with her young son—her husband's infidelity."

Rebecca caught her breath. "Seriously? Did Mr. B know about it?"

"Did he know? Oh my, yes, he knew. And he was livid."

"Sounds terrible." Rebecca could only imagine how her friend who valued honor and integrity above all else must have reacted to the betrayal.

"Terrible, indeed." Mrs. Larson threw her hands out to the side. "And then, when his daughter went back to her husband the whole family fell apart. Apparently, Benito told her that if she took back that lying, cheating scumbag of a husband, she was no longer welcome in his home."

Rebecca's knees nearly buckled. The Mr. B she knew would never have cut his daughter, his only child, out of his life. "I can't believe that. Are you sure?"

"Am I sure? Not entirely, and it was a long time ago." Mrs. Larson looked around the library as if someone might be eaves-dropping, which was silly because they were the only two there. "I hate to speak ill of the dead, but I heard it was Benito's temper that drove his Josephina away. Poor Antonia, she never saw her daughter or grandson again."

CHAPTER 18

"*I* need to talk to Nonna," Rebecca charged into Mariano's. "Do you know where she is?"

Tessa looked up from her computer. "Good afternoon to you, too."

"Sorry, hi." Rebecca tucked her backpack under the counter. "You can't believe how much Mrs. Larson knows. She must see and hear everything around here."

"Who are you talking about?" Patty came through the swinging door from the storeroom.

"The librarian," Rebecca said.

"Oh yeah, she's like the clearing house of gossip for this town," Patty said. "When I moved here a few years ago, she knew things about me even before I did."

Tessa laughed. "It's true. But you won't get any gossip out of my grandmother. Nonna is the epitome of discretion."

"I'm not looking for gossip," Rebecca said. "Just, well, confirmation. Mrs. Larson told me some stuff about Mr. B I can't believe, that I don't want to believe."

"Okay," Patty said. "Spill it."

Rebecca gave them a brief rundown of what Mrs. Larson had said. "I never once saw Mr. B lose his temper, except maybe with the realtor he couldn't stand."

"If there's one thing I've learned in my almost forty-four years," Tessa said, "it's that we never know what goes on in other families. And keep in mind, Rebecca, Mrs. Larson was talking about something that happened long before you met Benito. He might have been a different man back then."

"I guess." Rebecca had to sit on that thought for a while. If he had ever been anything less than wonderful, she didn't want to know it.

"I have to go meet a client," Tessa said. "But first I'll check to see where my grandmother is. It looked like she was heading this way about an hour ago." She tapped the screen on her cell phone.

"You track her phone?" Rebecca was impressed and surprised.

"Of course I do. What kind of granddaughter would I be if I didn't know where my eighty-seven year old grandmother was every minute?" Tessa studied the screen. "Hmm, looks like she's at Nutmegs."

"Aren't you clever," Patty said.

"That I am." Tessa tapped again. "And now she's on the move heading in this direction."

Patty grabbed Tessa's phone. "Boy, for an old lady she moves fast."

The three of them watched the little blue dot move on the map as Nonna made her way down Main Street. It landed at Betsy's Blooms a few doors from Mariano's.

"Without a doubt, she'll come here next," said Tessa. "See you girls in a bit."

After Tessa left, Rebecca put on her apron and went to work unpacking and shelving expensive Manuka honey from New

Zealand. Every few minutes she opened the door and glanced toward the flower shop to see if Nonna was on her way.

Patty poked her on the shoulder. "Go," she said.

"Go where?"

"To find Nonna. It's making me crazy that you keep opening the door and jingling the bell. Just hurry back."

"Thanks. I'll make it quick, I promise."

Rebecca jogged down the street, hopeful Nonna hadn't relocated in the last few minutes, and rushed into Betsy's Blooms. The flowery perfume permeated her nose. She sneezed twice.

"Rebecca, hello." Nonna held a bouquet of pink peonies and white roses.

"Hi, Nonna," Rebecca said, wrapping her long arms around Tessa's grandmother. "Where's Betsy?"

"She stepped out for a coffee. Told her I'd hold down the fort for a few minutes. Are you here to buy flowers?"

"No, I'm here to see you."

"How lovely." Nonna set her flowers on a sheet of newspaper. "How did you know where to find me?"

"Oh, um, I just saw—"

"Tessa's tracking my phone, isn't she?"

Rebecca quelled. "Maybe?"

Nonna laughed. "It's no secret dear, and I think it's sweet she likes to keep track of me. So, what might I do for you?"

"I have some questions about—about Mr. B."

"That's intriguing." Nonna rested a warm hand on her arm. "I'll certainly help, if I can."

Rebecca repeated the story she'd heard from Mrs. Larson. When she finished, she sucked in a big breath of air. "I didn't even know Mr. B had a grandson until the day of his funeral. I told him everything about my life, my parents' divorce and my insecurities and how shy I was at school..." she stopped and pressed her hands against her eyes to keep the tears at bay. "But he never mentioned his grandson."

"Perhaps it was just too painful for him," Nonna said.

"You don't really think he drove his daughter away, do you? Maybe Mrs. Larson was wrong about that. I mean, you know what a gossip she is."

"It's possible—our lovely librarian has never met a rumor she didn't want to repeat." Nonna clasped one of Rebecca's hands between both of hers. "What I do know is that Benito was not one to dredge up the past. Antonia was my friend for many years, and she didn't share much about their family troubles either. Regardless of that, I'm certain they both loved their daughter and grandson desperately. All those years ago, when Josephina returned to Clearwater with her son, Benito and Antonia were as happy as I'd ever seen them. And that little boy worshipped his grandpa. They were inseparable."

Rebecca struggled to make sense of it. The man she knew would have moved heaven and earth for his family. It pained her to imagine they'd had a terrible falling out and never made amends. "Nonna, I hate to ask, but do you know how Josephina died?"

"An accident." Nonna's lips tightened. "A senseless car accident. It was tragic."

Rebecca recalled the dates engraved on Josephina's headstone—Mr. B's daughter had been only forty-four, the same age Tessa was now. "But why is she buried here in Clearwater then? I mean, if they were estranged how did that even happen?"

A sad smile spread across Nonna's face. "That, my dear, remains a mystery. Somehow Benito brought his daughter home. I still recall Antonia telling me how grateful she was that when the time came, she would rest beside her daughter. It brought her a sense of peace."

Nonna turned silent for a moment. She took a quivery breath. "And then she never talked about it again, not even to me, a mother who had suffered the same loss." Her eyes filled with tears. Nonna's own daughter had passed away following a long illness when Tessa was a little girl.

"I'm sorry, Nonna," Rebecca said, holding back her own emotions. "I didn't mean to make you sad."

"Don't apologize, my dear. It's not like I don't think about my daughter every day. Although over the years I've come to recall the happier memories, which is part of healing, I suppose."

Rebecca nodded, hopeful her happy memories of Mr. B would eventually diminish the pain she felt now.

"One time," Nonna said, frowning as if conjuring up an old thought, "Antonia and I were on one of our long walks, and I asked how Benito was. I wasn't expecting a confession of any kind. But Antonia confided in me how worried she was. Said he'd fallen into a very dark place."

"That's awful," Rebecca said. "It breaks my heart to think about him being so sad."

"Sad, indeed. More than sad. He'd lost all hope for a while."

"Because Josephina died?"

"Yes, but I think it was losing contact with his grandson that truly broke him."

The puzzle pieces scattered in Rebecca's mind. "No matter how upset Mr. B was with his daughter, I don't think he would've cut off his grandson."

"Families can be complicated, and relationships can be damaged beyond repair. Maybe he did try to make amends, but to no avail." Nonna focused on the flowers she'd been arranging. She stroked a white rose with one finger. "All I know is that the two of them visited their daughter's grave every Sunday after church. Antonia had an abiding faith in God and in the belief that she and her daughter would reunite in heaven."

Rebecca reached for Nonna's hand. "Do you believe that, too? That souls can find each other after death?"

"I do, my dear." Nonna lifted her chin. "I have to believe that. Otherwise, loss is too hard to bear."

Rebecca turned, and her eyes fell upon a bucket of daisies. She imagined Mr. B and his wife bringing flowers to their daughter's resting place year after year. And now, the three of them together for eternity.

CHAPTER 19

*B*etween the news about Mr. B investigating the town charter and the heartrending story of his daughter's death, Rebecca was in a tailspin. The flow of information came at her from a faucet that went on and off, forcing her to reconsider her decision to move on.

Rebecca tried to find some semblance of equilibrium. Chris Harrington had checked out of the inn that morning without notice. He'd left his key in an envelope and dropped it through the mail slot. With it was a quick note scribbled on the back of his business card.

Rebecca, thanks for all the extra towels (happy face). See ya next time.

"What does 'see ya next time' even mean?" she asked Zack. "Did he book another reservation?"

"No. And it doesn't mean anything." Zack dusted a display of local winery wines. "It's like 'catch ya later' or 'take care' or 'gotta run' or—"

"Okay, I get it. Means nothing. But what about the happy

face, don't you think that's kind of a cute way of…" Rebecca glanced at Zack's blank face.

"Why do girls always read so much into things? Must be exhausting to think so much."

Exhausting, indeed. Still, Chris did take the time to pen the short, sweet note. And that had to mean something.

"I guess," Rebecca said, deflating.

"Oh no, you have a crush on him." Zack wagged his head. "Don't deny it. I've got four sisters, and I can spot a girl with a crush a mile away."

"Four sisters?"

"Yes, four, and every one of them is a hopeless romantic. I might be younger than you, but I know women."

"You do, huh?" His claim made her laugh.

"You bet I do. And don't forget Chris Harrington's got a freakin' hot girlfriend. I checked her out on Instagram and TicToc. Whoa. She's got this one reel where—"

"Stop!" Rebecca threw her hands up. "I get it. Jessica the party-planning, flower-arranging influencer is way more exciting than I could ever hope to be."

Zack put his palms up. "Don't flip out."

"I'm not," Rebecca said. "I'm—oh, never mind. But for what it's worth, I do not have a crush. Not even the least little bit. It's just that he's nice, and he kind of reminds me of Mr. B."

"That's actually sweet. But I still think you have a crush on him."

"Think whatever you want." Rebecca tucked Chris's business card in her overalls pocket. A crush on Chris Harrington? Ridiculous.

THAT SUNDAY, four days after Chris checked out of the inn, Rebecca drove to Mr. B's house to see if she could find the pages he'd copied from the town charter. Maybe she could figure out if he was on to something. Or better yet, confirm that he wasn't. Putting the matter to rest once and for all would allow her to move on with a clear conscience.

At the kitchen door, Mila charged into the house, dashing from room to room as if certain she'd find her beloved master hiding somewhere. It had been two weeks and two days—not nearly long enough for a dog as smart and devoted as Mila to forget.

Rebecca raised the windows to let in some fresh air. The house was hot and musty. Gone was the homey smell of cinnamon toast.

She opened the refrigerator, releasing the odor of spoiled food.

"Oh, yuck." Rebecca grabbed a trash bag and cleared the shelves then washed every surface inside and out with hot soapy water. Immediately, the house smelled fresher. On a roll, Rebecca swept the kitchen floor, dusted the table, and wiped down the countertops.

Mila wandered back into the kitchen, obviously disappointed. She settled herself under the kitchen table and drifted off like she'd done a million times before.

"You sweet girl," Rebecca said, patting Mila's warm head.

She was about to start clearing the pantry when the front door opened. Mila lifted her head and tilted it to the side. Then, heavy footsteps on the hardwood floor. Who would just walk into Mr. B's house without knocking? Mila rose slowly, her entire body on alert.

"Anyone here?" A male voice, inquisitive yet commanding.

Mila shot out of the kitchen, barking and growling at the same time.

"Whoa, hey, get back, you dirty mongrel!"

Rebecca ran toward the melee and released a high-pitched

whistle like Mr. B used to do. Mila halted. Her frantic barks quieted.

"Is that your dog?" A man with fair hair and piercing blue eyes stood behind the coat rack by the door. "What a menace."

"She's just protecting her house," Rebecca said.

"Her house?" The man stepped away from the coat rack but lingered close to the door. "What do you mean? This house is empty, or at least it's supposed to be. Mind telling me who you are?"

With no context or any idea who the stranger was, Rebecca hesitated, wondering how she'd explain her presence. Maybe he was another realtor. Or even more likely, Troy Dayton's client.

"I'm—I'm Mr. B's housekeeper." It wasn't a total lie considering she believed it was her responsibility to keep the house safe, and that, at least in part, justified the title of *housekeeper.*

"Mr. B? You mean Mr. Becerra. You do know he died, don't you?"

"Uh, yeah, I heard that. But he paid me in advance, so I figured I should still show up." Rebecca hoped the explanation would avoid a trespassing charge.

The man laughed. "Isn't that responsible of you. Very upstanding and honest."

They stared at each other a moment. In a timid voice, Rebecca asked, "Are you an old friend or something?"

The man cocked his head. "I'm Benito's son-in-law."

"Son-in-law?"

"That's what I said, yes. And I'm here to help my son untangle the disaster his grandfather left him." He said it as if he'd flown in like a super hero.

Rebecca pondered as puzzle pieces fell into place. He was Chris's father, Josephina's husband, the man Mr. B couldn't stand because he was a lying, cheating philanderer who tore apart the family. Rebecca wanted to tell him what a despicable cad he was and kick him out the door, but all she could do was utter a quiet, "Oh."

Again they eyed each other. She suspected that getting on this man's bad side would be a terrible idea.

"I met Chris when he was here for the funeral. And I—I just want to do what I can to help because, well, Mr. B was a friend of mine."

"I take it that's his dog." Mr. Harrington scowled in Mila's direction. "Benito always had an attraction to ugly mutts."

Rebecca clenched her fists behind her back. Calling Mila an ugly mutt was not only rude and offensive, it was incorrect. "Mila is actually a beautiful blend," she said politely. "And extremely smart."

As if aware they were talking about her, Mila approached Mr. Harrington, the hair on her back standing straight up. A low growl from deep within her throat sounded.

"Back, Mila," Rebecca commanded, and the dog retreated. "Anyway, I just was cleaning the kitchen."

"And I'm just checking things out. I haven't been in Clearwater since, well, in a very long time."

Rebecca wondered if he was going to visit his wife's grave while he was in town. "Did Chris come with you?"

"He'll be here." Mr. Harrington took a seat in Mr. B's recliner and crossed his legs.

Seeing the shifty son-in-law in Mr. B's chair irked Rebecca. If she could have pressed an ejection button to toss him into the air, she would have. But the awkward encounter presented an opportunity. Mr. Harrington might be a wealth of information. She tried to come up with a vague topic, perhaps about when he was last in Clearwater, but her rumination halted when the front door opened and Chris walked in.

Rebecca's heart did a little flip-flop. She took a closer look at his face. His features were a perfect combination of his grandfather's complexion and beautiful smile set into his father's chiseled bones, as if an artist had been commissioned to paint a handsome man and Chris's face was the finished product.

"Hey, Dad."

Mila scampered over to greet him. Chris knelt and petted the dog as she licked his face. "Hello, girl."

"Look at you," Mr. Harrington said. "Best friends with your grandfather's dog once again."

That was an interesting tidbit, especially Mr. Harrington's condescending tone.

Chris rose, unamused by his father's quip. "Rebecca, hi, I didn't see you there."

"Hi," she said, tapping her fingers on the back of a dining room chair. "Yeah, I was just doing some cleaning."

"How about that?" said Mr. Harrington. "Not like your grandfather to hire himself a cute, little housekeeper."

Ordinarily, being referred to as "cute and little" would have pleased her, but not the way Mr. Harrington said it.

"Housekeeper?" Chris cocked his head.

Rebecca pulled her braid over her shoulder and twirled the end with feverish speed. "I thought I told you that."

"Not exactly," Chris said.

"Evidently," Mr. Harrington said, "she's been prepaid for cleaning services."

Rebecca stammered an explanation. "The truth is, I helped Mr. B out with anything he needed, sort of like a personal assistant. And therefore I did stuff around the house. He had a cleaning service that came in once a month but I sometimes cleaned in between." Yeah, that was definitely a stretch. Rebecca justified the story to herself by recalling how they'd wash dishes together after sharing a meal or snack. "I came today to check on things and found there was some spoiled food in the refrigerator. So I thought it would be nice if I cleared it out and—"

"Rebecca, it's okay," Chris interrupted. "Just go ahead do what you need to do. Or want to do."

"Oh, okay then. I'll be in the kitchen." Rebecca started to leave but then turned back to him. "Are you, were you, um, staying here? Or do you need a room at the inn?"

"The inn?" Mr. Harrington asked. "You mean the place Jessica was talking about?"

At the mention of Chris's girlfriend, Rebecca wondered if she'd be showing up, too.

"Rebecca works at the—actually, Dad, don't worry about it." Chris turned back to her. "I'm not sure of my plans, yet."

"Okay, well, let me know." Rebecca backed into the kitchen, taking Mila with her.

To stick with her story, she had to keep cleaning the kitchen. Quickly too, because Curly was expecting a walk, and three other dogs were on the schedule.

As she cleared the pantry shelves, Rebecca strained to hear the conversation between Chris and his father. She only picked up a few snippets about the worn out furniture, all the clutter, and the hall closet full of boxes and moth-eaten coats.

Throughout the process, Mila marched back and forth as if supervising the activity.

Rebecca needed a better vantage point to see and hear. She moved from the kitchen into the dining room adjacent to the living room and started dusting the china cabinet.

"You don't need to bother with any of this crap," Mr. Harrington said to Chris. "Let the wrecking ball do the work."

Rebecca dropped a china cup. It shattered on the hard floor. "Oh my God, I'm sorry."

"Who cares?" Mr. Harrington gestured toward the broken china with a careless wave. "See that Chris—just let everything go."

"I don't know, Dad. What if there's something of value here?"

"The only thing of value your grandfather ever owned is this land." Mr. Harrington's tone was sharp. "And your grandmother collected junk."

Rebecca choked. The teacup she'd just broken was bone china from England. There was an entire collection of delicate cups and saucers as well as teapots, cookie platters, and dessert sets. "This isn't junk," she said under her breath, unable to resist defending Antonia's taste. Rebecca felt an odd kinship with the woman she'd never known. If Mr. B loved Antonia, then Rebecca loved her, too.

"Excuse me?" Mr. Harrington said. "Did you say something, Rebecca?"

"No, well, yes, it's just that..." she hadn't meant for him to hear her. "These dishes are beautiful and most likely antiques."

"Is that so? Do you have some expert knowledge when it comes to antiques?"

"Leave it alone, Dad." Chris moved closer to his father, almost as tall but not quite. "She's just trying to help."

Rebecca appreciated Chris's intervention. Despite her best efforts, she and Mr. Harrington had gotten off on the wrong foot.

"I don't know much about antiques, sir. But I have seen china like this in second-hand shops. All I'm saying is that it's not junk." Rebecca never stood up to authority figures. But speaking the truth, even if it was about something as minor as dishware, gave her a momentary flutter of confidence. "If nothing else, donating it to the charity store is better than letting it get smashed by a wrecking ball."

Mr. Harrington's eyebrows came together. "You do seem to be in the know about places around here. Maybe you'd like to help out."

"Dad, what are you talking about?" Chris asked, an edge in his voice.

"Take it easy, son. Clearly, your friend here is a hard worker."

Rebecca cringed at the way he said *friend,* emphasizing the word with heavy sarcasm.

"And seeing how she's familiar with Benito's house, she could do the work you're too busy to do." Mr. Harrington talked about her as if she weren't there. "We need to get going on this Chris. The property has to be sold and the money transferred into the business. We're running out of time."

CHAPTER 20

*M*r. Harrington hired Rebecca on the spot, instructing her to pack up the house, take anything she thought might be of value to the antique store, and deliver everything else to the charity shop or to the dump.

Rebecca considered it a win-win. Not only would she be paid for her time, she'd also be able to insure Antonia's possessions would be handled with respect, reverence even. Besides, what a waste it would be to demolish everything in the house with total disregard for people who could use a set of dishes or an old kitchen table.

The following day at the shelter, Rebecca told Willy about her new temporary assignment. Her initial enthusiasm for the project had waned as doubt in her ability to accomplish what she'd agreed to do set in.

"I might have over-promised," Rebecca said. "Do you think so?"

"Probably." Willy handed her a squirmy puppy in need of a bath. "You tend to do that."

"I do, don't I?" Rebecca said, wrangling the puppy under her arm.

"Yup. But I think you're doing a good deed seeing to it that the Becerra family treasures don't end up in a pile of construction waste."

Treasures, Rebecca thought. Yes, that house was full of treasures and the hidden story of a family that once upon a time had been happy.

"And geez-louise," Willy said. "Makes me livid when people disregard perfectly good housewares and treat them like trash. Not to mention how damaging it is to the environment. Did you know that landfills across the country are—"

"I totally agree." Rebecca interrupted Willy's rant. Whenever he got on his soapbox about an issue, he didn't stop. "Hey, maybe we could organize a yard sale and make it a fundraiser for the animal shelter."

"A fundraiser? That's a great idea. Anything you do to raise money for the shelter will be much appreciated." He gave her shoulders a squeeze. "That's some real initiative on your part."

She noted that her "we" turned into Willy's "you." As if she didn't already have a million things to do. But a twinge of pride boosted her confidence.

The puppy licked her chin. "I'd better get this little guy bathed before his new owners show up."

"Be quick," Willy said, pointing at her. "They'll be here in twenty minutes, and you're a slow bather."

Rebecca shrugged off the comment—that was Willy, always a bit of a grumbler.

She carried the adorable black and white mutt across the barn and ran warm water into the oversized sink. Although she'd regretted cutting back her hours at the shelter, Rebecca had no choice. Willy could barely afford to pay her minimum wage, while she made twenty dollars an hour for dog walks.

As far back as she could remember, making money had been a priority. When she and her mother moved to Clearwater, they'd been on the verge of homelessness. And while she worried and fretted, her mother stuck by the old adage: *It'll all work out, it always does.* At least that's what she said most of the time. Still, her optimism, on occasion, suffered from periods of doubt.

It had taken months for Rebecca to relax after they'd settled into their new town and cozy cottage. At one point, her mother suggested she should be hypnotized out of her anxiety. But time and calm and a rigid work schedule seemed to be the cure.

Still, however, at Rebecca's core, a persistent fear lay buried. And when Mr. B died, it flared like a flame hit with lighter fluid, reminding her of the instability of her teen years.

As she shampooed the little dog and tried to keep him from eating the lather, her mind filled with worries—everything from her dependence on her mother and the free housing the inn provided to whether or not she'd be able to fulfill her promise to Chris's father that clearing out the house would be a *piece of cake.*

Why didn't she just keep her mouth shut?

It was easy to be a follower, to have someone else tell her what needed to be done. That's what she liked about working at Mariano's—Patty and Tessa told her what to do, and she just did it. Even at the inn, she mostly followed her mother's instructions. And dog walking was easy, because dogs were dogs, and they all loved her no matter what.

Rebecca scrubbed the little pup until he disappeared inside a mound of suds and lather. Under a gentle spray of water, the dog's shiny, sleek coat emerged, reminding Rebecca of Mila. It was a beautiful thing when something that at first appeared hopeless and worthless turned out to be precious beyond measure.

Perhaps some of Antonia's collectibles would turn out to be hidden treasures. And just like that, Rebecca's resolve to make something from nothing returned.

~

"You what?" Alice dropped a scoop of tuna-noodle casserole on Rebecca's plate. "How on earth do you have time for a project like that? You already work twelve hour days."

"I'll do it at night and—and on the weekends." Rebecca rubbed her eyes. "I can fit it in." Once again, doubt blew in like a cold wind, putting a damper on the motivation she'd felt earlier.

"Weekends?" her mother said, feeding Mila a piece of noodle. "You work at Mariano's on the weekends."

"I'll manage, okay?" Rebecca snapped at her mother. "And please don't feed Mila from the table. You're undoing all of Mr. B's training."

Alice's lips formed a tight line. "You've been very testy lately."

Rebecca hunched over the table and ate a bite of gooey casserole. Her mother was not the greatest cook, but she did know her way around any dish that featured noodles. "I'm sorry, I'm very stressed. Maybe I did take on too much. But now that I agreed to do the job, I have to do it. Besides, I want to." She pictured a giant earth-mover scooping up massive amounts of debris containing everything that ever mattered to Mr. B and his wife.

"I understand." Alice said in a soft voice. She rested a hand on her daughter's wrist. "How much will they pay you?"

Rebecca glanced up. Was this one of her rare pessimistic moments?

"You're sending mixed signals again, Mom. First you're worried I'm working too much and now you're wondering how much money I'll make?"

Alice lowered her chin and nibbled a bite of noodles. "I know. I think I caught anxiety from you."

"Please don't tell me your carefree spirt is waning." Rebecca studied her mother's eyes, searching for reassurance. "I really do count on it."

"Of course not. I'm just over-thinking is all."

"Oh-oh," Rebecca said. Her mother over-thinking always spelled trouble. "What about?"

"It's nothing," said Alice, infusing her voice with false peppiness. "Well, not nothing, but probably nothing *much*. Forget I said anything."

Rebecca wanted to shake the information out of her. "Now you're really making me nervous. What is it?"

Alice huffed. "I was at the library the other day, and the knitting ladies were there talking like it wasn't a library at all. Very loudly, which is rather rude in a library."

"Please get to the point. What did you overhear?"

"One of them said there's a large hotel chain interested in building a resort on Mr. B's property."

"Yeah, well, I heard it could be condominiums, but what difference does it make? Either way, it goes against everything Mr. B wanted." Rebecca ate a large forkful of casserole, which was getting cold and clumpy.

"The difference is that a hotel could put our little inn right out of business."

Rebecca put a hand over her mouth and forced herself to swallow. "That would be terrible. I mean, what would we do? Where would we go?"

"Now you're overthinking." Alice offered a half-hearted, one-shouldered shrug. "It probably won't happen, and if it did it would take years to build."

"I guess." Rebecca pictured a bulldozer plowing through Mr. B's house, cement trucks and earth movers rolling up his driveway.

Alice flipped back to her optimistic self. "Cheer up, honey, no matter what happens we'll figure something out. We always do. Just have to hope for the best—"

"And plan for the worst," Rebecca said, finishing her mother's oft-used quip. She glanced at Mila snoozing in the window seat of their cozy cottage. For the first time ever, her mother had a job she loved and one she wanted to keep. But Lakeview Lodge was more than a job—it was their home. A new and even larger worry sent a chill through Rebecca's body.

The death of her friend had unleashed a tsunami of potential disasters, not only for Clearwater but now, it seemed, for her and her mother as well.

CHAPTER 21

On Saturday morning, Rebecca sat at a table outside of Nutmegs eating a sticky bun, or trying to. Her favorite food in the world stuck in her throat. After the conversation with her mother a few days earlier, her stomach had been twisted in knots. The prospect of change and the possibility of having to move had sent her anxiety soaring. Now, making and saving money was more critical than ever.

Rebecca shed her sweatshirt. The sunscreen she'd slathered on her fair skin carried the scent of the ocean, reminding Rebecca of the beach where she and her mother lived the summer after her parents divorced. They'd stayed in a tiny guest house owned by one of Alice's old friends.

It had been an idyllic few months as mother and daughter embarked upon the next phase of their lives, tightly bound by the reality that they only had each other. It was a summer Rebecca hoped would last forever, but of course it had to end. Alice and Rebecca packed their bags and entered a phase in which they never fully unpacked, literally or figuratively.

Rebecca never put down roots. How could she when those roots would be severed at any moment. She lived her teen years under a cloud of uncertainty and no sense of continuity. Her mother was the only constant in her life. Was it any wonder they were so attached?

The sun bathed her face. Rebecca closed her eyes, letting its warmth soothe her frazzled nerves, if only for a moment

A light touch on her shoulder made her bolt upright.

"I didn't wake you, did I?" Chris Harrington stood over her with a cup of coffee and a pink bakery box.

"Oh, no, I wasn't sleeping. I was just—just thinking." She dusted crumbs from her hands.

"May I join you?" He gestured toward the empty chair.

Rebecca had never seen him dressed so casually—shorts, t-shirt, flip-flops, like a guy on his way to the lake to go fishing.

"Oh, yeah, sure," she said, smoothing her curly hair which was unfortunately out of control, curls shooting in all directions. "I thought you went back to Seattle."

"I did, but then, well, some stuff happened, so I—I decided to come back here."

Well, that was vague and completely uninformative. Rebecca hadn't forgotten Mr. Harrington's admonition that they needed money asap. And evidently, a lot of it. A few million from the sale of a property, especially one that inspired no emotional attachment, was quite the lucky break.

"What happened?" Rebecca asked. The question had popped out of her without any thought to how intrusiveness it might be. "I'm sorry. That's totally none of my business. I didn't mean to ask. It just, well, you said something happened, and I thought it might…"

"It's okay. I'm pretty upfront with things. I figure if I'm not doing anything wrong, I got nothing to hide."

Rebecca's mind drifted. Mr. B had said something similar. Maybe that was why he never talked about his daughter—because his temper had driven her away, breaking Antonia's heart. And it shamed him.

"My dad and I had a big argument over how I'm handling things." He took a deep breath and crossed his tanned, muscular legs. "And that led to an argument with Jessica, because she thinks I'm dragging my feet."

"Are you?" Rebecca asked, hoping it was so. The more time he took, they more breathing room she had.

"No. I'm just being cautious, but some people mistake that for weakness. My dad makes decisions fast and never looks back, regardless of whether the decision is good or not. Somehow that works for him." Chris took a breath. "Even if he has to ram it down throats."

"Hmm, and he seems like such a nice guy." Rebecca didn't even try to hide her sarcasm.

Chris grinned at her. "You're a funny one. He is smart though, that's for sure. We're in business together—a software development company. We've been trying to raise capital to expand." He frowned, as if he were deep in thought. "This inheritance came along at the right time. It's a real game-changer for us."

Rebecca sensed those were Mr. Harrington's words, not his.

She pressed her lips together, thinking about Mr. B's useless notes stuffed in her dresser drawer and her inability to fulfill what had been his dying wish. All that money from the sale of his land invested in software development. Hardly the legacy Mr. B wanted to leave behind.

The subject annoyed her, a cruel reminder of how she'd failed her mission. "I, I've gotta go."

"You haven't even finished your sticky bun," Chris said with a faint note of disappointment.

"I have to meet a client at nine." She glanced at her watch.

"A client? What kind of clients do you have?"

Rebecca couldn't help laughing at herself. "The four-legged kind."

He grinned. "Animals are your clients?"

"Yep. I'm a dog walker, in addition to all the other stuff I do."

"Like working at Mariano's and at the inn with your mom. Oh, and you're a housekeeper, too." His brown eyes crinkled around the edges.

"I'm not really a housekeeper," she said, dipping her chin into her chest. "I kind of made that up on the fly."

"I thought you might have."

"Did you tell your dad? I'd hate for him to think I'm a liar. Although I wasn't really lying, not exactly."

"It's okay." Chris leaned back. "My father's opinion isn't all that important."

Rebecca gave him sideways glance. "That sounds kind of weird. You don't care what your dad thinks?"

"It depends on the subject." Chris lifted the plastic lid on his coffee cup and took a sip. "You remember I told you my mom and I lived in Clearwater when I was a kid?"

Rebecca nodded, her attentiveness heightened.

"I was maybe ten or eleven. We were here at least a year, and I went to school, fifth grade, I think. Anyway, I loved that old house. I used to hide in little nooks and closets, especially under the stairs. I kept a flashlight and pillows in there. It was my secret fort."

Rebecca pictured the cubby hole Mr. B had turned into a cozy bedroom for Mila when he'd first rescued her. The small space was stuffed with old blankets, creating a warm, safe sanctuary for the shy dog recovering from mange and starvation.

"It was a rough time. My parents had separated after my dad —well, after he cheated on my mom." His laugh was bitter. "What kid wants to think about that, right? Anyway, my grandparents' house was a haven for me. I'd forgotten about that until—until now. Being there actually brings back some good memories."

A flock of birds flew overhead, squawking, and Chris looked up.

"I don't know why I'm telling you all this," he said. "And please stop me if I'm boring you."

Boring? Hardly. Chris was the exact opposite of boring. "You're not at all."

"Well, thanks. Anyway, as far as my dad goes, he's a really smart guy and an okay father. But not a good husband. He's on his third wife now, and she's not much older than I am."

"Third, wow," Rebecca said, figuring that Chris's mother had been his first. She responded with the only story that showed she could relate at least a little. "My parents divorced when I was young. But my dad had never been around much anyway, so to be honest I didn't miss him. Then my mom went through some crazy phase where she couldn't, or wouldn't, stay in one place for long."

"You lived like nomads, huh?"

"Exactly. I was always the new girl at school, so it was hard to make friends. Guess that's why my mom and I are so attached to each other." The relationship sounded like codependency. "I've been told I have failure to launch syndrome."

"I loved that movie." Chris laughed lightly.

"Never saw it," Rebecca said, doubtful she ever would. Too close to home.

"Do you think you do?" Chris asked.

"Do what?"

"Have failure to launch syndrome."

"Maybe. But I actually like living with my mom. We get along, and we're really close. I almost moved out a few months ago, but that plan fell apart when my friend moved away. I was devastated at first but then kind of relieved. Another excuse to stay with mommy."

"You know, that's not necessarily a bad thing. In some cultures, the parents and grandparents and kids live together forever. My grandfather said his family always had multiple generations living together. He grew up in a house with both his grandmothers. *La vida con tres mamas,* he used to say."

Hearing Chris speak Spanish, using Mr. B's accent, made Rebecca dizzy. An image of Mr. B as a little boy surrounded by the love of three doting women made her smile. But the happy thought gave way to the dark reality that her friend ended up alone in old age, his wife and daughter gone and his grandson lost to him for reasons Rebecca would never find out.

"What's in the bakery box you got there?" she asked, lightening the mood.

Chris lay a hand on top of the box as if it contained something precious. "One of those sticky bun things. I hear they're really good."

"You haven't had one yet?"

"This will be my first." He opened the box and removed the pastry. "Should I try it now?"

"Yes! I can't wait to see your reaction." Rebecca scooted her chair in close and watched him take a big bite. "What do you think?"

"I think," Chris licked a spot of caramel glaze off his thumb. "This is the most delicious thing I've ever had in my life."

"Thank God, because I could never be friends with someone who doesn't love them."

"Friends, huh?" Chris's expression softened. "Good to know, especially since we'll be working together for a few days."

Rebecca clasped her hands in her lap. She thought she'd be sorting the house on her own. Learning Chris would be helping alongside her made the job much more appealing.

The alarm on her phone chimed, startling her. She'd completely forgotten about it. "Now I really do have to go."

Chris packed up the remainder of his sticky bun and secured the lid on his coffee. "Can I walk you to your car?"

"You want to walk me to my car?"

"Is that too old-school?"

"No. It's nice of you." Rebecca struggled to keep her enthusiasm in check. "The only man who ever walked me to my car before was your grandpa."

They fell in step next to each other and left the bakery patio, heading down the block to where Rebecca's Suburban was parked.

"Where's Mila, today?" Chris asked.

"I left her with my mom, which might be a problem because whenever I'm not there Mila tries to escape and run home." Rebecca, who usually paced herself to slower walkers, lengthened her stride to keep up with Chris.

"Home being my grandfather's house?"

"Yeah, I don't think she'll ever stop waiting for him to return. She's the most loyal dog I've ever known, and I've known a lot of dogs."

As they passed the pizza place, Rebecca waved to Gerardo who was tossing dough in the air. When the pizza maker saw Rebecca, he grinned widely, threw the dough extra high, and blew her a kiss.

"You know everyone around here, don't you?"

"Pretty much. That's what it's like living in a small town, and one of the reasons I love it." Rebecca slowed her steps. "Well, here's my car."

Chris stepped off the curb and opened the door for her, just like Mr. B used to do.

"Thank you," she said, a blush heating up her face.

He closed the door and leaned into the open window. "I'll see you this afternoon."

"I'll be there." She watched him walk, his steps long and certain, as if he knew exactly where he was headed.

CHAPTER 22

Chris went about ten feet before he stopped and looked back. Her car was already halfway down the block. He didn't move until it was out of sight. There was something about her that intrigued him. A genuineness, as if she'd come from another era. They'd had an entire conversation, and she never once glanced at her cell phone. And neither had he.

When he saw her on the patio at Nutmegs with her face turned toward the sun, he'd hesitated to disturb her. And normally he wouldn't have. But for some reason he was drawn to her.

His cell vibrated in his pocket—he'd forgotten it was there.

"Hello?"

"Hey, Chris, Adam Hawk calling."

Adam Hawk had been his best friend the year he lived in Clearwater. They'd spoken briefly at the funeral and exchanged numbers with an off-hand *it'd be great to catch up sometime.*

"Rumor has it you're back in town," Adam said. "Are you free for lunch today?"

"Yeah, I am," Chis said, surprised by how much the invitation appealed to him.

"Great. There's a burger place just outside of town. I'll text you the address. How does twelve sound?"

"Sounds good. See you then." Chris might have guessed Adam would follow through on catching up. Most people in Chris's world were full of empty promises, meaningless offers, and cheap talk. Clearwater people were different.

THE RESTAURANT WAS LOCATED off a rural road in the midst of some wine tasting rooms and random small businesses. He searched the crowded dining area and spotted Adam in a corner booth. His old friend stood. His handshake was solid and heart-felt. After dispensing with the usual, mundane greetings and ordering burgers and beers, Adam offered a tight-lipped smile.

"It's been a long time," he said.

"It has." Chris felt a flood of emotion. "I wish we'd have stayed in touch."

"Hey, we were just kids."

"I know," Chris said. "But that year, you were like a big brother to me. You probably don't remember, but I was kind of shy back then, and our friendship, well, I want you to know it really mattered."

Adam sipped his beer. "Mattered to me, too."

Chris hesitated, unsure of how to explain why he'd vanished without saying goodbye to his best friend. "I don't know what you've heard about me over the years, but it—it was complicated."

"I just wondered where my friend had gone. And all anyone would tell me was that you'd moved away." Adam's eyes shifted toward the window. "About a month after you left, I rode my bike to your grandfather's house. It was early summer, and I hoped you'd be coming for a visit. All I remember is that when I asked your grandparents about it, your grandmother started to cry.

A twinge of sadness pinched his chest. "I wanted to stay in Clearwater, but, well, my parents decided to get back together, and I had to go along with it."

"That's what kids do," Adam said. "Never have much choice when it comes to parents' decisions."

"Yeah, but not staying in touch, that's on me. You wrote me letters, and I never wrote back." Chris had no desire to go into how unhappy he was in Seattle, but he owed his friend an explanation. "As soon as my parents and I got home, they started fighting again, mostly about my grandpa. My dad thought he'd tried to poison me against him."

"That doesn't sound like Benito."

"It wasn't. He never said anything bad about my dad to me. He did to my mother though." Chris glanced at the ceiling, reluctant to revisit one of the worst days of his life. His father had come to Clearwater to take his wife and son home. A huge fight broke out, and by then Chris spoke enough Spanish to understand what his grandfather had said—*if you return to that man after all the times he's betrayed you, you are no longer my daughter.*

"Kids overhear grownups arguing all the time."

"Yeah, of course," Chris said, sorry he'd mentioned it. He was there to catch up with a friend, not revisit old wounds and childhood drama.

"All I can tell you is that I had tremendous respect for your grandfather. He and I became pretty good friends over the years."

Chris dipped a French fry into ketchup. "You and my grandfather? How'd that happen?"

Adam swallowed the beer left in his glass. "He helped me out. And that's one of the reasons, the main reason actually, I wanted to meet with you."

Chris pushed his half-eaten burger to the side, his hackles up. Adam didn't care about 'catching up' at all. His old friend was there on business. "Alright. I'm guessing you want something from me, so let's hear it."

"Whoa." Adam's shoulders went back. "I'm not going to ask you for anything, Chris. I want to tell you that I owe you money."

Chris paused. In his world, people didn't usually offer up that kind of information unsolicited. "Why do you owe me money?"

"Because my grapevines are growing on your land. Benito let me plant there but refused to take any money. He did accept a nice bottle of wine now and then." Adam chuckled. "And he always called to tell me how the grapes tasted, when they'd be ready for harvest. He was better at that than my vineyard manager."

A mental image of his grandfather's property came to mind, but not a present day one. It was one from his childhood, when he and Adam ran through the fields sneaking grapes from the vines.

Adam's voice brought him out of the reverie. "Now you're the landowner, and I'm your tenant."

Chris pressed his lips into a tight line. "Sorry I barked at you, Adam. Truth is, and I hate to admit it, but I don't know what the hell I'm doing. Talk to me about software and power points and venture capitalists, that's my knowledge base. Farming and land management, not so much."

"Agriculture, grape growing, winemaking—all that's my area of expertise, so I'm here to help."

"I appreciate that," Chris said. "But the property's going to be sold, so anything we agree to is only short term."

Adam rubbed the scruff on his cheeks. "After you sell, I'll work something out with the new owner. Leasing out land around here for growing grapes is profitable, a good deal for everyone. Who wouldn't want that?"

A developer, that's who. But Chris kept that possibility to

himself. He hadn't even signed a contract with Troy Dayton yet, let alone entertained offers. "Let me think about it, Adam. And since you're already using the land..." his thoughts trailed. Would it be ethical to withhold the fact that whoever bought the land was most likely going to destroy it? Although that hasn't been decided on either at this point. Regardless, monthly income for the use of his land would help with cash flow until he and his father secured financing to launch their business.

"Nothing needs to be decided right now," Adam said. "We know where to find each other."

Chris relaxed. Even as a kid, Adam had been genuine and kind with an unflappable sense of fair play. "You know, you're probably the most upstanding, honest person I've ever known. I'll never forget that basketball game when you called a foul on yourself. Even the ref said it wasn't. But didn't matter, you made sure the other team got their free throws."

"Oh, yeah." Adam laughed. "And then the other team won by two points."

"You're the kind of guy who does the right thing even when nobody's looking."

"I try," Adam said, a slight redness on his cheeks. "Hey, are you around tomorrow? My girlfriend and I are having a casual Sunday barbecue. We'd love for you to come."

"Really?" Chris said, thinking it would be a good distraction to hang out, have a beer, relax. "Yeah, thank you."

They finished eating, and Adam insisted on picking up the bill. "You can get it next time, buddy. I have no doubt we'll do this again."

Chris headed back toward town, wondering what this unlikely reunion might lead to. Either way, he was grateful to have his old friend back in his life.

CHAPTER 23

*R*ebecca's heart pitter-patted. While walking dogs, she had fantasies of working side by side with Chris —his hand brushing up against hers, a shared smile, a moment of awkward attraction.

"Just stop!" She chastised herself as the dogs sniffed a tree trunk. Her imagination was out of control.

At Mariano's, she was distracted and antsy as the clock ticked toward three.

"Rebecca!"

She spun around to face Patty. "What?"

"You look like you're in another world. Did you hear me?"

"I'm sorry." Rebecca continued printing out price tags. "What did you say?"

"Adam and I are having a party tomorrow, it's kind of a last minute thing. Can you come?"

Rebecca chewed her cheek. "Maybe, what time?"

"Late afternoon. A barbecue, summer casual, not a big crowd. Cece and Brad, Natalie, a few of Adam's winery friends —you know, the usual."

"It's nice of you to invite me."

"Are you kidding?" Patty pinched her arm playfully. "You're always invited. Besides, you deserve to have a little fun, and I promise you will."

Rebecca wasn't sure what fun was anymore.

"And do me a favor." Patty pulled on the waist band of Rebecca's plain black pants. "Could you dress up a little?"

"I thought you said it was casual." Rebecca's wardrobe was limited at best.

"*Summer* casual," Patty said. "And there'll be cute guys there, some of Adam's business friends."

Rebecca was acquainted with the men who worked with Adam—winemakers, distributors, vineyard managers. Cute was an understatement. "Pants, shorts, and denim overalls are practically all I have. I had to borrow a skirt from my mom for the funeral, remember?"

"I'm afraid I do," Patty said.

"Should I wear that?"

"Oh, God no. A black skirt to a barbecue? Don't you have a sundress or something?"

"No." Rebecca tried to picture the clothes hanging in her closet. "I do have a cute blouse that I wore in high school. It's got this little scalloped neckline."

"You need to get rid of that along with anything else you wore as a teenager. Maybe Cece has something that would fit you."

As if on cue, Natalie and Cece entered the shop with cheerful greetings.

"Do either of you have an outfit Rebecca can borrow?"

"I probably do," Cece said, poking a toothpick into a square of cheddar on the sample platter. "What's it for?"

"A barbecue on Sunday, which you both are invited to." Patty waggled her head. "Sorry it's so last minute."

"Wait," Rebecca said. "You already told me they were coming."

"They are. They just didn't know it until now."

"How do you know we're not busy?" Cece asked.

Patty grunted. "You'd better not be busy."

"I'm not," Natalie said. "Sunday is my only day off, and a summer barbecue sounds delightful."

"I'll check with Brad." Cece threw a wry smile in Patty's direction. "But I'm pretty sure we're free. Hopefully my parents can babysit."

"I'll babysit," Rebecca said.

Patty looked at her in disbelief. "No you won't."

"Oh, right. I forgot."

"Geez, you really make me nuts," said Patty. "Which leads me back to the problem. Rebecca has nothing to wear, so you two are going to have to dress her."

"Fun!" Natalie leapt off her stool. "It'll be like styling a life-sized Barbie Doll."

As the youngest of the four girlfriends, Rebecca was often treated like a little sister, a role she relished—except for when it came to her appearance.

"A Barbie Doll? You are not forcing me into some slinky dress with four inch heels and giving me a new hairdo."

Cece intervened. "Of course not. All we'll do is elevate your style a little. We're really good at it, too. You know how many little girls we've turned into glamorous princesses? Come on, you have to let us."

"She will." Patty wrapped an arm around Rebecca's waist. "I promised her some of Adam's hot friends will be there. Since Cece's married and I'm with Adam, you two will be the only available women in attendance."

Natalie held up her hands. "No, way—wine guys are not my type. They tend to be, I don't know, too interested in wine."

Rebecca puzzled for a second. "That's like saying I'm too interested in dogs."

"Sorry, but you are too interested in dogs," Cece said.

"But dogs are what I love most in the whole world. They have every quality I admire—loyalty, devotion, intelligence, the ability to sense what you need when you need it."

"You've just described the perfect man," Natalie said.

Rebecca slapped her forehead. "You're right. I'll never meet a man that measures up to a dog, will I?"

"Don't even start thinking that way," Patty said. "You'll only depress yourself."

"And me, too." Natalie's shoulders slumped. "Maybe I should give up on men and get myself a dog."

"Yes!" Rebecca veered into her favorite subject. "You'd be the perfect dog-mom, Nat. And adopting an animal who needs—"

"Stay focused!" Patty shouted at them.

"Come on, ladies, we have work to do." Cece pushed Natalie and Rebecca together like a pair of mannequins. "Look at that, you're almost the same height, but Natalie's legs are longer."

"That shouldn't matter," Natalie said, sizing Rebecca up from head to toe. "One of us will find something that'll fit her."

"See?" said Patty. "I knew this would work."

"I'm not so sure," Rebecca said. The idea was becoming less appealing every second. "I'll look so—so not me."

"That's the plan," Patty said. "If we let you look like you, you'd wear overalls and hiking boots."

"Not nice, Patty," Cece said.

"I'm just being honest."

"It's okay." Rebecca's arms hung heavily at her sides. "I know I have no fashion sense. Even my mom would tell you that."

"Don't you worry," Cece said, moving a lock of hair off Rebecca's face with gentle fingers. "I am an artist, after all, and you are my blank canvas."

A blank canvas—now that was a concept Rebecca could embrace.

CHAPTER 24

*R*ebecca knocked on the front door of Mr. B's (now his grandson's) house.

Mila sat at attention beside her foot, panting and tail thumping. When Chris opened the door, she bolted inside and ran up the stairs to Mr. B's bedroom. A moment later, she scurried down the stairs and into the kitchen.

"She sure is excited to be here," Chris said, watching her sniff around the living room and into the bathrooms. "And there she goes."

When Mila reappeared, she had a chewed up rubber ball in her mouth. Rebecca recalled how Mila never tired of chasing the ball around the yard as Mr. B threw it for her over and over again. The memory had surfaced suddenly, bringing with it a twinge bittersweet nostalgia.

Mila went to her spot in front of Mr. B's recliner, turned in circles, and settled on the rug with the ball tucked between her paws.

Chris sat and stroked Mila's head. "You're a good girl, aren't ya?"

The sight stirred Rebecca, and she allowed another memory

to surface. In a dream-like state, she watched as Chris morphed into Mr. B. The vision lingered, like the words of an old song that could take her back in time.

In a flash, the bubble burst when Chris stood and morphed back into himself. "We should get started, don't you think?"

Rebecca forced her brain to reset. "Yes, let's start."

They'd been working only a few minutes when Chris's cell phone rang. He put one earbud in and disappeared into the other room. No sound for a minute. Then she heard him speak, his tone sharp.

"No, I didn't plan on that. And we never settled it anyway."

Rebecca wrapped newspaper around china plates, straining to hear every word he was saying.

Chris emerged from the other room. He paced and shook his head, eyes closed. "I can't do anything about that now, Dad. We'll deal with it when I get home." A long pause. "Fine... whatever... I know it!" Another long pause. Chris opened the hall closet, the one with all the boxes. He stood there a moment, his profile dark and jaw twitching.

Rebecca held her breath, worried he might start yelling. Not that she cared about him arguing with his dad. But it might be awkward when he got off the phone. On the other hand, he knew she was there. If he didn't want her to hear, he'd go outside.

"No, I told you no, not yet. I'll handle it..." he glanced at Rebecca but without focus, as if he were looking straight through her.

The call ended. Chris flung his phone onto the couch and fell into his grandfather's chair, head in hands. "Sorry you had to hear all that."

"I didn't hear any—well, yeah, I heard a little. I'm going to get some water. Want some?"

"Sure." He followed her.

Rebecca filled two glasses with ice cubes and water from the tap.

Chris guzzled, his Adam's apple sliding up and down his smooth neck. He set the glass on the counter. "I'm not handling this well."

Rebecca stepped closer, catching a whiff of cologne. Or maybe it was his natural scent—masculine and woodsy. "Why do you say that?"

"Because I'm not," he said. "I wasn't prepared for how hard this is. The whole situation is a lot to deal with, and I'm under some—some pressure."

"Time pressure, right." Rebecca gripped the back of a chair. She'd always felt so comfortable in Mr. B's house. But it wasn't his house anymore. And she wasn't there as a welcome, beloved pseudo-daughter anymore either. Only a worker who was there to do a job.

"It's not just about how long this is taking." Chris's shoulders slumped forward. "It's more than that. Do you ever feel like you don't have control over your own life?"

Rebecca squeezed the chair back so hard her knuckles turned white. *Only every single day of my life since as long as I can remember.* "Sometimes, yes. A lot of the time, to be honest."

One side of his mouth ticked up, and a dimple she'd never noticed before appeared. A light sheen of perspiration on his forehead. "It's hot in here. I don't think my grandfather believed in air conditioning."

"He totally did not believe in air conditioning." Rebecca laughed. "Every summer we'd sit on the porch in the late afternoons savoring even the smallest hint of a breeze. Mr. B made the best horchata, so cool and smooth and sweet." She closed her eyes and summoned the memory, the taste, the scent of grapes growing in neighboring fields.

When she opened her eyes, Chris's intense gaze drew her in, destabilizing her.

"I completely forgot about horchata," he said. "Abuela made it by the pitcher."

"Abuela?" she asked.

"Spanish for grandmother. I called her Abuela, but I called my grandfather Papa. I'm not sure why, probably because that's what my mom called him."

Rebecca shivered, unable to comprehend how much heartbreak Mr. B had endured in his life, the regrets he must have had.

"I'm sure this…" Rebecca paused to choose her words. Poking a stick into Chris's wounds would be cruel. "This process, you know, having to deal with the house is hard."

"Maybe I need to recalibrate. I think I'm letting it be harder than it should be." He knelt in front of Mila and gathered her against him. "Like my father says, I'm a little soft sometimes."

Rebecca shook her head. "I don't see that at all. You're—you're thoughtful, just like your grandfather. He was the most thoughtful, kind, intelligent man in the whole world."

"Was he though? I mean really?"

Rebecca sensed he was challenging her, as if he thought she'd been deceived or misguided. Or maybe that she was a poor judge of character. "Yes, really. Mr. B was all that and more."

"If that's the case," Chris said. "We knew two very different men."

Rebecca didn't understand the sudden change in his demeanor. She thought they were getting along well. She was trying to be supportive, but it was like he'd flipped a switch.

"I just want you to know the man that I knew, because if you—"

"Why?" he snapped. "Why are you so intent on being right about him?"

Rebecca tried to dial back her emotions, but she was unable to contain her reaction. "Listen, I didn't know him twenty years ago, but I knew him these last five years better than anyone else did."

Chris seemed to bristle at her claim. "That's a bold statement."

"Maybe, but it's true. There's a lot of things I question about myself, and I mess up all the time. But I would bet every last penny I had on your grandfather's integrity."

"That's a bet I'd take in a heartbeat." Chris crossed his arms over his chest. "You think because you knew him recently, that makes you right and me wrong? That's pretty presumptuous."

Rebecca backpedaled to diffuse the tension. "I don't mean to presume anything."

"Well you did, and you are." The accusation stunned her.

"That is totally unfair." Defensiveness surged through her. "I don't even know what we're arguing about. All I can tell you is that your grandpa was a gigantic part of my life, and losing him has practically crushed me!" Her attempt at containing herself gave way. "I don't know what happened to you twenty years ago, but you seem to have landed on your feet just fine, with your fancy software business, a gorgeous girlfriend, and a father who, despite being kind of a jerk, is helping you succeed. And now your grandfather, a man you didn't even know anymore and apparently couldn't care less about, just made you a freakin' millionaire!"

Chris backed away from her, his face dark and serious.

"I'm going to let that go, Rebecca, except to say that you know nothing about me or my life or what I lost as a kid."

Mortified at her outburst, Rebecca stood still as a statue. Now *she* was turning into a person she didn't recognize. Even so, every word of what she said was true.

"I can't even believe how ungrateful you are." The words hurt as she said them. Not because they weren't true, but because she'd trusted him to be better, to be like his grandfather.

Chris closed in on her personal space. "You need to leave."

"Good, I will. Are you firing me?"

"I believe I am."

"Well you can't, because I quit!"

"Fine." Chris sneered. "You quit. I'll pay you for an hour."

His dismissal and indifference infuriated her. "It's the weekend, so you have to pay me time and a half."

"Fair enough. Time and a half."

"Good." Rebecca pushed past him. "Mila, let's go!"

The dog followed her to the door, glancing back at Chris as if unsure where her loyalty belonged.

"Wait. Your backpack." Chris held it toward her.

Rebecca snatched it out of his hand and stood as tall as she could. "And if you change your mind about needing my help, don't bother calling. Because it's too late. I'm—I'm done."

"Don't you worry. I won't change my mind, because I'm done, too. This whole—whole thing," he swung his arms through the air, "isn't worth it. I'll do exactly what my father and that realtor guy said to do—sell the land and make this house and everything in it someone else's problem!"

CHAPTER 25

*C*ece sat on the edge of her bed beside Natalie as Rebecca paced back and forth, recounting the story of her fight with Chris. In the twenty-four hours since she'd stormed out of the house, Rebecca relived and regretted every word she'd said countless times. "And that was it. I quit and he fired me and we'll never see each other again.

"Sounds awful," Natalie said.

"It was awful. I don't know what's gotten into me." Rebecca fell into a soft chair in front of a set of French doors that opened onto a balcony. The bedroom, decorated in soft hues of cream, gray, and sage, inspired a sense calm and relaxation, like a spa. But it wasn't enough to reduce Rebecca's agitation.

"I used to be so lighthearted and easygoing and—and happy." She dug her fingertips into the arm of the chair. "Now I'm an anxious, stressed out wreck looking for an argument."

"Come on, sweetie," Cece said. "Don't be so hard on yourself."

"What did your mom say?" Natalie asked.

"I didn't tell her yet. When I got home yesterday, there was an invasion of ants in two cottages. I had to put on my hazmat suit and play exterminator while my poor mom tried to shuffle guests around." Rebecca rubbed her eyes. "Then I had to walk Curly at the crack of dawn this morning because Tiffany had some, I don't know, some overnight thing."

Cece took her hands and pulled her to her feet. "Okay, enough. Let's focus on getting you ready for the BBQ. Brad just left to take Noah to my parents, so the house is empty except for us girls."

"That means we can turn on *Mamma Mia*." Natalie jumped on the bed like a little girl.

"Right you are." Cece turned on the music. "Ready to dance?" she asked Rebecca.

How could anybody stay dreary when she had two fabulous friends by her side and *Dancing Queen* blasting through the house?

For the next half-hour, Natalie and Cece played with their life-sized Barbie doll, making Rebecca try on one dress after another. Too tight, too loose, too sexy—nothing worked until Cece dug deep into her closet and found a pale blue floral slip dress with spaghetti straps and a handkerchief hem. She draped it over her arm with a flourish.

"It's gorgeous." Rebecca ran a finger over the silky fabric.

"With your red hair," Natalie said, "you'll look like a mermaid."

"I love mermaids." Rebecca marveled at the dress. She'd never worn anything so feminine. "I feel like Cinderella."

Cece unzipped the dress and slipped it over Rebecca's head. "Which makes us your fairy-godmothers."

The material slid over Rebecca's warm skin, skimming her hips and thighs. In the full length mirror, she hardy recognized herself. "It's perfect. I love it."

∽

THE SPRAWLING RANCH home of Adam Hawk sat at the top of a long driveway on a hill surrounded by vineyards. It had been built over one hundred years ago when most of Clearwater was nothing but open space and groves of fruit trees. Rebecca got out of the car, and a warm breeze blew through her hair.

"Ready to do this?" Natalie asked.

"Do I have a choice?" Rebecca checked her reflection in the side mirror. Her wild red mane had been tamed with some product that made her curls soft and bouncy, and Natalie had applied just the right amount makeup, sophisticated yet natural. The dress made her blue-green eyes almost turquoise. "Are you sure I don't look too—too different?"

Cece cupped Rebecca's elbows. "You look the right amount of different."

"The right amount of different." Rebecca repeated her friend's appraisal of her appearance. "That's good."

Natalie, Cece, and Rebecca, all of them nearly six feet tall, strode into Adam's backyard like models on the runway.

Patty's mouth dropped. "Oh my God, you guys look just like Charlie's Angels!" She grabbed Rebecca's hand. "And look at you. I never knew you were actually pretty, like super pretty."

"Little missy," Cece said. "You have mastered the art of the back-handed compliment."

Rebecca set her shoulders back. The back-handed compliment suited her fine. "I've never had my make-up and hair done by experts before."

"So…" Patty, in a tangerine colored mini-dress and platform sandals, did a little two-step hop. "What do you think of the new you?"

"I feel like the girl in Princess Diaries."

And with that, Rebecca was swept into the party. She stayed close by Natalie's side, sipping wine and chatting with people she knew, until Adam intercepted her.

"Wow, girl, you clean up nice."

"Why thank you, sir." Rebecca made a little curtsy. "It was all Patty's idea. She made Natalie and Cece dress me up. I just stood there and let it happen."

Adam gave her a warm, tight hug. They'd met ages ago and bonded over a mutual love of dogs. Adam's rescue pup, Tipsy the little brown mutt, was one of her first walking clients.

"Where's Tipsy?" Rebecca asked.

"On a doggy playdate," Adam said. "Hey, see that guy by the barbecue? The chef wearing the apron."

Rebecca peered over his shoulder. The chef held a spatula in one hand and beer in the other. Tall and broad-shouldered with short hair the color of wheat.

"I see him," Rebecca said.

"He's the new hot chef at some restaurant in Napa. And he's asking about *you*."

Rebecca's pulse ticked up. "Me? What'd he ask?"

Adam chuckled. "He wanted to know your story."

"Oh." Rebecca took a gulp of her cool chardonnay. "Does he have a dog that needs walking?"

"Come on, you know what that means. He thinks you're pretty and would like to meet you. You've attracted a number of stares since you walked in."

"Seriously?" Rebecca couldn't believe her friends had turned her into the kind of woman men notice.

"Seriously," Adam said.

"Um, okay, I'll meet him. Just need to run inside and use the bathroom first."

"Alright. Then come find me, and I'll introduce you."

Rebecca headed into the house, stunned to have caught the attention of someone like a new hot chef. She hurried through the living room to the powder room. With the door locked, she checked herself in the mirror. "Oh, no." Red blotches had risen on her neck and chest. No surprise considering how antsy she was.

She soaked a guest towel in cold water, pressed it against her chest, and took a few deep breaths. The bright pink flush on her pale skin faded.

Rebecca gripped the edge of the sink and put her nose close to the mirror. "You can do this," she said to her reflection. "You can meet a cute guy without freaking out or turning red as a strawberry. Or acting like a total idiot."

Fortified by her self-administered pep talk, Rebecca fluffed her curls with the sweep of her hands and marched outside.

The crowd had grown by a few more people, most of them dressed in shorts and flip-flops. Rebecca searched for her equally overdressed friends.

Brad and Cece were seated at one of the tables, and Natalie stood beside Patty and Adam, all of them laughing as if someone had told a joke. Rebecca smoothed the front of her dress.

The hot chef, supposedly waiting for her, remained at the grill. He turned over a steak with a pair of tongs. Rebecca moved toward him, catching his eye. He winked at her and tipped back his beer. Okay, that was cute, kind of flirty, but also a little bold. He certainly was confident in his ability to attract women.

Rebecca dialed back on the over analysis; he only wanted to meet her, not marry her.

She picked up a fresh glass of chardonnay and moved forward, aware of how the skirt of her dress swirled around her legs. What's the worst that could happen? She'd say something stupid, make a fool of herself, and go spend the rest of the night hanging out with Natalie and Cece. She'd had worse nights— way worse.

"Rebecca?"

She turned and came face to face with Chris Harrington. The red blotches sprang to life and goosebumps tingled on her arms. He'd trimmed his dark beard close to the skin. His musky cologne wafted into her nose like an elixir.

"What are you doing here?"

"Adam invited me." Chris pushed his hands into the pockets of his navy shorts. "I didn't recognize you at first."

"That, well, that's because..." Rebecca glanced at the chef who now was engaged in a conversation with an adoring audience. "Because I'm wearing a dress."

Chris laughed. "It's very pretty."

She started to explain it wasn't her dress but corrected the impulse to overshare. "Thank you." She gulped the cool white wine. A day ago, she was furious with him and certain they'd never speak again, but now, here they were.

"Rebecca," Chris said.

"Yes?" Her reply was frosty.

"About yesterday, I shouldn't have said that you—"

"Let's forget it." Rebecca interrupted him. "It doesn't really matter anymore, does it? Since we no longer have an association."

"I just wanted to say I'm sorry."

"Oh, well, then I guess I'm sorry, too." Rebecca didn't believe she had anything to be sorry for, but one sincere apology deserved another.

Chris motioned with a slight turn of his head. "Would you come sit with me?"

Rebecca forgot all about the chef and followed Chris as if he were the Pied Piper. They sat on a bench at the far end of the patio away from the crowd. Rebecca set her wine glass on a table, worried it might slip from her sweaty hands.

"I overreacted to something, I can't even remember now, but I was wrong to get angry with you. No excuse, but I did have a pretty hard week. My dad is all over me and I'm late on a project and Jessica's upset because, well, because I—"

"You don't have to explain anything to me," Rebecca said, sensitive to his obvious discomfort. "And if you want me to go back to helping you pack the house, I can do that."

His head snapped up. "Could you?"

Despite her emphatic announcement that she'd quit, Rebecca dismissed the incident.

"Yeah, tomorrow's Monday," she said, mentally reviewing her schedule. "I can be there in the afternoon. Will you still be here?"

Chris nodded. "I'm staying at least a few more days. I really do have to wrap this up fast. There are things I have to—to take care of in Seattle."

"I guess we have our work cut out for us then." Rebecca wondered what those *things in Seattle* might be. She knew next to nothing about his regular life. "So, how do you know Adam?" She picked up her chardonnay and took a big drink, holding the cool, tangy liquid in her mouth.

"We go way back," Chris said. "The year my mom and I lived here, Adam was my best friend. Even though he was few years ahead of me in school, he kind of took me under his wing."

Adam appeared in front of them and interjected. "That's because you were the best basketball player in the neighborhood." He gave Chris a squeeze on the shoulder. "It's good to see you here. Nothing like rekindling an old friendship."

"That's for sure." Chris stood and reached around Adam's shoulders. They slapped each other's backs.

"Hey, I really enjoyed lunch yesterday," Adam said. "Thanks again for meeting me."

"Of course. And we'll figure something out with the land."

Rebecca's antennae went up. It was one more tidbit of information she had no idea what to do with. The puzzle pieces were increasing and scattering.

"Okay, you two," Adam said. "Those steaks are done to perfection, so you'd better eat before they get cold. And have fun." He cracked a smile and gave Rebecca a quick wink, as if telling her to forget about the chef.

She wondered if Adam knew his old friend had a gorgeous

girlfriend and that his only interest in Rebecca was as the hired help.

"Probably should jump into the line and get food," Chris suggested. "We could eat together, unless you have some friends here."

"No, nobody at all, I'm on my own. Well, sort of on my own. I came with Natalie and Cece but they're..." Rebecca trapped the rest of the sentence behind tight lips. "Let's go check out those steaks."

They picked up plastic plates and silverware wrapped in napkins. Chris filled his plate with all the side dishes, but Rebecca, who would normally have done the same, helped herself to a dainty serving of salad, a few green beans, and one skinny breadstick.

They reached the barbecue where the chef stood offering filet mignon, beef ribs, and teriyaki chicken.

Chris opted for a steak then moved on to the next food station.

"What's your pleasure, pretty lady?" the chef asked her.

Wide-eyed, Rebecca opened her mouth but the words stuck.

"I recommend the filet." He tapped one with his pointed fork. "Cooked to a perfect medium rare."

"Gee, I'm not sure. It all looks so good."

"Well, you look like a girl who might want to try a bit of everything."

Rebecca shrank. Was he talking about food, or something else?

He sliced a few pieces of steak and cut a strip of meat off a rib bone. With tongs and a long fork, he arranged the meat on one side of her plate then added a small chicken thigh, the skin brown and crispy.

"This looks delicious."

"It is delicious. I hope you'll come back for more." The tip of his tongue brushed his upper lip.

"Thanks. I'll eat all this, I'm sure it's fantastic, and then if—I, okay, yeah. I'll come back." She giggled, sounding like a foolish girl, and headed to the table where Chris was sitting with Cece and Brad.

As she took her seat, Rebecca's arm grazed Chris's, and a jolt of electricity struck. Her attraction to Chris was undeniable, but also a dead-end. Not only did he live two states away, he was taken. The last thing Rebecca would ever do was pursue someone else's boyfriend. But there was no reason they couldn't be friends, or at least *friendly* while they finished the task that lay ahead. And maybe in the process, Rebecca would discover the peace of mind she needed to move on with life.

"Doesn't this look totally yummy? I'm starving," she said.

"What it looks like," said Cece, "is that you got some special attention from the handsome chef over there."

"Not really." Rebecca took a bite of her perfectly done steak. "I mean, he just thought I'd like to try a little bit of everything." She stuffed her mouth with another bite to prevent herself from saying another word.

"That is a little suggestive," Cece said. "And if I were—"

"Come on, honey," Brad said. "You know how celebrity chefs are. Big egos, think they can get away with anything."

A slight smile played on Chris's lips as he licked barbecue sauce off his fingers. His cell phone, face up on the table beside Rebecca's arm, vibrated and a stunning photo of Jessica appeared. Chris declined the call and flipped the phone over.

The friendly chatter about the lovely weather and delicious food continued. Chris's phone buzzed again. This time he didn't ignore it.

"Excuse me a minute," he said, leaving the table.

The moment he was gone, Cece tapped her fork on Rebecca's plate. "Hey, now I'm beginning to think there's something between you two."

"There's not. We're—we're just friends, and he hired me

back, so I'm going to keep sorting stuff at Mr. B's house and keep Antonia's beautiful things from ending up in a dumpster. It's just a job, that's all."

"A job with a purpose," Brad said, his voice reassuring. "Benito would be pleased to know you're helping his grandson."

Cece leaned against her husband's arm. "I sensed a hint of enchantment going on, but maybe I'm immersed in the fairytale moment we created. You are my Cinderella tonight."

"That I am." Rebecca tasted the rib meat, tender and bursting with flavor.

She swallowed hard when Chris returned to the table but did not sit. "I'm afraid I have to take off."

"Oh, okay," Rebecca said, disappointed. "See you tomorrow then."

"So nice to meet you both," Chris said to Brad and Cece. He touched Rebecca's shoulder so lightly she barely felt it. "Would you mind walking with me to my car?"

Her stomach flipped over as she looked up at him. His face drew her in like a museum painting—the more one viewed it, the more they could discern. His dark eyes held a mysterious depth, something akin to wonder, anticipation, longing.

"Sure."

They reached the edge of the patio, and Chris faced her. "So tomorrow we'll get back to work."

Rebecca had expected him to say something more serious, but he'd only wanted to confirm their schedule. "Yep, tomorrow afternoon. I have dog walks all morning and then I'm at the shelter until about two. After that, I'll head over."

"Great." Chris rocked on his heels. "Do you still have a key to the back door?"

"I do, but not with me. Do you want it back? I can bring it tomorrow."

"No. I just want to make sure you can get in the house. I'm not sure of my timing, so I might not be there. Of course, I can leave the door unlocked. Crime rates in Clearwater are pretty low."

"Virtually nonexistent," she said.

Chris laughed. Somehow his fingers brushed the back of her left hand, accidental of course, but it still made her heart flutter.

Then he touched her hand on purpose. It had to be on purpose, because he gently squeezed the tips of her fingers. "Thanks again for being so nice about yesterday. I was a real jerk."

"It's okay." Rebecca pulled back her hand and reset her brain in order to form a coherent thought. "I wasn't on my best behavior either. I know I'm pushy and way too talkative. I'll try to stay quiet tomorrow."

"You don't have to be quiet. I like talking to you."

Rebecca's mouth went dry. She took a step back creating an invisible barrier between them. "You do?"

"Sure, I do." Chris fiddled with his keys. "All right then, see you tomorrow."

"Yes you will," she said with a jaunty shake of the head.

He lingered a moment, as did she. Without thinking, Rebecca reached out and hugged him.

Chris's entire body stiffened, but he didn't pull away. Instead, he returned the hug with unexpected fervor.

CHAPTER 26

*R*ebecca returned to the table, her heart in her throat.

"What was that?" Patty slapped the table with both hands. "Did I see you hug Chris?"

Brad had relocated, thank goodness, and the seats were now occupied by her three best girlfriends.

Rebecca covered her face. "I don't know. I think I like him. And I can't like him. That would be so totally stupid!"

"Stupid or not," said Cece. "You can't help how you feel."

"He has a girlfriend and lives in Seattle." Rebecca lamented the truth. "I'm an idiot if I let myself have a crush on him."

"I agree," said Patty. "A real idiot."

"Patty," Natalie said, wagging a finger. "Not nice."

"Don't care." Patty smacked the table again. "Rebecca, you should quit that job at Mr. B's house. You're very impulsive. I saw that hug, and it probably mortified him."

"Geez, Patty," Cece said. "Talk about impulse control. Do you have to say everything that pops into your head?"

"Yes. And I can tell Rebecca she's too impulsive because my impulse control sucks, too," said Patty. "Still, she hugs much too freely. Not everyone's like us, Rebecca, not everyone likes to be hugged."

Natalie poked Patty's arm. "And not every truth needs to be spoken."

Rebecca had heard that admonition many times from Nonna. But none of it mattered now—the only thing she could do about her mistakes was try not to repeat them. "Patty, you're right. I've made a mess of things. But now that I un-quit the job, I can't quit again."

"Fine," Patty said. "But you'd better control your mouth and your hugs before you step into a pile of you-know-what. Crush that crush right now, stomp out the flame before it turns into a forest fire."

"Whoa," said Cece. "That was an impressive metaphor."

"I know, right?" Patty said, pleased with herself.

Rebecca dropped her head into her hands, her stomach as knotted up as an old ball of yarn. "I want to go home."

"You can't go yet," Patty said. "What about the chef? Nothing dampens a crush on a cute guy better than attention from an even cuter guy. He's been looking over this way ever since you got back to the table."

"It's true," Natalie said. "He keeps glancing in your direction."

Rebecca turned to Cece, the most level-headed of the bunch. "What do you think?"

Cece shook her head. "He might be alluring, and boy can he cook. But he's a player for sure. Anyone can see that."

"I'll bet he could teach our young, naïve Rebecca a thing or two." Patty's eyebrows waggled at her. "Maybe a summer fling is on the *menu*."

Rebecca chuckled at Patty's clever comeback, well aware of her own lack of experience. "I get what you're saying, but a fling is totally not for me. As Mr. B always said, I'm an old soul. And it's one of my better traits."

"I agree," Natalie said. "I think being an old soul suits you."

Rebecca stifled a yawn. "I really should go home. My day starts super early tomorrow."

"Come on, you're the only one of us still in her twenties," Patty whined. "The one who should want to party all night. You might be an old soul, but that doesn't mean you have to be an old fogey."

"I know," Rebecca said. "But I'm so confused. I didn't mean to hug Chris, it just happened. And then he hugged me back."

"You think it meant something?" Natalie asked. "I mean, did it feel like an obligatory hug or a friendly hug or a genuine *I-like-you* hug?"

"I have no idea. But what does it matter anyway?" Rebecca's mood plummeted. "I don't think it's right for me to be at a party. It's not even a month since Mr. B died."

"Is that what Mr. B would tell you?" Cece asked. "That you should stop living your life?"

Rebecca rested her chin on her hand and stared beyond the patio, the wide green lawn, and the acres of grapevines. The summer sun had begun its descent, turning the sky orange and pink. Adam's home was miles from the lake, but high enough to see it. The water shimmered like glass far in the distance, reminiscent of the countless sunsets she'd watched with Mr. B.

A strangled sob caught in her throat. She jumped out of her seat and ran inside before anyone could see her fall apart.

Sucking up her onslaught of emotion, she willed herself to maintain control as she entered the house.

A few people had gathered in the kitchen where Adam was pouring wine into bowl-shaped goblets and regaling his guests with stories from the vineyard.

An empty hallway lead to the bedrooms. Rebecca slipped into the first one, closed the door, and curled up on the bed. She clutched a hand-knitted blanket to her chest and released her sorrow. Mr. B would want her to acknowledge her heartbreak, but he wouldn't want her to mourn him forever

Ah, querida, one cannot use loss or regret as an excuse for not living.

It was a year or so after Antonia had died, and they were down by the lake. Mr. B threw a ball into the water, and Mila scampered after it.

"But how do you stop missing someone you loved so much?" Rebecca had asked.

Mr. B stared at the lake, as if the answer lay in the ripples on the surface. *You never stop missing them or loving them or wishing for one more moment with them. But you honor them by living your life in a way that would make them proud.*

He then rested his strong, heavy hands on Rebecca's shoulders.

Because of you and Mila, I am still living, perhaps even making a difference.

A loud rap on the door yanked the memory away.

"Just a sec." Rebecca rolled off the bed. She looked at herself in the mirror above the dresser. Mascara had left black smudges under her bloodshot eyes.

It was definitely time to go home.

She opened the door, not caring who was about to see her tear-stained face, and bumped right into the chest of the handsome chef. "Oh, sorry."

"No problem," he said.

Rebecca tried to squeeze between him and the doorway.

"Hold on there," he said, coaxing her backwards. "You've been crying." He closed the door without making a sound.

"I'm fine." As Rebecca backed up, he moved forward, his face only inches from hers.

"You sure?"

"Yep. I'm leaving now."

"Slow down, Rebecca."

He knew her name? And he was being nice, as if genuinely concerned for her.

"Why are you upset?" He stroked the side of her bare arm. "Maybe I can help."

"I don't think so," she said, her flesh reacting. "And please don't touch me."

He ignored her request and lifted a curl. "Your hair caught my attention the moment you waltzed in with your two friends. Man, the three of you…" his voice trailed, and his hand traveled toward her shoulder. He carried the scent of smoke and grilled meat on his clothes and skin. His masculine presence came on strong, like an unexpected storm, fascinating and frightening at the same time.

Rebecca bumped into the dresser. "I need to go. My friends are waiting for me."

"They can wait a few more minutes, can't they?" It wasn't a question, the way he said it, more of a statement of fact.

She put her hands on the edge of the dresser as he moved in closer. There were voices out in the hallway, people milling about the house.

"Someone could walk in here any second," Rebecca said, infusing her voice with a false lilt.

"Come on, Red, you can't deny the chemistry between us."

Although Rebecca had far less experience with men than most women her age, she knew a phony when she met one. She pressed her hands against his shoulders, not too hard but firmly enough to send the message. "To tell you the truth, there is no chemistry between us, at least not on my end."

A wry smile played on the edges of his lips. "Now you're just lying."

"Actually, I'm not, and you need to step back." She pushed harder against on his shoulders, but he didn't budge. Adrenaline fueled her. Her arms, strengthened by years of lifting large dogs, shot like torpedoes into his chest and propelled him toward the door.

The chef stumbled backwards and landed on the floor just as Adam opened the door.

"What's going on in here?" Adam asked.

"Nothing," the chef said, scrambling to his feet.

"Not nothing!" Rebecca's face burned. "Your chef is an egotistical jerk." She pushed past him and exited into the hallway where half a dozen people had congregated. "And I don't care how good his ribs are."

CHAPTER 27

*A*fter the guests were gone, Natalie, Cece, and Rebecca stayed to help clean up.

As Rebecca picked up a tray of dirty dishes, Adam took it from her. "Gimme that," he said. "You'll get your dress dirty."

"It's not actually my dress." Rebecca had no need to keep anything from Adam. He knew all about the makeover. "Natalie and Cece turned me into somebody I'm not. It was fun for a while, but this whole glamour look doesn't suit me."

Adam set the tray down and faced her. "I disagree. I think you pull it off perfectly."

Rebecca raised a shoulder. "Thanks, but it feels like all it got me was a very awkward encounter with the chef. And I didn't mean to shove him that hard."

"You're stronger than you look, I'll give you that much." Adam chuckled. "Listen, I am sorry about what happened. I never would've encouraged you to meet him if I'd known he was such a creep."

Rebecca waved off his apology. "It's fine."

"You definitely put him in his place."

Putting someone in his place hadn't been her plan. But the

chef had left her with no other option. And it felt good to do it. Really good.

NATALIE DELIVERED Rebecca home around midnight. The cottage was still except for the rhythmic tick-tick-tick coming from the oven clock and Mila's soft snores.

The dog lifted her head as Rebecca sat beside her on the cushion and stroked her silky ears. Mila still seemed to be struggling to adjust to Mr. B's death. Her new routine, three weeks old now, changed almost daily. Dogs thrived on consistency and expectations met.

"Such a good girl," Rebecca said, scratching Mila under the chin. "You want to sleep in my bed tonight?"

The dog rose and stretched and followed Rebecca into her room.

Warm breezes blew in through the open window, ruffling the filmy curtains. The bright moon cast a beam of light onto the wood floor.

With an arm draped over Mila, Rebecca stared at the yellow circle as she drifted off. She dreamed about kissing Chris, but just when their lips were about to touch, he became the chef, and the delicious dream turned into a nightmare.

THE SUN WAS BARELY UP when Rebecca began her Monday walk in Town Square Park with Mila and four other dogs. Thankfully, it was a well-behaved crew. Rebecca could manage the leashes in one hand and an extra-large coffee in the other.

After three walks in four hours, exercising eleven dogs in addition to Mila, Rebecca inhaled a peanut butter sandwich on her way to the shelter.

Mila collapsed in a sunny spot on the grass, ignoring her rambunctious playmates.

"You really wore that one out, didn't you?" Willy said, filling a giant metal dish with water from the hose. It splashed around his feet, and a young boxer jumped in circles trying to catch flying water droplets.

"She's exhausted. We went about twelve miles this morning." Rebecca carried the giant pooper scooper out onto the lawn and cleaned up the mess that had accumulated over the weekend.

"How long you been working here, Rebecca?"

"Over five years I guess. Why?"

"Just thinking I might hire a kid to do the grunt work a few days a week. Relieve us of doodie duty." He laughed.

"That would be totally amazing." Rebecca's mood lifted. The less crap she had to manage the better.

Rebecca spent the next couple of hours at the desk answering the phone and reviewing adoption applications and over-thinking the previous night's hug. She'd practically thrown herself at Chris. How would she explain it? She tried meditating him out of her head, but her focus was weak. And the fact that he'd kind of hugged her back was even more confusing.

She dropped her head onto the desk with a thud. No matter what unfolded when she saw Chris, she'd act as if nothing had happened. Hopefully he would, too.

Rebecca finished her shift at the shelter and loaded Mila into the Suburban. Her jitters, which had subsided with the distraction of work, returned with renewed force.

Her cell chimed with a call from her mother.

"Hey, mom, what's up?"

"My goodness, I haven't seen you since yesterday morning. How was the barbecue at Adam's house? Did you have a good time?"

It was a complicated question that required a simple answer. "Yeah, it was fun."

"And how did your makeover go? You never even sent me a photo."

"I looked super different."

"Well, that's intriguing. Can't wait to see a picture. In the meantime, I need to borrow your car. My battery died again."

"But I'm already on my way to work at Mr. B's house." She pushed the key into the ignition and started the motor.

"Well, just swing by here, pick me up, and then I'll drop you there on my way into town."

Rebecca considered the logistics. "I guess that'll work. But I'm in a hurry so be ready."

At the cottage, Mila jumped out of the car and trotted inside. She took her spot on the cushion in the window seat and rested her head on crossed paws.

"Mom, are you ready?"

"Be out in one minute," her mother called from behind her bedroom door.

With time to spare, Rebecca washed her face and studied it in the mirror, her eyelashes were as pale as the flesh on the inside of an apricot. Rebecca swiped a few layers of mascara over them and highlighted her cheekbones with light pink blush.

She peeled off her denim overalls, opting for white cut-offs and a light green tee-shirt—nondescript at best, but better than dirty overalls. And the green top did match her eyes.

"What is wrong with you?" Rebecca asked herself. "He is the most unavailable man in the world."

"Who are you talking to?" Her mother opened the door. "Ah, yourself."

"Yep, myself." She slipped her feet into flat sandals. "I'm my own best company."

At the door, Rebecca whistled for Mila to come. The dog raised her head, stared at her for a moment, then looked away.

"She's still terribly glum, isn't she?" Alice said.

"She is. I think she can't give up on Mr. B. Every time we go to his house, she races around looking for him. I probably shouldn't bring her there anymore."

Alice sighed. "I guess she needs to learn that that house is no longer her home."

"It's nobody's home, is it?" Something shifted in Rebecca's mind. She needed to cement her memories of Mr. B in her heart, because the house would soon be gone, flattened and broken and carted to the dump.

Rebecca left Mila behind and followed her mother out to the car. While Alice drove toward the main road, Rebecca ate two granola bars.

"Is that your lunch?"

"Kinda." Rebecca shook crumbs from the wrapper into her mouth.

"Maybe we should go out to dinner tonight," her mother said.

That was Alice's way of getting Rebecca's undivided attention so she could pepper her with motherly questions.

"I thought we were trying to save money. A week ago you made tuna casserole."

"I know. But it's been forever since I've had a night off, and Zack is working reception until ten, so we can sneak out for an hour or two. What do you say?"

Rebecca hesitated. What if she and Chris were making so much progress they wanted to keep working? What if he suggested they order pizza? What if they made horchata and sat on the back porch and watched the sunset?

"Yes, let's go out to dinner." Rebecca slammed the window on her overactive imagination.

"That's my girl." Her mother squeezed her knee.

When they arrived, the driveway was empty except for Mr. B's old truck that hadn't been moved in weeks. No sign of Chris's rental car.

"I'll text you when I'm ready to be picked up," Rebecca said.

Inside the house, two floor fans circulated the hot air. For the first time, she was able to view Mr. B's home with a different perspective. Everything looked the same, but it wasn't. The aroma of toasted bread, the sound of boots on the hardwood floor, gone as if they'd never been real.

Mr. B's cowboy hat rested on the hook by the door. It had been there since the day he'd dropped it and Rebecca had picked it up and put it where it belonged. She lifted it off the hook and inhaled the scent of the warm, soft fabric.

An image of Mr. B the day she'd met him at the shelter jolted her emotions to the surface. She put the hat on her head, sat in his recliner, and allowed herself one more cry over the loss of her friend, her mentor, her soulmate.

Rebecca wept, as if she could empty herself of all the emotion preventing her from accepting reality.

Finally, she finished her cathartic episode. Rebecca blew her nose, wiped her eyes, and got to work. There were empty boxes strewn about, their flaps open, waiting to be filled. She zeroed in on Mr. B's desk. The drawers were jammed with ancient office supplies—dried out pens, sticky notes that had lost their stickiness, rusty paperclips, and a lifetime supply of Scotch tape. Rebecca set aside anything usable, which wasn't much, and dumped the rest of the contents into a plastic trash bag.

A bunch of papers and notes and files sat in a tall stack on the edge of the desk. Rebecca checked the little tabs where Mr. B had labeled them: *Receipts, Bills, Statements, Land Use Restrictions*

"Land use restrictions?" Rebecca flipped open the folder. Inside were two pages out of the Town Charter—the two pages he'd asked Mrs. Larson to photocopy for him! One of the paragraphs was highlighted in bright yellow—and he'd underlined terms like *restricted residence zoning, ordinances, petitions.*

Despite the mind-numbing, esoteric legalese and language,

Rebecca was able to glean the broad message that interested Mr. B, especially the part about residents having authority over the approval of large scale construction projects.

A loud, obtrusive knock interrupted her reading. She hurried to the door, expecting to see Chris's handsome face.

It was anything but.

"Hello, Red." Troy Dayton stood on the porch as if he were a welcome guest.

"What are you doing here?" she asked.

"I could ask the same of you, but I already know." His eyes drifted upward. "Nice hat."

Rebecca yanked the cowboy hat off her head and returned it to its spot by the door.

"I'm here to see Chris," Troy said.

"What for?" Rebecca asked.

"Not that it's any of your business, but to have him sign some documents so we can get this place on the market."

He was so full of himself Rebecca half expected him to buff his fingernails on the lapel of his sport coat. She knew the property had to be sold, but she'd hoped Chris wouldn't involve the slimy real estate agent. Mr. B didn't like him, and neither did she.

"Well, he's not here. And I don't know when he will be."

"Maybe I'll just hang out and wait." Troy's cell buzzed in his hand. He glanced at the screen. "Ah, dammit."

"What's wrong now?" Rebecca sounded flippant on purpose.

The suave realtor loosened his tie. "Again, not your business, but it appears I can't wait. I've got a major deal that's about to close, and my client needs me. No worries, I'll give Chris a call, catch him another time." He waved it off as an insignificant annoyance.

"Well then, goodbye." Rebecca tried to close the door, but Troy stuck his foot out.

"Hold on a sec. It's a scorcher out there. Do you think I could get a glass of water before I go?"

He did look overheated with his red face and sweat trickling from his hairline. And although she couldn't stand him, Rebecca was not the kind of person who would let a fellow human dehydrate.

"Fine."

Troy stepped into the house, his head swiveling. "Is that dog around?"

"If she were, she'd have attacked you already." Rebecca led him toward the kitchen and filled a glass with water and ice.

He drank like a man lost in the desert then set the glass in the sink. His eyes fell upon the page from the Town Charter which she'd placed on the counter.

"What's this?" he asked, picking it up.

Rebecca snatched it from him. "It's nothing."

Troy leaned against the refrigerator, arms crossed. "Too late, I already saw. Why are you interested in zoning and ordinances?"

"I'm—I'm not. I was just..." she pressed her lips together. What difference did it make if he knew that she knew what was in the town charter? "Actually, I've been doing a little research."

"I see." The realtor rubbed his palms together. "Now it makes sense."

"What does?"

"Your little project. I ran into the librarian the other day. She mentioned you'd been snooping around."

"Snooping?" As gossipy as Mrs. Larson was, Rebecca knew she wouldn't have used that word.

"Well, I believe inquiring was what she said. And that our friend Benito had been looking into it right before he died." He made it sound like some kind of conspiracy.

"Mr. B was not your friend. And neither of us did anything

wrong," she said, wishing she had the nerve to splash ice water in his face.

"Hey, I'm not suggesting you did. Just wondering why you're interested. I mean, no offense here, but you're just a dog walker."

Whether he intended to offend her or not, it sure sounded like an insult.

Rebecca straightened her back and glared at him. "Land usage happens to be a subject in which I'm quite interested."

"Is that so?"

Not really, she thought. At least not until recently.

She ran a finger along the edge of the paper. "Did you know that—that in order for certain construction projects to be permitted, the town council must approve them? And that any citizen can move for an objection?" She impressed herself with the succinct summary of what she'd just learned.

"Hmm," the realtor said, wiping perspiration from his brow. "And did you know ordinances that haven't been enforced have a de-facto expiration and cannot be brought before a town council due to the here-to-fore otherwise aforementioned abandonment statute?"

Whoa. That was the most convoluted run-on sentence she'd ever heard. But still, it could be true. Either way, Rebecca could tell she'd ruffled his feathers by the way his jaw jetted with indignation. She folded the paper in half twice and tucked it into her back pocket. "Whatever," she said with a benign lift of her shoulders. "Do you want more water?

"No, thank you." His lips spread out over his too-large teeth, part grin—part sneer. "I'll just be on my way."

"I'll escort you out."

He crossed in front of her and headed through the living room. "I can manage."

Troy opened the door then turned. "Listen, Rebecca, I'm not

sure where or why we got off track with each other, but I have no issue with you. You seem like a nice person."

"Okay." Rebecca didn't know what to make of his sudden conciliatory tone. He couldn't possibly think she had any influence over Chris's decision about the property. Or might he? If he did, she had no reason to make him think otherwise.

Troy Dayton swung his jacket over one shoulder. "And as far as those zoning ordinances go, they're rather complicated. I've been in the real estate business a long time, so if you have any questions about it let me know. I'll be happy to educate you."

"Educate me?" It sounded indecent, or at least mocking.

"Anytime you want." He handed her a business card, just like he had the first time they met, and skipped down the steps toward his fancy Lexus.

CHAPTER 28

The moment Troy's car was out of sight, Rebecca locked the door and texted Chris to tell him the realtor had come by to see him.

She watched her screen, waiting for his response. Nothing. Maybe he was driving. Maybe he'd turned off his phone. Maybe he didn't want to see or talk to her ever again. Maybe he was as mortified by the hug as she was.

The house felt even hotter since Troy left. Rebecca stood in front of the box fan and let it blow directly into her face. The encounter with the realtor had her mind spinning.

She sat at the table with the photocopied pages from the town charter and reread the sections Mr. B had highlighted regarding zoning and ordinances. Rebecca had no way of knowing if the restrictions would even matter anymore, especially after what Troy had said about a *de-facto expiration*.

She was about to start emptying the china cabinet when another loud knock interrupted her.

Chris, finally. She braced herself for whatever awaited and opened the door.

Jessica burst into the house. "Chris! Where are you?"

Rebecca jumped out of the way. "He's not here,"

"Where is he?"

"I'm not sure. Is something the matter?"

Jessica whipped around. "As if you don't know." She spat the words at her.

Rebecca faltered. "I don't know anything. When I got here, the house was empty, and that was like an hour ago. Chris was supposed to meet me here. You think something happened?"

"You bet something happened." Jessica flung her large tote onto the couch. "He's lost his mind."

"Lost his mind? What are you talking about?"

Jessica squinted at her. "You really don't know?"

"Know what?" Rebecca threw her arms to the side. Why did everything with this woman have to be so difficult?

Jessica swayed, as if deciding how to proceed. "Well, if Chris didn't mention it, then I..." she covered her face with both hands. "Forget I said anything, okay?"

What a strange girl Jessica was. She could be mean and offensive, yet vulnerable at the same time. Whatever she meant by Chris having lost his mind, it obviously distressed his girlfriend.

"Okay, I'll forget it." Rebecca agreed just to be polite. "You seem awfully upset though."

"How perceptive of you." Jessica mocked her with a disdainful glance.

"Why are you so mean?" Rebecca asked. "And pushy and downright rude?"

"Goodness me," Jessica said, derisive laughter erupting. "Who are you and what have you done with the innocent dog walker?"

"See?" Rebecca, more than half a foot taller, straightened her back. "Super rude. Didn't your mother teach you any manners?"

A pale blue vein on the side of Jessica's neck pulsated. "Don't ever bring up my mother."

Well, that warning packed a punch. Obviously, some heavy baggage existed between this girl and her mother. "I apologize," Rebecca said. "I didn't know it was a sore subject."

Jessica waved her off. She circled the room, her hands on her hips, as if checking on Rebecca's progress, then stopped. "Why is it that ever since Chris met you he's been—different."

Rebecca softened her voice. "Don't you think his grandfather's death and dealing with this house might have more to do with it?"

"Maybe," Jessica said, sliding her gold 'J' charm along the chain. "Maybe not."

The tiny woman, as pretty as a Disney princess, stared at Rebecca with big, round eyes. She pursed her naturally pink lips. "I know you think you're doing something heroic, fulfilling a death-bed promise or something like that. But here's the thing, Rebecca," she paused as if her words needed time to sink in, "you're in over your head. You know nothing about business or real estate. And you definitely know nothing about Chris."

The house, already hot, grew stifling. In a physical match-up, Rebecca could flatten Jessica. But in a meeting of the minds, she was sorely disadvantaged. Less educated, less experienced, less informed. Troy Dayton was right—she was *just a dog walker*.

"Wait." Rebecca pinched her lower lip. "Did you talk to Mr. Dayton?"

"I did. You need to understand that both he and I are doing what we can to help Chris wrap things up and unload his grandfather's property so he can focus on what matters. And what matters is his work and his life in Seattle. It's the best thing for everyone, even you. Don't you just want to put this whole ordeal behind you?"

Old insecurities flooded Rebecca's system. Jessica was sending a firm message, telling her to get out of the way and quit poking around in things that do not concern her. She should go back to doing what she knew how to do, as insignificant as those things might be.

Rebecca wasn't meant to challenge people. She was meant to please them.

Mr. B's faith in her was undeserved. She should have given up when Chris rejected his notes the first time she'd brought them to his attention.

Rebecca cowered under the scrutiny of the Disney princess. Sweat dripped into her eyes. She squeezed them tight against the sting. What in the world made her think she could climb a mountain when she was barely equipped to walk up a hill?

"Are you alright?" Jessica asked. "You look awfully pale. And you're pretty pale to begin with."

"I need to go." Rebecca grabbed her backpack and ran out the door, only to realize she had no car. She stopped in the driveway and texted her mother.

> COME GET ME NOW!

She tapped send just as Chris drove up. Timing was everything, and her timing was off in a big way, any escape now foiled.

Chris got out of the rental car, another nondescript compact, and halted at the sight of his girlfriend standing on the porch. "Jessica, what are you doing here?"

"I came to see you," she said sweetly. "We need to talk about, well, you know."

"No, we don't. There's nothing left to say." He turned to Rebecca. "Are you leaving?"

"Yeah. I gotta go." Rebecca couldn't wait to flee the scene, although she did wonder why Jessica's appearance had surprised her boyfriend.

"Hold on just a sec," Chris said to her. "Okay? Just wait."

Jessica marched down the steps. "Chris, please come inside. We—we need to talk privately."

Rebecca's curiosity flickered to life.

"If this is about the money, I'm done talking about it." Chris opened the water bottle in his hand and drank, then he wiped his mouth with the back of his hand. "It's not my father's decision what I spend it on or how I distribute it."

Rebecca's cell buzzed with a return text from her mother:

On my way!

She texted back:

No rush, take your time.

The back and forth between Chris and Jessica was too good to miss, and no doubt it had something to do with Jessica claiming he had lost his mind.

"I completely agree." Jessica stepped closer and clasped his hands with hers. "Now let's just go inside and—"

Jessica's phone rang, and she held up one finger. "I've got to take this." She threw a warning glance in Rebecca's direction before zipping into the house.

Rebecca reached for her braid and twirled the end into a tight ringlet. "Did you tell me to wait?"

'I did," he said, rocking on his feet. "I just wanted to mention that, well, about last night."

"Last night?" Rebecca responded as if she had no memory of it.

"Yeah, when you, I mean we hugged. I hope I—"

"It was my fault." Rebecca jumped in before he could tell her it didn't mean anything. Patty was right about her propensity to over-hug, and now she'd created the most awful, awkward situation with Chris. "I hug without thinking, and I should never have done that. I'm so sorry if I embarrassed you or made you uncomfortable. Really, it was nothing but—but an impulse, like a reaction. Like when you touch a hot stove and yank your hand away."

"Oh, okay." Chris nodded, his face void of expression. "I understand. And I'm sorry, too, I guess."

"Good. You're sorry, I'm sorry, we're all good," Rebecca said in sing-song fashion. She glanced down the driveway, now sorry she'd told her mother not to hurry.

"You're probably wondering what that was all about, you know, the part about my money?" Chris cracked his knuckles.

"Not really, no," she said, one shoulder inching upward toward her ear. "None of my business anyway."

He glanced back at the house, as if to be sure Jessica wasn't standing over them. "You must think this whole situation is crazy. I mean, even I think it is."

"Yeah, it's—it's a lot." Rebecca was hardly in the position to judge anyone else's family drama.

"Exactly. It's a lot, and I'm doing the best I can."

His vulnerability touched her heart. Rebecca almost reached out to hug him but caught herself just in time.

"I'm not sure why I'm telling you this," Chris said. "I guess I just need to talk to somebody who can understand why I'm being cautious."

"And you think I understand?"

"I think you do." Chris seemed to be searching her face for confirmation.

Rebecca gave him a sidelong glance. "No wonder Jessica thinks you've lost your mind."

Chris stifled a laugh. "Is that what she said?"

Rebecca hunched and covered her eyes. "Oh, geez, I don't know why I blurted that out. Besides, I probably heard it wrong."

"You didn't," Chris said with matter-of-fact lightness. "She does think that. And I frustrate her."

"Oh, well, that happens. My ex-boyfriend totally frustrated me. But then he was a real jerk." Rebecca wished she could sink into the ground. What was it about Chris that made her speak without thinking first? Mentioning her ex-boyfriend? She might as well have shouted *I'm single and available and have a crush on you!*

"Well, I'm glad you think I'm not a jerk, if that's what you were saying."

"Yes, that's exactly what I was saying. I mean, you are like the opposite of a jerk."

"Thanks." Chris pushed his hands into jeans pockets. "Anyway, right now she and I have a difference of opinion, you know, conflicting priorities."

Conflicting priorities, the reason some people want Clearwater to grow and some people don't.

"I get it," Rebecca said.

"I know you do." Chris seemed to find more meaning her words than she did. "Well, I'd better get inside."

He turned and walked up the steps like a man heading somewhere he didn't want to go.

Rebecca stood in the middle of the driveway in front of a house that once was filled with comfort and love. Mr. B would've been heartbroken to know that his home, his grandson's inheritance, had become the centerpiece of nothing but trouble and strife.

CHAPTER 29

*C*hris entered the house and steeled himself for another argument with Jessica. She was seated at the dining room table texting or posting or doing whatever she did on her phone. Chris closed the door loudly, and her head sprang up.

"Hey," she said, her tone conciliatory. "I know you're surprised to see me. Please don't be mad."

Chris paused to formulate a response. He and his girlfriend had been on the brink of breaking up the other night. But after tears on her end and exhaustion on his, he'd decided not to make any rash decisions. Too many balls in the air—not a good time to make a drastic, life changing move. And part of him did love her. Their relationship had been a whirlwind at first, fun and exciting, both of them caught up in the thrill of infatuation and being the most attractive couple in any room. But as soon as they were tested—the demands of work, petty jealousy, and Chris's realization they had practically nothing in common—the arguments began.

And here they were, about to embark upon another.

He kept his voice even, hiding his annoyance at being blind-sided by her sudden appearance. "I'm not mad, just surprised."

"Can we talk about the other night?" Jessica asked. "I mean, I never intended to hurt you."

"I know that." He took her hand and guided her to the couch. They sat side by side. "But you can't unsay what you said. And you meant it. You don't believe in me."

"But that's not what I said," she argued.

"It's what you implied. You think I'm dragging my feet and being indecisive, as if I don't know what the hell I'm doing. And then I find out you and my father are discussing me behind my back?"

"We weren't." She pressed both hands against her chest. "We were just—just talking about your grandfather's estate and how the money will—"

"I'm not going to be railroaded into a decision about this property or my money. Not by my father and not by you." Chris had no problem delaying. He was an information gatherer, the kind of person who needed to analyze every aspect of a situation before making a move. His father saw this as weakness, and evidently so did his girlfriend.

Jessica scratched her upper lip with a pink fingernail. Everything about her was perfect, maybe too perfect. It's what attracted him initially—physical beauty. Then she turned out to be ambitious and driven, qualities he admired. But eventually, the line between ambition and greed blurred.

Jessica's eyes pooled with tears. "All I want is for us to get back to our lives in Seattle, to move forward. A month ago we were looking at apartments together."

Chris swallowed hard. His stomach clenched. How could so much change in such a short time? "I know we were, but then my grandfather—"

"Our living together has nothing to do with your grandfather." She stiffened. "It has to do with us. And we are so good together, you and I, we're the perfect couple."

On social media, they were. Every photo, post, and story—

they appeared to be perfect, both of them beautiful and success-ful. Her highlights were full of fancy food eaten in expensive restaurants, weekend getaways to the mountains and resorts, spa days. But half of it was staged. Most of the meals Jessica photographed weren't even hers. The glorious weekend in the mountains was a trip she'd taken with girlfriends. And the photos of the two of them? She'd posted those even though he didn't want to be featured like a puppet in her social media world.

Chris drew back. How had he never noticed the life she was living was not his life? It was a show, a sham, a play in which he had no part.

"We just need to get back on track," Jessica said, reaching for his hands. "Tell you what, you'll be done here in a few days. When you get home, we'll start looking at places again. There's a condo you're going to love, right near downtown. I'll schedule an appointment for next—"

"Jessica, slow down." Chris kept his tone measured. "Let's just hold off until I get things settled here, okay?"

Her chest expanded, and her collar bones stuck out as her chin lifted. "And when will that be, Chris? When will you get things settled? In a week or two? A month? Three months? You haven't even listed the property, even though Troy Dayton has offered to handle everything. Why are you resisting it?"

"I don't like that guy."

"I don't care if you like him or not. He can fast-track the sale." Jessica stood. "You need to get this done. Your business is suffering, our relationship is—is off track, and I'm losing patience. It's time for you to make a decision."

That's exactly what he needed to do. Make decisions, move forward, get the work done. And change what needed to be changed. The path he'd been on for as long as he could remember had brought him to a fork in the road, a turnoff he'd never expected, and there was no way he could ignore it.

. . .

CHRIS SAT on his grandfather's porch overlooking the lake. Jessica had driven into town, supposedly to buy a few things at the drug store, but Chris knew she was angry with him. She probably was on the phone with one of her girlfriends complaining right now. At this point he didn't even care. The sunset mesmerized him, a mix of colors that reminded him of the orange and cherry ice pops he'd eaten with his grandfather that one perfect summer. He closed his eyes and imagined sitting on the swing, gliding it back and forth with Rebecca by— *Rebecca?*

"Whoa," he said aloud, shaking his head as if to rid himself of the thought.

His phone beside his leg vibrated with a call from his father. He declined it. They'd talked enough in the last few days. A minute later, a text appeared:

You need to get home!

Chris ignored it. He left his phone on the swing and walked through the tall grass down to the lake. Cool water lapped at his feet. The faraway sound of laughter, a dog barking. He squinted into the distance toward Lakeview Lodge.

'*Get home,*' his father had demanded.

Chris didn't know where home was anymore.

CHAPTER 30

*R*ebecca waited at the reception desk on pins and needles for them to arrive. When Chris showed up, she noticed his pinched face and downturned lips.

"Thanks for arranging a room at the last minute," he said.

"You're welcome. I'm afraid the only cottage we have left is the smallest one. It's still nice, though."

"I'm sure it's fine for one person," he said, setting his credit card on the counter.

"One person?"

Chris's dark expression implied something had changed. "I'm staying at the house. Jessica and I are, well, we had a…"

Rebecca pressed her knees against each other to keep her legs still. The idea that the beautiful couple might have had an argument sent her mind in a dozen directions. Although she wasn't surprised, not after the interaction she'd been privy to earlier.

"I'm sure it'll all work out," Rebecca said. Of course she no idea—it just sounded like something she ought to say.

"Where's Mila?" Chris asked. "I was hoping for one of her exuberant greetings."

"I left her with my mom."

"Oh, well, that's good. She's a lucky dog to have you after losing her master."

"Yeah, I'm lucky to have her." Rebecca was still thankful Jessica had stepped in and refused to let Chris take Mila back to Seattle.

"She's adjusting pretty well then?"

"We're getting there." She wondered why he was making small talk. "I can show you to the cottage."

"I'll find it. I think I know my way around here by now."

"I guess you do." Rebecca handed him the key. "It's Rosewood, down the first path to your right. You'll run right into it."

"I assume there are plenty of towels," Chris said with mock seriousness.

"Plenty." She mirrored his glibness.

Chris tapped the counter. "Alright then. Thanks, Rebecca."

"Sure," she said, now wishing he'd linger a bit longer.

And then he did.

"One more thing…"

She caught her breath.

"…do you know of a shredding place around here? I found a couple boxes of old bank statements and stuff. I think that kind of thing should be shredded."

"Oh." Her breathing returned to normal. "Yeah, there's one by the office supply store. I drive by it all the time. Why don't I take the boxes for you?"

"You don't mind?"

"Part of the job, isn't it? I'll pick them up tomorrow or the next day, whenever you want."

"There's no rush. It's all just trash anyway."

"Right. Trash."

"I'd better go, Jessica's waiting in the car. Have a good night." Chris backed up a few steps then stopped and squeezed his forehead with one hand. "Rebecca, I'm really sorry I dragged you into this mess. I mean, it's gotten so much more complicated than I ever expected it to. I thought this inheritance was going to be the greatest thing that ever happened to me, but—but now I'm not so sure."

Rebecca ached to be close to him, to touch his hand, caress his cheek—but she planted her feet where they were and spoke with reverence. "You know, your grandfather used to say there's a very thin line between a blessing and a curse."

Chris revealed the trace of a smile. "Wise man," he said. "I wish I'd known him better."

REBECCA SPENT the night talking herself out of falling for Chris. She revisited every boyfriend and crush she'd had starting with the little curly haired boy who couldn't tie his shoes in kindergarten all the way to the most recent failed relationship. Her track record with men was sorry at best. Falling for Chris would lead to a broken heart for sure.

Finally, she fell into a deep, dreamless sleep that ended at sunrise with Mila nudging and whining at her to wake up. The poor dog had been confined to the cottage all day yesterday, so she was wound up and in need of exercise.

Rebecca wished she could let her loose. In her old life, the faithful dog could run free and would always return home at the sound of Mr. B's whistle.

The outside air smelled especially fresh. Birds chirped, and lizards skittered in the bushes. Rebecca waved at her mother who was already setting up coffee on the patio by the lodge.

With Mila on a long lead, Rebecca let her romp in the water chasing sticks and balls. A few early risers were out in rowboats and paddle boards.

Mila dropped a stick at Rebecca's feet and barked.

Rebecca picked it up. "Can I trust you?

Mila barked again.

"I hope you're not lying." She removed the leash and threw the stick into the water. Mila retrieved it and came right back. She was learning, getting used to her new life, adjusting.

Rebecca peered in the direction of Mr. B's property. In the distance she could just make out the little dock bobbing on the water, the old rowboat tied to its mooring. Her worries, which had been pushed aside last night when she couldn't stop thinking about Chris, returned. What would happen in Clearwater if developers moved in to build hotels and condos and horrible strip malls? The town, the lake, the neighborhoods, the vineyards—all would be changed, if not destroyed. And there was nothing she could do about.

Chris would unload his inheritance eventually, whether he dragged his feet or not. And Rebecca was ready, too. Although she wanted Mr. B's intentions to be granted, trying to represent them was becoming a burden. She was exhausted, frustrated, disillusioned. She was over it.

CHAPTER 31

*B*rad Redmond read the pages from the town charter with keen interest. He even made notes in the margins. Rebecca, sitting across from him at a small table inside Nutmegs, stuffed a large bite of sticky bun into her mouth and washed it down with a gulp of milk.

After her romp at the lake with Mila, Rebecca had called Brad and told him about the pages Mr. B had copied from the town charter. It was her final card, her last chance, the only thing preventing her from giving up. She half-hoped he would advise her to quit. All she needed was a tiny nudge.

The other half of her held her breath, clinging to a thin rope. Regardless of who ended up buying Mr. B's property, the esoteric language in the town charter could prevent Clearwater from becoming one more overbuilt, overcrowded victim of misguided progress.

Brad looked up. "Interesting," he said.

"Really?"

"Very." He tapped the point of his pen on the paragraph Mr. B had highlighted. "I'll tell you, Benito knew what he was up against. And this makes complete sense now. I'm rather embarrassed I didn't think of it before. There's little doubt that this ordinance could tie up a major project for months if not years."

Rebecca leaned in. "So that might make a builder less interested in Mr. B's land?"

"Exactly. The problem is, it has to be tested. And without a proposed project I don't know how, or if, the town council would deal with the ordinance. Their job is to balance many interests, including the desire of those who want growth."

"I can't imagine anyone who'd want to see Mr. B's property turned into a giant condo complex."

"You'd be surprised how many people would. Big projects mean big money."

Rebecca pinched her lips between her fingers. "So what am I supposed to do now?"

"Start attending the town council meetings. There might be an opportunity for you to make a motion on the subject."

"Me? I've never even been to a town council meeting. Besides, I'm a nobody. I have no skills or knowledge or influence. I'm just a girl who walks dogs."

"Let me turn that around for you, Rebecca." Brad pointed the pen at her face. "What you are is a concerned citizen of this town. And that, my friend, is power."

BRAD'S PEP talk did little to change her mind. Rebecca doubted that any random concerned citizen wielded power. She was beginning to hope Troy Dayton was right, that the ordinance Mr. B had discovered was expired due to whatever mumbo-jumbo reasoning the realtor had used. That would be the nudge she needed to call it quits with a clear conscience.

After ten miles of dog walks and a couple hours at the shelter, Rebecca drove to Mariano's. She found Patty in the storeroom opening boxes.

"Perfect timing," her boss said.

"You want me to take over unpacking?"

"I sure do. I'll go clear a couple of shelves for a new display. We'll have room for about half of everything, and the rest you can put in storage."

"Sounds good," Rebecca said, slicing a strip of packing tape with scissors. Working alone in the back room suited her mood. She had some deep thinking to do.

She'd been unpacking jars and wiping them off when a hunger pang rumbled in her stomach. Had she eaten lunch? She couldn't even remember.

One of the great benefits of working in a gourmet shop was the availability of tasty snacks. Tessa was fastidious about expiration dates, so foods nearing the end of their shelf life were transitioned out of the shop and into a cupboard in the back for general consumption. Rebecca opened a jar of perfectly good but out-of-date peach preserves and spread it on crackers.

The back door of the storeroom rumbled open, and Tessa entered with Buttercup, the sweet St. Bernard Tessa rescued from Furry Friends a few years back.

The dog romped toward Rebecca. She kissed the top of Buttercup's basketball sized head and hugged the top half of her body.

Tessa laughed. "What? No hug for me?"

"Oh, sorry, did you—," Rebecca realized she was kidding. "Yeah, I'm supposed to work on less hugging."

"So I heard. For what it's worth, I don't mind an occasional hug." Tessa offered her one, and Rebecca accepted with gusto.

"Thanks for that. Are you hungry? I just opened some peach preserves."

"Perfect, I'm starving," Tessa said. "And how about some green juice? You look like you could use one."

Green juice, the grassy nutritional drink Tessa pushed on

everybody in need of a boost. She took one from the industrial refrigerator and poured it into two plastic cups.

"Here you go. I know you don't like it, so I'm only making you drink half."

Rebecca forced down a gulp of the grassy juice and shivered. "I don't think I'll ever get used to this stuff."

"It's like stinky cheese, an acquired taste." Tessa gave her an appraising look. "You want to tell me what's going on?"

"It's kind of a long story." Rebecca hesitated to unload her drama on Tessa. "And you're so busy."

"Just a sec." Tessa got up and pushed open the swinging door into the shop. "Hey, Patty, everything under control in there?"

"All good!"

"I'm here if you need me." Tessa returned to the stainless steel counter where Rebecca was working and made another cracker with peaches. "Alright now, you have my attention."

"I'll try to be brief." Rebecca licked a remnant of preserves from her thumb. "I know you prefer quick stories to long ones, and plus you have tons of—"

Tessa pressed her hand. "Shorter is definitely sweeter. Get started."

Rebecca told her everything, the entire story, from her run in with Jessica to the possibility that Chris is for some reason dragging his feet to Brad Redmond's suggestion that she, as a citizen of their town, has a voice and the right to speak.

When the story ended, Rebecca pressed her lips together and folded her hands in her lap.

Tessa exhaled a breath of air, as if she'd been the one talking non-stop. "I must say, it sounds like you've learned a lot in the last few weeks."

Rebecca nodded. "I have, not that I ever intended to."

"To be honest, I'm impressed by how you've handled the situation you stumbled into. I may have underestimated you."

"I'm not sure if that's a compliment or not."

Tessa finished her green juice. "Probably a bit of both. You do have a reputation for being a little flighty."

"I know." Rebecca had never been in denial of the impression she gave, accurate or not. "For some reason it suits me—keeps expectations low."

"That's one way to avoid disappointing people." Tessa raised an eyebrow.

Rebecca stared at her. Tessa was right—Rebecca always did her best to not disappoint, because disappointing people led to conflict, the main thing she truly wanted to avoid. Although in the last few weeks, she hadn't been very successful at that.

Tessa patted her on the back. "I've known you a long time, Rebecca, ever since you and your mom came to Clearwater. And although it doesn't seem like it, you and I have a lot in common. Both of us suffered losses at a young age."

Rebecca nodded. Tessa's mother had died young, and then her father abandoned her, leaving her to be raised by Nonna.

"We had childhoods fraught with upheaval and uncertainty. In my case, I became a control freak. You, a pleaser."

A pleaser, that's exactly what she was. She wanted everyone to be happy with her, and the idea of making anyone mad threw her into a state of debilitating anxiety.

"Here's the thing, Rebecca. There's nothing wrong with being a pleaser. Although I find it annoying now and then, especially when you can't make a decision, your pleasing nature makes you likable."

"I like to be likable," Rebecca said. "It was so hard for me to make friends when I was a kid, moving around and changing schools all the time. I—I at least wanted to be liked."

"Doesn't take a degree in psychology to figure us out, does it?" Tessa said with a wry smile. "Most of us are the way we are for a reason."

Rebecca toyed with a curl beside her ear. "Is there a reason you're telling me this now? Are you suggesting I need to change or something?"

"Honestly, I'm not sure. I just see a difference in you lately."

"Good or bad?" Rebecca asked.

"Definitely good. Ever since Benito died and left you with a —a purpose."

Rebecca twirled the curl around her finger. "But it's not something I wanted. All it did was take me down a rabbit hole into ordinances and restrictions and—"

Tessa's mobile phone, vibrating on the stainless steel, lit up with a text. Tessa glanced at the message. A deep frown creased her forehead. "Well, how about that."

"What?" Rebecca asked.

"Looks like you're ruffling feathers all over the place." Tessa slid her phone over. "From our friendly neighborhood landscaper, the one who owns the gigantic nursery."

Rebecca read the message aloud:

> Tessa, does that dog walker still work for you? She's stirring up a whole heap of trouble. Might be time to cut her loose.

"Oh my God," Rebecca's heart dropped. "Why would someone say that? And how does anyone know I'm stirring up trouble? I don't mean to be, I swear I don't."

She felt like Dorothy in The Wizard of Oz after her house dropped on the wicked witch. An innocent girl who intended no harm, but harm she caused none-the-less. "Do you want me to quit, Tessa? I will if you need me to. The last thing I'd want is for your shop to suffer because of something I did."

"Good heavens, no! You think I've gotten as far as I have by caving into threats or competitors who had it out for me?" Tessa tapped her screen and typed her response:

> I have no intention of cutting Rebecca Sparks loose. And by the way, cancel that 25K landscaping job on my house. I'm not interested in working with a bully.

Rebecca gasped. "Did you really just do that?"

"I sure did," Tessa said, waving both hands as if it were a minor decision. "No big deal. Her design wasn't all that great."

Rebecca threw her arms around Tessa. "Thank you, thank you, thank—"

"Okay, okay." Tessa disentangled herself. "Enough hugging."

"Sorry." Rebecca locked her arms at her sides.

"You're being challenged," Tessa said. "Brad is right—not everyone is on the side of keeping Clearwater the way it is. The further this goes, the uglier it will get. You need to stay the course on this. It might have been something Benito started, but for better or for worse, it's been left to you to finish."

"Do you mean his property? Or his digging into the town charter? They're two separate things—aren't they?"

"Separate but connected, it doesn't matter. What matters is that a strong woman never runs from a fight worth fighting."

FORTIFIED by Tessa's support and conviction, Rebecca plowed forward. After her shift at Mariano's ended, she crossed the street and sprinted through Town Square Park to the library.

Without a word, Mrs. Larson handed her the town charter.

Rebecca carried it to the table and spent the next hour studying and taking notes on land use, building restrictions, and citizen approval. To her surprise, she found her investigation to be more interesting than expected. Evidently, being a concerned citizen carried plenty of weight.

"You're sure busy over there," Mrs. Larson said, her rainbow framed glasses perched on the tip of her nose. "That town charter hasn't received this much attention in decades."

Rebecca brushed a few wisps of hair off her face. "What do you mean?"

"You're the third person today reading it. First one was that nosy realtor, what's his name, Troy something. And then just a few hours ago, the owner of the landscaping business dug into it." Mrs. Larson laughed at her own joke. "Pun intended. Get it? Dug into it, like with a shovel, like when you dig in dirt?"

"I get it," Rebecca said with a polite laugh. No surprise that the landscaper had an interest in Clearwater expanding. New construction required new landscaping. It was all about money. "Did either of them say anything about it? Or have any reaction?"

"Not that I could tell." Mrs. Larson glanced at the old-fashioned school clock on the wall. "My goodness, it's late. Afraid I have to close up. You can always come back tomorrow."

Rebecca closed the book. "I probably won't have time tomorrow, maybe the day after. But if anyone else is involved in the town charter, will you let me know? Unless it's some kind of violation to reveal who's reading what, you know like private information. Is it?"

The librarian twisted her mouth to the side. "It could be, but I'm not worried. Everybody knows everybody's business around here anyway. So, where are you off to now?"

"I think I'm heading home, unless I'm needed at the shelter. Sometimes we get strays dropped off at odd hours."

"Goodness gracious, you really are everywhere, aren't you? I've never seen anybody with so many jobs. And now you're the *Champion of Clearwater*, defending the charter upon which this town was built." Mrs. Larson pumped a fist in the air.

CHAPTER 32

The next morning, rays of light shined through the branches on the giant oak, and long shadows stretched across the grass at the park. Rebecca jogged on the path with three dogs, her first walk of the day. A few early risers passed by with waves and smiles.

After one lap around, she stopped by the gazebo and turned on the spigot to let the dogs lap up some water before they started their second loop.

"Come on guys," Rebecca said, tugging the leashes. "Back to our workout."

She'd taken only a few steps when Nonna appeared in a powder blue jogging suit and wide brimmed hat.

"Hi, Nonna!" Rebecca didn't hesitate to hug the woman who accepted her affection with equal enthusiasm. "How are you?"

"You know me, grateful for every day, especially one as beautiful as this. Although I dare say it's a good thing we're out early. I've barely been walking ten minutes and already I'm perspiring." She slipped off her jacket and tied it around her waist. "May I join you and your little pack?"

"Sure, I'd love it."

They fell into an easy conversation about mundane matters before Nonna brought up the rumor mill.

"I hear you've tip-toed into a bit of an awkward situation, my dear."

Rebecca grunted. "I hope it's only that, but I think I've really made some people mad around here. I never meant to, you know, I only want to do what's right."

"Ah, the dilemma of the peacemaker." Nonna's lips tightened. "People think doing the right thing should please everyone, but it never does. That's why we must have clarity and commitment. Otherwise, it's too easy to quit."

"I want to quit," Rebecca said. "I hate stirring up trouble, and I never wanted to study the town charter. And I for sure didn't want to get sucked into the problems Mr. B's grandson has with his father and girlfriend."

"Oh, dear, that does sound messy." Nonna slowed down the pace. "But it's your choice."

"My choice?"

"Yes, dear."

"Not really. This all landed in my lap when Mr. B died. I can't just pretend it didn't. And now that I've made such a mess of things, I feel like it's my responsibility to clean it up."

"It's your choice," Nonna repeated.

Rebecca stopped to let the dogs sniff a tree trunk. "But I didn't choose this. The whole thing started off so small—a couple of pages of notes Mr. B wrote for his lawyer. And then he died, leaving it to me to handle."

Nonna grasped Rebecca's elbows. "Benito did not leave it to you. He died unexpectedly, you know that."

"I know," she said, her head dropping forward. "I guess you're right. It was my choice to try to finish what he started. I just never thought it would get so out of control."

"Control is a complicated thing—a mixed bag you could say." Nonna straightened the brim on her hat. "Pay closer attention to the little decisions, the option to go one way or a different way. You'll come to find out how much control you actually have. My guess is it's more than you think."

CURLY WAS WAITING by the back door when Rebecca let herself into Tiffany Pressman's fancy townhouse. The kitchen was immaculate, as if the cleaning crew had just been there.

"Oh, Rebecca, good morning." Tiffany wore a silk robe, and her hair was wrapped in a terrycloth turban. She poured coffee into a tall white mug.

"Hi," Rebecca said. "I thought you'd be at work by now. It's after eight."

"I took a day off," Tiffany said, tapping her red fingernails against the white porcelain. "My sister and I are going out for her birthday."

"That's nice."

"Yes, well, she's a stay-at-home mom, so I'm treating her to a massage and high tea in the city."

Rebecca could only imagine how much an outing like that would cost. She picked up Curly's leash and began to strap him into the harness when Nonna's advice struck like a gust of wind.

"Tiffany, did you see I resubmitted the Venmo request? I know how busy you are, and I hate to keep asking, but I really need to—"

"I've been meaning to do that. When I get to the office tomorrow, I'll catch up." She started for the stairway.

Rebecca's breathing sped up. Choices, decisions, control—all within her power.

"Tiffany, wait."

The intimidating business woman in the silk robe turned. "What? I'm in a hurry."

"I'm sorry, but I can't walk Curly until you pay your bill. I've been waiting for weeks."

"I said I'd take care of it tomorrow."

"No," Rebecca said, loud and firm. "Unless you pay me now, I won't walk Curly. Which is really sad, because he obviously needs his walk. And if you don't pay me now, you'll have to find a new dog walker."

Tiffany's face turned as red as her nails. "You're not serious."

"I'm totally serious," Rebecca remained resolute but polite. "I love dog walking, but it's my work and how I earn money. Would you go to work if your boss didn't pay you?"

Tiffany blinked at her, as if she were looking into the face of a stranger.

Rebecca removed her phone from the front pocket of her overalls and opened the money-transferring app. "As soon as I receive the money, Curly and I can be on our way."

PATTY'S MOUTH GAPED, and she slapped both hands against her cheeks. "You really said that? To Tiffany Pressman?"

"Can you believe it?" Rebecca's heart still pounded, hours later. "And it wasn't even that hard. I mean, once I realized it was up to me, I just went for it. And I told her she needed to pay me a week in advance from now on."

Patty grasped Rebecca's upper arms. "I'm so proud of you. It's liberating, isn't it?"

"It really is." Rebecca tightened the sash on her Mariano's apron, her chest high and proud, and got to work, recalling Tiffany's deer-in-the-headlights look when Rebecca demanded her money. With the rush of adrenaline in her system, she'd taken Curly on an extra-long walk, figuring the poor dog who came perilously close to losing his dog walker deserved added attention. It wasn't his fault he belonged to a woman like Tiffany Pressman.

Halfway through her shift, Rebecca's energy returned to a normal level, and she went about her tasks as usual—carrying cases of wine to cars, dusting shelves, and cleaning up after a customer who had dropped a jar of the most expensive honey they carried. Although the woman offered to pay for it, Patty assured her it wasn't necessary.

"Good thing Tessa isn't here," Patty said, plucking pieces of glass out of the puddle of golden goo. "That Manuka honey is one of her favorites. And you know how she can't stand waste."

"At least the customer bought a bottle of wine." Rebecca pushed the lever on the bucket to squeeze water out of the mop.

"Exactly," Patty said. "And she'll probably come back some day."

Rebecca mopped with vigor until every bit of stickiness was gone.

At four o'clock, she removed her apron and tucked it under the counter. Her day had begun at seven and she hadn't had a break. "See you later, Patty."

"Oh, wait, I just need to run to Nutmegs to pick up some cookies for a gift basket order. Can you stay another fifteen minutes?" Patty asked, one foot already out the door.

"Sure." Rebecca yawned as she put her apron back on. She helped herself to a snack from the sample charcuterie tray—cheese and salami on a sourdough baguette with roasted red pepper spread. Her mouth was full when the door opened, bells jingling, and a customer walked in. She swallowed quickly.

"Hello." Rebecca said, her tongue catching a crumb on her upper lip. "Welcome to Mariano's."

"Is Tessa here?" The woman wore Khaki pants, a white sleeveless top, and slip on sneakers. She had straight dark hair with severe bangs that sliced straight across her forehead.

"I'm afraid she's not," Rebecca said. "Is there something I can help you find?"

The woman dropped her keys into her purse. "You're Rebecca, aren't you?"

"Yes, ma'am." Rebecca tucked her hands into her apron pockets. "I'm sorry, but I don't think I know you. We have so many customers that sometimes I don't remember everyone who—"

"We've never met, so don't worry about that. My name's Stephanie Carter. I own a landscaping business, and Tessa is one of my clients."

The owner of the landscaping business who tried to get Tessa to fire her? Rebecca set her jaw and said nothing.

"I hear you've been pursuing the resurrection of some old ordinances in the town charter."

Rebecca blinked and held her breath, thinking it best she neither confirm nor deny.

"Benito Becerra and I were old friends, and we had a lively discussion about this very subject. He was dismayed to learn the ordinances were no longer enforceable. Ah, such a good, kind man, but he wasted time on an issue that was long since over. I wouldn't be surprised if the stress he brought upon himself contributed to his heart attack."

Rebecca's stomach churned.

"Anyway, I realize you're young and idealistic. Most people your age think business is evil and development is bad, but that's just not true."

Rebecca didn't know if she thought that or not. But whatever this woman stated as fact, Rebecca was inclined to think the opposite.

"Do you understand what I'm saying, Rebecca?"

"Um, I think so." Rebecca's fingers entwined around each other inside her apron pocket.

"Good then." Stephanie clutched her hands in front of her

chest. "Because I'd hate to see you waste your time, what with how busy you are working all your different jobs."

How did this woman know so much about her? Probably from Mrs. Larson, the nosy librarian who couldn't keep her mouth shut. Rebecca wondered if she had tipped off Stephanie to Mr. B's investigation as well.

"I am very busy." Rebecca knew Stephanie could not care less about how busy she was or how much time she might waste. "And I appreciate your concern," she said in a most sincere tone.

"Exactly. We're all busy with our jobs and families and community activities. Look at me—just like Tessa, I run my own business, and that business depends on growth. Imagine how you could grow your business with more people moving into the area." Stephanie's smile widened. "More people means more dogs. You could double or triple your client base. And then you'd hire others to do the walking for you while you sit back and collect the money."

"I never thought about that," Rebecca said. She'd never farm out her beloved dogs, but the idea of making more money did appeal to her.

"Well, you should." Stephanie took a small step closer. She was shorter than Rebecca, but not by much. "Anyway, as long as you realize the town charter is just an archaic, meaningless document. That's what Benito found out—that his pursuit was completely pointless. And then he died."

Why did everyone keep reminding her that her friend had died? Geez, as if she didn't know it. Rebecca had a sudden urge to strangle the woman, but the bells on the door knob jingled, interrupting her indignation.

"I'm back." Patty placed a large Nutmegs bag on the counter.

The landscaper turned. "Hello, Patty."

"Stephanie." Patty glanced between Rebecca and the land-scaper, as if gaging the situation. "It's been a while."

"It has," Stephanie said, her voice aloof.

Rebecca blanched at the chilliness between them. How was there so much discord in Clearwater that she knew nothing about? Less than a month ago she was living in blissful ignorance, and now she encountered hostilities and dissension at every turn. Rebecca had spent her entire life avoiding conflict and animosity. But there were *mean girls* everywhere, not just in high school. Bullies came in all shapes and sizes—men like Troy Dayton, women like Tiffany Pressman. People who used armtwisting and clever manipulation to intimidate others.

Then there were those who stood up to them—and those who didn't.

"Are you here to buy wine?" Patty asked.

"She's not," Rebecca said. "Stephanie came to see me."

"She did?" Patty asked.

"I didn't, actually." Stephanie wagged her head. "I came to talk to Tessa about her landscaping project."

"The one she cancelled?" Rebecca asked with false innocence.

"Excuse me?"

Rebecca stood firm. She'd wandered into the mud, and now the only way out was to walk right through it. "I was there. She cancelled the project after you advised her to fire me because of all the trouble you think I'm stirring up."

Stephanie's eyebrows lowered. "Well, it appears I may have misjudged you, Rebecca. You're not the sweet little thing I thought you were."

Sweet little thing—that's how people had viewed her most of her life. Adrenaline pumped through her system, but the red blotches she expected to flush her skin remained beneath the surface. "I guess I'm not. But I'm certain Mr. B's pursuit was not pointless, and I won't be bullied into letting it go."

Stephanie planted her hands on her hips. "There's nothing you can do about it. I know Troy Dayton told you the ordinances were dead the other day."

Rebecca could not believe she'd been a topic of conversation between the realtor and a woman she didn't even know. Her discovery of Mr. B's research into the town charter had sparked quite the controversy.

The bells jingled, and a man entered the shop.

"I'll be right with you," Patty said to him before moving toward Stephanie. "You need to leave. You're disrupting business."

Rebecca opened the door and motioned with an upturned palm.

"Fine." Stephanie rolled her shoulders back. On her way out, she pointed at Rebecca's chest. "You're out of your league, young lady. Way out."

CHAPTER 33

*C*hris entered the attorney's office, located in a stately home in Napa. His grandfather's lawyer, Mr. Nash, greeted him with a warm handshake.

"It's nice to finally meet you, Chris. I've heard a lot about you over the years."

Chris returned the shake, but not the sentiment. Up until a few weeks ago, he didn't even know the man existed.

Mr. Nash gestured toward a leather club chair. Chris seated himself on the edge and glanced around the room, more of a cozy den than an office. Tall windows that looked out to a manicured backyard, over-stuffed bookshelves, and an old-fashioned cart with crystal bar glasses and decanters of amber liquid.

"This is a nice office." Chris clasped and unclasped his hands. The antique desk and paintings of ships were reminiscent of another era. "All the lawyers I deal with in Seattle work in skyscrapers, and their offices are as sterile as operating rooms."

Mr. Nash released a hearty laugh. "Don't I know it. I used to have an office like that. Couldn't wait to get out of there. I'm semi-retired now, but I keep a few select clients. Figured when I turned seventy-five last year, I deserved to surround myself only with people I liked and respected." He paused. "Men like your grandfather."

Chris picked up the hint, as if he didn't already know how respected and admired his grandfather had been. He squeezed the supple leather on the arms of his chair, waiting for the lawyer to get down to business.

"Can I offer you a drink? I got the good stuff right over there."

"No, thanks," Chris said, unable to relax. The great inheritance, the windfall that would change the trajectory of his business and the rest of his life, had resulted in the unintended effect of derailing him. "So, you have papers for me to sign?"

"I do." The lawyer placed a few sheets of paper on the coffee table. He explained what they were for then handed Chris a fancy pen. It felt substantial and weighty between his fingers. "Your grandfather had the property in his trust, so there's no probate. It's a rather seamless transaction."

Chris signed his name. "So that's it?"

"That's it, unless you have any questions."

Chris set the pen down. He had nothing but questions.

"I can see you're uneasy, which is understandable," Mr. Nash said. "This kind of situation is always difficult. I'm here to help. And in case you were wondering, I'm off the clock. Your grandfather was my favorite client, and he always paid his bill on time."

"I wish I could say that that sounds like him, but to be honest, I—I didn't know him all that well." There was something about the old lawyer that made Chris want to talk. "I mean, I did when I as a kid, but we lost touch a long time ago."

"Yes, Benito mentioned that." Mr. Nash's lips formed a tight line.

Chris sensed an opening in what had been a locked door for

most of his life. Maybe this man could tell him why his papa who had loved him so deeply had abandoned him.

"Do you know what happened? Why my grandfather stopped talking to me? Did I do something wrong?" Chris exhaled. Here he was, a grown man now, sounding like a child.

Mr. Nash uncrossed his legs then crossed them the other way. "No, that wasn't it at all. In fact—well, let me start with this. Benito became my client shortly after your mother died. It's what brought him to my office in the first place. He was considering..." the lawyer stopped. His jaw tightened, and he broke eye-contact.

"Considering what?" Chris's pulse sped up.

Mr. Nash stood. He went to the bar cart and poured a splash of scotch into a glass. "I hesitate to tell you."

"Mr. Nash," Chris said. "Please, for most of my life now I've been—been tormented because my grandfather abandoned me. If there was a reason, I need to know what it was."

The lawyer sipped his scotch. "Benito hired me after your mother's death because he wanted to seek custody of you."

If Chris hadn't been sitting, he would've fallen over. "Custody? Are you serious?"

"Completely."

Chris pressed his palm to his forehead. His stomach twisted. How different his life would have been if he'd spent his teen years with his grandparents in Clearwater. Instead, he ended up isolated with a father who traveled for business and a step-mother who, although not fairy-tale evil, was incapable of caring for an angry teenage boy whose mother was dead. "Well, what happened? I mean, I never knew anything about it."

"We were about to file the papers," the lawyer said, "when your grandfather changed his mind."

"Why did he do that?"

"Probably because I told him the likelihood of winning was slim to none. You had a father, and unless there had been evidence of abuse or neglect, no judge would have removed you from your home."

Home? Is that where he'd been? Not after his mother died. She was his home. "If I'd had the choice, I would've lived with my grandparents."

"You were too young to make the choice."

Chris glanced out the window, losing focus. The leaves and branches of the trees blurred. "But why did my grandfather stop calling? It was sometime after my mother died, and I never heard from either of my grandparents again. I called and called, and they never answered…"

Except once… One time his papa picked up, and it sounded as if he'd answered by mistake.

Papa, it's me!

Ah, mi hijo, we cannot speak anymore. I will write to you, and you will write back. That is the best we can do. I love you, my boy, always know I love you.

The memory caused a sharp pain in his chest. Chris swallowed a gasp of air, as if he'd been startled. "He said he couldn't talk to me anymore. I mean, why would that be? Why would my grandfather be unable to talk to me?"

The lawyer lowered his chin. "When your mother passed away, your grandparents were devastated, your grandmother in particular. She—she refused to eat, wouldn't even go outside. Fell into a kind of delirium. Benito was terrified she'd die of a broken heart. It wasn't until he brought Josephina's body here for burial that Antonia found a modicum of comfort. It brought her back to life, gave her a purpose I suppose, a place to put her heartache."

Chris pictured the graves he'd seen the day of his grandfather's funeral—mother and daughter side by side, together for all eternity. It made sense that his religious grandmother would want to be buried by her child who had died tragically. "It still doesn't explain why my grandparents cut me out of their lives."

Chris gave him a hard stare. The lawyer knew more than he was saying.

"It does not." Mr. Nash smoothed his gray mustache. "I wish I could help you, Chris."

What a curious statement, Chris thought, wondering how to interpret it. Maybe he knew nothing; maybe he knew something but couldn't say. The latter seemed more likely. After all, Nash was a lawyer, a trusted confidant. Even after his client's death, he would want to keep information private, err on the side of discretion.

"I wish you could, too." Chris started to stand, but then he changed his mind. If he dug a little deeper, perhaps he'd come up with something the lawyer would be able to talk about. This was his one opportunity. After today, he and Mr. Nash would probably never see each other again. "Do you know anything more about my grandfather's property?"

"Other than the fact that it's now yours?"

Chris proceeded with care. "My grandfather had, well, I guess you'd call her a friend. A young woman who helped him out with stuff around the house, kind of like a personal assistant."

Mr. Nash perked up. "You mean Rebecca. He loved that girl, talked about her every time I saw him. I think they kind of shared a dog. Have you met her?"

"Yes, a few times." Chris wasn't surprised to hear that his grandfather had loved Rebecca. From what he'd seen, everybody in town loved her. And with good reason. "I'm asking because she said something to me about my grandfather wanting to subdivide his property."

"Huh, interesting. I'd forgotten about that." Mr. Nash's bushy eyebrows moved inward. "Right before he died, he asked about donating a piece of land to the conservancy for public gardening or something. Said he'd had a run-in with a slick real estate agent that sparked a concern of some kind."

Slick real estate agent, no doubt Troy Dayton.

"What did you tell him?" Chris asked.

Mr. Nash scratched the back of his head. "Not much. It was such a quick conversation. Benito said he'd get back to me after he thought it through and made some notes. Of course, I never saw any notes because, well, you know…"

Chris pictured the crinkled pages Rebecca had shown him that night a few weeks ago, the notes he'd dismissed. Her devotion to his grandfather was steadfast, unflinching. And he'd accused her of having an ulterior motive.

"Are you okay?" the lawyer asked.

"I think so. Thanks for—for your time." He stood on shaky legs.

"Of course, and if you need me for anything, please don't hesitate. Your grandfather truly was one of the finest men I've even met, more integrity in him than ten men combined."

"Thank you," Chris said, because what else what else could he say? Benito Becerra was revered by everyone. And in death, even more so.

They walked through the foyer to the front door and shook hands.

"Mr. Nash," Chris said, "the thing you said about my grandfather wanting custody of me."

"Yes?"

"One of the things I remember about him was that he could be pretty stubborn. He didn't back down, even if he thought he'd lose."

The lawyer rested a heavy hand on Chris's shoulder. "You need to understand that a child at the center of a custody battle is an untenable situation. Nobody wins, everyone suffers, the child most of all. Your grandfather realized that. All he cared about in this world were you and his wife. You were the only two who mattered."

Chris thanked Mr. Nash again and took his leave. The entire

drive back to Clearwater he dwelled on those last words. The implication was clear. Had his grandfather sought custody, Chris would've been caught in the middle. And although he was too young to choose with whom he wanted to live, he'd been old enough to make his preference known. And it would have torn him apart. His family was already in shambles.

Still, a sliver of 'what if' disquieted him. What if his grandfather had gone forward and tried to take him away. The idea chilled him, wondering what his father might've done, the lengths to which he would have gone to make sure his father-in-law lost in a battle of Shakespearean proportion.

CHAPTER 34

*R*ebecca opened the back of the Suburban. She shoved aside an embarrassing pile of random stuff to make room for the two boxes headed to the shredder. Over the last few days, Rebecca had packed up all of Antonia's dishes and collectibles and put them in a storage shed at the lodge.

Chris maneuvered the boxes into the car. He reached up to close the trunk, his taut muscles visible. "Thanks for taking these. And whatever time it takes for you to shred all this paper, just add it to the hours you've already worked."

"Honestly, I've hardly worked at all." Rebecca's eye drifted toward the house. "Seems we keep getting interrupted. But I've cleared this weekend, so I can get all the clothes bagged up. I know you're in a hurry to put up the 'for-sale' sign."

Chris pushed a hand into his overgrown hair. "It's not really all that pressing."

"What do you mean?" Rebecca asked. "Troy Dayton seems to think it is."

"Troy, huh." Chris frowned. "You talked to him?"

"Yeah, the other day when he came by to meet you." Rebecca wished she hadn't brought it up—big mouth strikes again. "I hope I didn't say anything wrong, but he was so pushy about something that I, uh, I thought—"

"It's okay, Rebecca. None of this matters. When I do list the property, he won't be the realtor. I've already found someone else."

That was the best news Rebecca had heard all day.

"Do me a favor and keep that between us." Chris leaned against the back of her car. "I don't want to ruffle any feathers, at least not yet."

Now, they shared a secret. A pretty meaningless one, but a secret nonetheless.

"Who would I tell, anyway?" Rebecca said, trying to make light of it. A trickle of perspiration dripped into her eye, and she blinked. "So, do you want me to come back later?"

"I'm sorry, what?" Chris seemed far away, as if his mind and body were in two different places.

Rebecca was tempted to hug him. He looked like he could use a hug. But she wasn't hugging so much anymore. And she definitely wasn't hugging him. "Are you okay?"

"I have a lot on my mind."

"You want to talk about it?" she asked, hoping he would.

"Nah, it's not a big deal. Just, well, I met with my grandfather's lawyer earlier, and he told me some stuff that has me kind of perplexed."

That didn't sound like a small deal to Rebecca. "Perplexed is a good word. I think I live in a constant state of perplexation."

A slight smile, barely noticeable, but enough to make Rebecca think she'd amused him.

"Perplexation." It rolled off his tongue. "I like that word."

"I'm not sure it's actually a real word."

"I believe it is." His focus sharpened, and he beheld her with an intensity that made her heart skip. An invisible force drew them toward each other. Rebecca held her breath. She brushed some hair out of her eyes and moistened her lips.

"I'd better get inside," Chris said. "I have a conference call to get ready for."

"Oh, okay, see you tomorrow then," Rebecca said, flustered and embarrassed. What a foolish girl she was to think he'd wanted to kiss her.

"I probably won't be here. I'm flying back to Seattle."

"You're really racking up those miles, aren't you?" Rebecca laughed to cover up her disappointment. "When will you be back?"

"I'm not sure. I'll text you though." Chris picked at some chipping paint on the railing. He'd said he had to prepare for a call, but he made no move to go inside. "I really have to thank you, Rebecca. You've been a huge help, especially the last few days."

"Hey," she said lightly, "that's what I was hired to do."

"It's more than that." A wistful, almost melancholy, expression crossed his face. "You—you're special. Genuine and caring. We never really got to know each other that well, but something tells me you're the kind of person one can count on. No wonder my grandfather loved you."

This time she didn't initiate the hug. He did. And it felt like goodbye.

THE SHREDDING TRUCK was parked behind an office supply store at a strip mall a few miles outside of Clearwater. Rebecca hoisted the first box out of the back of her car and handed it to a man who dumped the contents into the gaping mouth waiting to be fed mounds of paper.

"I have one more," Rebecca told him. She wrapped her arms around the box and lifted it out of the car.

"Hey," the man shouted. "Careful there, looks like the bottom's about to—"

The box split open, and its contents spilled onto the ground. Her head flopped forward. "I can't believe this."

The man grabbed an empty box off a pile of boxes and dropped it by her car. "You'd better hurry," he said. "I'm out of here in a few minutes."

"Okay, thanks." Rebecca chased a few pages rolling over in the wind.

She scooped several handfuls of paper before noticing a stack of envelopes secured by a red rubber band. Just as she was about to fling it into the box, Mr. B's familiar handwriting caught her attention. She flipped through the stack. Every envelope was addressed to *Christopher Harrington,* an address in Seattle. On the front of each one in severe block letters 'RETURN TO SENDER.' The postmarks were decades old. Rebecca checked the seals. Not one letter had been opened. There were four stacks, sorted by years, at least twenty in each stack.

"Hey," the man shouted. "You gonna bring me that last load? I gotta get going."

His voice jolted her.

"No, it's okay." She called to him. "You can go."

The truck roared to life, and the man drove off. Rebecca could hardly breathe as she filled up the box, lifted it back into her trunk, and sat beside it with her arm across the opening. Now what? Once again, she was in possession of something she had no idea what to do with, as if it were some kind of curse. If the box hadn't collapsed on her, the letters would've been destroyed. Nobody would've known they existed.

But for some reason, fate and chance had dealt her a new hand and an even bigger decision to make.

THAT NIGHT, sleep eluded her. The box in the back of her car haunted her. The letters were a huge complication. She rolled over and found herself nose to nose with Mila. The dog yawned and licked her face.

"What should I do?"

Mila let out a tiny whine, as if to say she had no idea either.

Rebecca closed her eyes and prayed for a dream that would reveal something meaningful, a dream in which Mr. B appeared and told her exactly what *he* wanted her to do. In his deep, soothing voice he would speak to her, and then she'd be able to proceed with confidence and certainty.

But instead of Mr. B, it was Tiffany who appeared in her dream, yelling at her because Curly was sick to his stomach and insisting it was all her fault.

CHAPTER 35

*R*ebecca parked the Suburban behind the office supply store, got out of her car, and scanned the area. The shredding truck was nowhere to be seen.

She stomped into the store. "Where's the shredder guy?" she asked the young woman at the register.

"It's Saturday," the cashier said. "He's only here during the week."

"Oh." Rebecca had spent the last few hours in a tailspin, making herself crazy. But then she made a decision that the letters needed to be shredded as intended. If the box hadn't broken, they'd be gone. And she never would've known they existed.

However, another glitch had thwarted her plan.

"If it's just a few pages, we have a shredder in the back."

"It's more than a few pages," Rebecca said. "Like a half box of —of stuff."

The cashier raised one shoulder. "Doesn't matter. It's just one of those trashcan shredders, you know the kind you feed in a few sheets at a time? I can let you use it."

Rebecca couldn't imagine watching Mr. B's letters get sliced by razor sharp teeth one by one, hearing the grinding scrape of metal. "That's really nice of you, but I'll just come back on Monday."

She returned to her car, mission unaccomplished, and slammed the door. Now she'd have to drive around with the box in the back of her car for two more days.

Her cell phone, which she'd left on the passenger seat, buzzed. Curly's cute face lit up the screen.

"Ugh." Rebecca swiped to answer. "Hi, Tiffany."

"I need to talk to you. Where are you?"

"In my car." Her pulse quickened as she remembered her dream. "Is Curly okay?"

"He's fine, but I need to see you. Can you come by my house?"

Rebecca's most difficult and demanding client sounded off her game. "Now?"

"If possible, yes."

What on earth could be so important? "Are you sure Curly is okay, because last night I had a dream that—"

"I told you he's okay. When can you be here?"

Rebecca started her engine. "In like ten minutes, I guess."

"Fine. See you shortly."

Tiffany ended the call without saying goodbye.

CURLY TROTTED over and greeted Rebecca by pushing his nose into her stomach.

"Hi, you sweet boy." Rebecca stroked his sleek fur, relieved to see that he was, in fact, fine.

"Thanks for coming." Tiffany, wearing her overpriced workout attire, leaned against the kitchen counter. "I don't have a lot of time to explain, and I wanted to tell you this news in person."

"Okay." Rebecca toyed with the ragged threads on the hem of her cutoffs.

"I'm afraid I have to let you go," Tiffany said.

Rebecca almost laughed. "You're letting me go? You don't want me to walk Curly anymore because I made you pay me for my services?"

"God, no, that's not why. To tell you the truth, I was impressed when you did that. You seem to be toughening up lately, a trait I admire."

"Then why?" Rebecca wondered if she could change Tiffany's mind. Curly was one of her favorite dogs, and now that Tiffany's bill was current, Rebecca didn't mind driving the extra distance. "Did you find somebody else?"

"No, Rebecca. It's a different matter entirely."

Rebecca nearly burst into tears. "Did I do something wrong?"

Tiffany crossed her arms and shook her head. "Do you know what I do for a living?"

Rebecca had no idea—only that it must pay well. "I'm sorry, I don't."

"I work for what's called a private equity firm. And I acquire properties for large-scale developments—resort hotels, luxury housing, that kind of thing." Tiffany waved a hand. "I know this probably means nothing to you."

Rebecca pulled out the chair and sat. She didn't completely understand what Tiffany was saying, but she certainly recognized the buzz words. "Wait. Does this have something to do with my research into the town charter?"

Tiffany clicked her nails on the granite counter. "It does. Apparently, you've stirred a very large pot and pissed off some people."

Rebecca was dumbfounded. "You mean Troy Dayton and that landscaper lady, Stephanie someone?"

"I don't know who the landscaper lady is. And Troy Dayton

is a little weasel. Neither of them matter. The bottom line is, my firm is looking at properties in Clearwater, so it's a bad optic should your name come up in association with mine."

"This is unbelievable," Rebecca said, twisting and squeezing her fingers together. "All I ever wanted to do was keep Mr. B's property from being turned into something he didn't want. I never meant to cause trouble or make people mad or have any effect on anything else. And now people I don't even know are talking about me, probably saying horrible things."

Tiffany took a seat beside her. "Listen to me, Rebecca. I know I'm not the nicest person, and I can be a real pain, but I'm going to give you some advice. You can take it or leave it, but I hope you'll take it."

Rebecca stiffened. She knew exactly what was coming—the same patronizing warning she'd heard multiple times before.

Tiffany put her hands flat on the glass table. "You need to be more like me."

Rebecca choked so hard she had trouble catching her breath. Tiffany filled a glass with water and set it in front of her. Rebecca sipped the cool liquid. Her voice came out weak and raspy. "Why would I want to be like you?"

"Because I'm a fighter."

"I'm not though. I'm a—a pleaser."

Tiffany scoffed. "Oh sure, your exterior is that of just a sweet, agreeable dog walker. But you stood up to me the other day. And I know that scared the crap out of you."

Rebecca had to agree. Standing up to Tiffany was terrifying.

"There's a fighter in you, and I'm telling you to keep going. Fake it 'til you make it. If you ever want to be more or do more or change the status quo, you'd better get used to making people mad. Quit worrying about being liked. Look at me. Nobody likes me, and I do not give a flying you-know-what."

"Nobody likes you?" Rebecca couldn't imagine that, although Tiffany was pretty unlikable.

"Well, my sister likes me, but she has to because I buy her stuff." Tiffany's smile looked surprisingly genuine. "Don't worry, people will always like you because you're a good, honest person."

"I really am." Rebecca could hardly wrap her brain around the current situation—sitting at Tiffany Pressman's kitchen table where the high-power executive was telling her to stay in the game and fight the fight.

"Here's my final piece of advice—if you're determined to pursue some mission on behalf of your dead friend, you'd better be all in. Because if you aren't one hundred percent committed to it, your opponents will squash you like an annoying little bug. So make a decision. Quit now—or plow forward with everything you've got."

The ominous warning shocked and bolstered her at the same time. "So you're *not* telling me I'm in over my head?"

"Oh, you're in over your head alright. I'm just telling you don't drown."

Rebecca wondered if Tiffany was setting her up, telling her to 'plow forward' only so that she could see her fail. "I have to ask, I mean you're obviously on the opposite side of—of what I'm trying to do. Why don't you want me to give up?"

A wry smile played on the corners of Tiffany's glossy pink lips. "Two reasons. First, I'm a bit of a gambler, and I like to bet on the dark horse. And second, which if you tell anyone I'll deny it, is that I have a soft spot for underdogs. And you my friend are the most under-underdog I've ever met."

CHAPTER 36

*R*ebecca gripped her steering wheel with sweaty hands. Tiffany Pressman had pushed her down, pulled her up, then pushed her down again. Rebecca's head swirled in a hazy mix of contradictions, and the only way for her to make sense of it all was to focus on the one particular tidbit of advice that rang truest.

If you want to be more or do more or change the status quo, you'd better get used to making people mad.

REBECCA SLAMMED her brakes at the sight of Chris's rental car parked in the driveway at Mr. B's house. She'd expected him to be long gone by now, but there he was, walking out the front door. He looked like a surfer in his swim trunks and a white t-shirt with the sleeves cut off.

"You're still here," Rebecca said, stating the obvious. It was early afternoon, the sun high. Perspiration trailed down the back of her neck.

"Yeah, my flight was delayed. Decided to take a quick swim in the lake."

She pictured him shirtless, hair slicked back, water dripping down his chest.

"That must have felt amazing," she said stupidly.

"Uh, yeah, it did."

This would be the last time she'd see him. She'd known him less than month, but in that small amount of time she came to realize he was much more than a young version of his grandfather, he was the kind of man Rebecca wanted—thoughtful, steadfast, caring. Maybe now, going forward, she'd know what to look for. To see beyond the pretty wrapping paper and find out what was inside the box.

"I don't want to be in your way. I'll come back tomorrow to finish bagging clothes. Have a safe flight home."

"Okay, thanks."

Rebecca was disappointed, and a little surprised that he didn't stop her. Last night he seemed reluctant to part ways. Then again, in the light of day, one's sense of purpose was illuminated. Chris needed to get his life back on track as much as she did, perhaps even more. And because she cared about him, she wanted him to be able to do just that, sort of.

But the letters were in her car, intact and not yet shredded. She'd discovered them by chance. She'd missed the shredder this morning by chance. Chris's flight had been delayed by chance. Three events that changed the scenario. It meant something. But even if it all meant nothing, Rebecca had to give Chris the letters. Deep in her heart, she was certain Mr. B would want his grandson to know he had never forgotten him, didn't abandon him, always loved him.

She turned. He was still on porch, as if he'd been watching her.

"I have something that you should—should see."

He stepped down one step. "Okay."

Rebecca chewed on the inside of her cheek. She opened the back of the Suburban, praying she wouldn't regret it.

He walked toward her. "What is it?"

"It's some of the papers that were supposed to be shredded. But I found something—unexpected." Her pulse pounded like a pinball, and her nervous rambling began. "You might already have seen them, but then maybe you haven't. And I don't know if they'll mean anything to you at all. I mean, they would to me, but you're not me, obviously, and I'm a little—"

Chris peered into the box. "It's a bunch of old bank statements. That's all."

"It's not."

"Are you telling me you went through the boxes?" There was no anger in his voice, only—*perplexation.*

"No, I totally didn't. One of the boxes broke." Her response sounded lame, even to her. "Everything fell out, and when I was picking it all up, I found—I found the letters."

He reached into the box and removed one stack and thumbed the envelopes. He turned white, really pale, as if his blood had been forced down to his feet. Shock turned to disbelief, which rolled toward anger. "Oh my God." He mumbled it under his breath, talking to himself. "Oh my God."

"Are you alright?" she asked.

His mouth hung open. "I can't believe this."

"I'm sorry if I've done something to make you mad." She fought back tears. "I—I just wanted to do the right thing."

Chris pulled the cardboard box out of her car. "That's what everybody says when they screw up. It's like a mantra that neutralizes even the most egregious acts."

Rebecca shrank. His words stung. She started to explain what her intention was, but she didn't even know. She'd merely reacted to a chain of events that resulted in her believing—hoping—that he'd want the letters.

She closed the back of her car and took one last look at the grandson of her beloved friend.

Chris opened the front door and flung the box into the house. "I gotta go," he said without looking at her.

"Okay, well, goodbye."

Rebecca turned away, clinging to a thin thread of hope that he'd stop her.

He didn't.

CHAPTER 37

*a*s the plane approached Seattle, Chris leaned his head against the window. The city lights blurred. He closed his eyes. His life as he'd known it was over.

The letters, neatly folded and stacked, were tucked into his backpack. He'd read every one of them, some twice. In the early years, the letters were frequent, the first one dated about three months after his mother had died. It didn't take a detective to figure out what Mitch Harrington had done. Or why.

It was the handwriting that struck Chris first, so familiar and consistent. Then the words, the cadence of his grandfather's sentences. Chris hadn't heard his voice since that one last phone call, but it was in every letter, as if he were speaking aloud.

The airplane landed with a hard jolt.

Chris exited the terminal into a cool Seattle evening. He slipped on a sweatshirt before heading to his car, a BMW he and Jessica had picked out together a year ago.

Nobody knew he was back. He sat in the driver's seat, unsure of where to go first. He was about to blow up his entire life. The only decision was where to start.

. . .

LIGHT SPILLED out of his father's house, a modern split level home with more windows than walls. Chris rang the doorbell. It was the house his father bought a few years ago with his new wife, so Chris was a visitor, not a grown-up kid returning to his childhood home.

His stepmother, Donna, answered the door. Her face registered surprise.

"Chris, hi." She ushered him into the wide foyer. "Is everything okay?"

"Is my dad here?" he asked.

"He's upstairs in his office." Donna was in her forties, attractive but not a typical trophy wife. As far as stepmoms go, she wasn't bad. And because Chris was in his twenties when she'd married his father, she'd never tried to be a mother figure. Although she did like to feed him. "Did you have dinner? I have some delicious pasta leftover from last night."

"I'm fine, thanks." He had no appetite, despite the fact he hadn't eaten anything since a sticky bun that morning. It was hard to believe that twelve hours ago he was sitting at Nutmegs sipping coffee and half-hoping he might bump into Rebecca. He was sick to his stomach about the way he'd responded to her when she gave him the letters. How he would make that right, he had no idea.

"Christopher," his father said, coming down the stairway. "I thought I heard your voice." His expression shifted. "What's going on?"

"You tell me." Chris unzipped his backpack and turned it over. The letters spilled onto the floor. He said nothing, just waited for his father's reaction.

Donna picked up one of the envelopes. "Isn't this your printing, Mitch?" She pointed at the spot where he'd written 'return to sender.'

Mitch took the letter out of his wife's hand. "It's nothing."

Donna looked from her husband to Chris and back to her

husband. "I'll leave you two alone." On her way out, she gave Chris's shoulder a squeeze.

"So, you found them," his father said.

No reply necessary, just stony silence that hardened Chris's resolve to have the confrontation they both knew was a long time coming.

"What do you want me to say?" his father asked. "What's done is done. Your grandfather wrote to you, big deal. If I'd let you have the letters, it wouldn't have changed anything."

Anger and disbelief rose from his gut up to his throat. "It would have changed everything!" Chris struck the foyer table so hard the flowers in the centerpiece trembled. "I thought he'd forgotten me. I begged you to let me go visit him. I called his house a thousand times, and he never picked up. What did you do to him that he wouldn't talk to me?"

His father's jaw jetted out the way it always did when he became defensive. "I didn't do anything to him. Benito hated me. Never thought I was good enough for his precious daughter."

"You weren't." Chris spit the words. "I've always known that. And if my mother knew you'd cut me off from my grandfather, she'd hate you. She'd hate you and curse you. You think I don't know what you did to her—that you cheated again and again? I heard the arguments, Dad. I was a little kid with my head under the pillow trying to drown out the yelling and fighting. But I heard it all."

Mitch went to the bar in the dining room. He poured himself a shot of whiskey and knocked it back. "I think," he said slowly, "we should talk about this tomorrow. It's getting late. You've had a long day. I think in the morning we can have clearer heads."

Chris snickered at him. "My head is clearer than ever. So much that I never understood, I do now. Papa kept writing to me month after month, hoping one of his letters might slip through. Quite the conspiracy that you were able to intercept all of them. And then, instead of just throwing them out, you sent them back to him unopened. That way he'd know I'd never gotten them. You couldn't resist having the final dig."

"Oh, please, Christopher." He poured another shot. "You're taking this too far. I did it for you. I wanted you to have stability, to not be torn between us. You deserved a normal childhood."

"Normal? My mother was killed in car crash the same day she found out you were having another affair. I put it all together years ago. You are such a pitiful cliché."

"That's unfair," his father said through clenched teeth. "I made mistakes, yes, but I loved your mother more than you know."

Chris's upper lip twitched. His father's words were meaningless and trivial. For most of his life, Chris had maintained a healthy amount of respect for his father. Now, even that had been taken from him.

"Why is she buried in Clearwater?"

His father didn't answer. But Chris had already figured it out. What Mr. Nash had said about Antonia finding peace when her daughter was returned to her.

"Because I thought it was what she'd want."

Chris couldn't contradict that. His parents' marriage was doomed regardless. His father couldn't help himself when it came to other women. If Josephina hadn't died, they would have divorced eventually.

"Here's what I think, Dad. I think you let my mother go back to Clearwater as part of a deal." Chris knew his father well. He always needed to get something in return. "How much did my grandfather pay you?"

"That's absurd, Christopher. I didn't want your grandfather's money."

"Not until now." Chris threw the accusation at him, and it hit hard. "You're chomping at the bit for me to sell the property and sink my inheritance into your business. Wow, the ultimate revenge—his money becoming yours."

"You're crossing the line." Mitch Harrington's face contorted. "It's not my business, it's our business. And it's going to succeed no matter what."

"It might." Chris agreed. "You still haven't answered my question. What deal did you strike?"

"For God's sake, why are you questioning me about an event that occurred so many years ago? It's ancient history. I allowed your mother to be buried there because it was the right thing to do."

There it was—the right thing to do. A derisive laugh erupted from Chris's mouth. "I don't buy it. You never give without getting something in return. How many times have you told me that everything is a negotiation? So if it wasn't money that exchanged hands, what was it?"

His father's chest expanded. He seemed to grow taller, like a bear in the wild. "What are you trying to do? Get me to admit to something you already know? I'm sure your grandfather exposed every lurid detail in those damn letters you found."

Chris collected his letters and stacked them on the table.

Benito Becerra had never written a word against his son-in-law. His letters were full of wonderful stories about his childhood, his family in Mexico, his youth as a cowboy wrangling cattle. He wrote about his love of animals, nature, and warm grapes eaten from the vine. He talked about quiet days and simple joys—fishing, horseback riding, tending to his fields, and watching sunsets. He even mentioned a new friend, a red-headed girl who came into his life at its darkest moment. And every letter ended with *I love you, my grandson, 'te amo mi nieto.'*

"You were holding something over him, something so important that even he wouldn't cross you."

Chris wrapped the rubber bands around his letters. He could

tell he'd touched a nerve. The temple on the left side of his father's head pulsed, as if a tiny bug were trapped under the skin. Again, Mr. Nash's words came back to him—how desperate his grandfather was to rescue his wife from despondency for fear she'd die of a broken heart.

The reason revealed itself, dawning like a sunrise. "It was my mother, wasn't it? God, I know you so well." Chris shoved the letters into his backpack. How could his father have been so cruel? "It's what you taught me about business, *'go for the juggler, son, find the one thing they can't live without and let 'em know you have the power to take it away.'* Winning trumps everything, and you were hellbent on winning against my grandfather. It makes me sick. I know the deal you struck—no contact with me or you'd dig my mother out of the ground and take her away." Chris's stomach roiled. "Except you let him write letters, because that you could control."

Mitch Harrington didn't deny the charge. And if he had, Chris wouldn't have believed him. His Papa had had no choice. He would've done anything to save Antonia, the love of his life.

Chris closed the zipper on his backpack slowly, deliberately, as if sealing off part of himself. His father's eyes clouded over. To Chris's astonishment, he looked almost defeated.

"What are you going to do?" his father asked. "You can't walk away. We're building a business together. We're on the verge of making it a huge success."

Chris's heart cracked in another spot. He had no idea a heart could break in so many places. "You can have it, all of it. Do whatever you want."

"Come on, son, you don't mean that."

"Oh, I do. It's the easiest decision I've ever made."

His father reached for him, but Chris jerked away. "You know what, I just thought of something." The memory chilled him. "When you came to Clearwater to take Mom and me home with you, I was what, maybe twelve? And Papa wanted to give me his dog. He begged you to let me take the dog, and you refused. I always thought it was because you didn't want a dog, but it wasn't. You just couldn't give him one win, could you? That's why you returned the letters unopened. You wanted him to know I never saw them. And the ones I wrote to him, the ones you said you'd mail from the office. What happened to those? You were obsessed with hurting him."

His father sank into a chair. "You make it sound as if I were downright evil."

Chris took a few deep breaths to calm himself. "Only when it came to my grandfather. But you know what really kills me? It was all so pointless, Dad. There was more than enough love in me for you both."

The pain in his father's face registered. It gave him no satisfaction to have caused it. But it didn't bother him either. He'd gone numb.

As Chris passed through the foyer, Donna stood on the stairway landing, her eyes red and cheeks wet. She raised a hand goodbye, and he did the same.

CHAPTER 38

*I*t was Sunday, exactly one month since Mr. B died. Rebecca was in a fog, still in disbelief at the way Chris had reacted yesterday when she'd given him the letters. And while she was devastated by how they'd parted ways, she didn't regret what she'd done. She'd thought it through enough times to know that Mr. B had hoped his grandson would someday find the letters—it's why he'd kept them all these years. Whatever Chris felt about the letters or did with them now, well, that was his choice.

Finding strength in her convictions had become easier, chipping away at insecurities. Her fear of making people mad was diminishing, freeing her to move forward into unchartered spaces.

DAYS PASSED, blending into one another as July rolled into August. The lake grew warmer, the rooms at the inn were booked solid through summer, and Mila stopped trying to escape to her old home. In fact, she loved living at Lakeview Lodge. She was the official greeter of all the guests, rewarded with so much attention she seemed to wear a constant grin. When Rebecca wasn't around, Mila trotted after Alice or Zack or her favorite maintenance man who always had treats in his pocket.

Rebecca's schedule was more packed than ever. She added another shift at Mariano's, continued at the shelter a few times a week, and took on two new dog walking clients that were local and more convenient than Curly. Rebecca hoped Tiffany had found a new dog walker who could handle him and wouldn't mind the unpleasant order to check his 'business' on every walk.

The skirmish over land use and ordinances appeared to have been put on hold. According to Mrs. Larson, nobody had been to the library to review the town charter in over two weeks. So Rebecca set it aside. The conflict and tension that had kept her on tenterhooks all summer faded like a storm that had run out of steam.

"HELLO, RED, HOW'VE YOU BEEN?" Troy Dayton placed a bottle of Zinfandel beside the register.

Rebecca, busy wrapping a gift for another customer, ignored him.

"Hello?" he said, his tone sarcastic.

Rebecca turned. "I'm sorry, were you talking to me?"

He smiled his toothy grin. "I get it. Lemme start over. So, *Rebecca*, how've you been?"

"Very well, thank you." She held herself up straight. "Would you like me to ring that up for you?"

"If you don't mind."

"I don't mind. It's my job."

"One of your many." Troy gave her a sly look. "Will I be seeing you at the town council meeting tomorrow night?"

Rebecca nearly dropped the wine on the counter. "Tomorrow?"

"First Thursday of every month." He shoved his credit card into the machine. His arrogance was as insufferable as his overly pungent cologne. "I would think you'd know that."

"I totally do. Just forgot that tomorrow was Thursday. But yeah, for sure I'll be there." Regaining her composure, she bagged his expensive bottle of wine and handed it to him. "See you tomorrow, Troy."

"No more 'Mr. Dayton,' huh? That's cute." He snatched his bag off the counter and left the store, giving the bells an extra jingle on his way out.

The moment she could take a break, Rebecca ran across the street to the library. There it was on the public announcements bulletin board:

TOWN COUNCIL MEETING THURSDAY NIGHT
7 pm Library Community Room

REBECCA CHARGED in and found the librarian in her usual spot behind the counter, hot pink glasses on her face.

"There's a town council meeting tomorrow night?"

"Hello to you, too."

Rebecca took her outburst down a notch. "Sorry, Mrs. Larson, but I just heard about it."

"If you paid closer attention, you wouldn't be caught off guard."

"You're right, I've just been super busy." She made a mental note to be more aware. "So it's in the community room? Where's that?"

Mrs. Larson gestured toward the children's reading corner at the back of the library. "Right there. We push the bean-bag chairs and tiny tables out of the way for the meetings which take place on the first Thursday of every month."

"First Thursday, got it."

"Except holidays of course, but rarely does a holiday fall on a first Thursday. Sometimes New Year's Day does, so in that case we have to reschedule. But tomorrow is just a regular old first Thursday in August. So, yes, town council, tomorrow night seven o'clock, here at our lovely Clearwater library."

"Okay." Rebecca was out of breath just listening to her. "Do you know who's in charge of the meeting?"

"The mayor of course, who else?"

"I guess that makes sense." Rebecca was ashamed by how little she knew. She recalled her conversations with Brad Redmond. "Mrs. Larson, if I ask you a question, can you please please pleeeease keep it between us?"

The librarian placed both hands on her chest. "My dear, of course I can. I know everybody thinks I'm a gossip, and maybe I am. But when it comes to a true confidence, I am a steel trap."

Rebecca had no choice but to trust her. "I might want to ask —ask the town council about the ordinances Mr. B was looking at. Find out if they're enforceable or not. Is that a topic I could even bring up? I mean, I've never been to a town council meeting. Are there rules and stuff?"

"Of course there are rules." Mrs. Larson removed her pink glasses. "And to bring up a subject you need to place your name on the agenda."

That sounded easy enough. "Okay, cool."

"Not cool. The agenda is already set. Requests to speak must be submitted a week ahead of time."

Rebecca's energy fizzled. "So that's it? I can't do anything?"

"You can submit your request for next month's meeting."

"I can't wait that long," she said. "I think Troy Dayton is going to, I don't know, propose something that might affect Mr. B's property."

Mrs. Larson's face lit up. "In that case, all you have to do is voice your objection. If he makes a motion, that's your opening. Every motion has to be discussed before it's put to a vote. You, my dear, need a civics lesson." She curled a finger at Rebecca, led her down an aisle, and pulled a book from the stacks. *The Governance of Small Towns, Villages, and Rural Communities.*

"You want me to read this?" Rebecca asked, thumbing the pages.

"Cover to cover."

"It's over a hundred pages."

"If you want to make your voice heard tomorrow night, you need to know what you're talking about. And you should download *Roberts Rules of Order* cheat sheet. Get the lingo right." Mrs. Larson pushed the book into Rebecca's chest. "Now go learn something."

Rebecca stayed up most of the night. The book wasn't quite as boring as she'd expected, but it wasn't riveting either. She selected pertinent sections and wrote notes on a yellow legal pad. Then she studied Roberts Rules until her vision blurred.

It would take weeks if not months for her to absorb all the information. But she all she had was a few more hours.

Rebecca fell asleep on top of her bed with the book on her stomach and Mila curled up at her feet.

CHAPTER 39

"*O*rder, order, please!" The Mayor, Mrs. Kilpatrick, owner of the fancy gift shop next door to Nutmegs, pounded her gavel on the hardwood table. Betsy from Betsy's Blooms sat on one side of her, and a man Rebecca didn't know sat on the other.

Sandwiched between Patty and Mrs. Larson on rickety folding chairs, Rebecca spun in her seat as chaos broke out. "I can't believe they're arguing over cookies."

"Yep." Mrs. Larson scrolled through her phone. "Happens almost every month."

The woman who brought up the subject, Marge, continued to complain. "These packaged cookies are horrible. If we can't afford to buy from Nutmegs, we at least should get the bakery cookies from Costco."

Patty interjected, feigning indignation. "And who's going to drive all the way to Costco? The closest one is an hour away."

Marge sneered at her. "Oh, I don't know Patty. Maybe you could go. Unless you're not allowed to drive anymore."

"Hey!" Patty shouted. "That accident was not my fault."

"You ran the stop sign," Marge said.

"I did not. I had the right of way, and you were—"

Rebecca tugged Patty's arm. "You're making a scene."

"I know," Patty grinned. "Isn't it great? Somebody's got to stir it up to keep things exciting."

If anybody could stir things up, it was Patty.

"Ladies, please," said the mayor. "We're not here to discuss your car accident."

A man down the row waved at the mayor. "I move we table the cookie debate until next month's meeting, or better yet, until the end of time."

Someone shouted. "Second!"

At least they were following Roberts Rules.

"So moved," the mayor said. "Discussion?"

Marge stood again. "I do not want to wait until—"

"For God's sake," said the man next to her. "Give it a rest, Marge."

She huffed and sat.

"All in favor of tabling the cookie debate?" said Mayor Kilpatrick.

Fourteen of the fifteen attendees shouted 'yay.'

Rebecca said it along with the others, bolstered to have her voice heard, even if it was only about cookies.

"Any opposed?"

Marge raised her hand. "Me."

"Motion carries." The mayor struck the gavel. "Marge, if you want to go to Costco for cookies, knock yourself out. You can submit a request for reimbursement. Just coordinate with the refreshments committee. Now let's move on."

A flurry of other topics were bandied about. Rebecca listened with fascination—they elected a chair for the fall festival, approved the purchase of new playground equipment for Town Square Park, and granted permission for Nutmegs to expand their patio seating.

Patty dozed off and Mrs. Larson played Sudoku on her

phone, but Rebecca was riveted. She paid close attention to the proceedings, enjoying the rhythm of motions, discussions, and voting. She made note of who spoke intelligently (and who did not) and admired the mayor's ability to maintain some semblance of control.

"Wake me up when something good happens." Patty rested her head on Rebecca's shoulder.

"Are you kidding? It's all good. It's amazing. Small town politics—I love it."

"Well, you're the only one," Mrs. Larson said.

"Why aren't there more people here?" she asked.

"Because," the librarian said, continuing her game, "it's boring and usually unproductive."

Rebecca found that hard to believe.

"Next on the agenda is, let's see, a construction project over on Shorewood Lane." Mayor Kilpatrick removed her glasses. "Who's speaking on that?"

"I am."

Rebecca snapped to attention at the sound of Troy Dayton's voice. She hadn't seen him earlier, so he must have slipped in after the meeting was called to order.

"Ah, Mr. Dayton," said the mayor. "We meet again. Do you own the property in question?" Her cynical tone indicated she already knew the answer.

"I do not. The owners are out of town and asked me to speak on their behalf." The realtor, dressed in khaki pants and an orange polo shirt, removed a folder from his briefcase. Sitting next to him was Stephanie Carter, the landscaper.

Rebecca hooked an elbow over the back of her chair. He caught her eye and winked. It incensed her to see him acting so smug. Mayor Kilpatrick invited him to the center of the room to speak at the podium in front of the council members. Troy launched into what sounded like a prepared speech, using fancy words like *infrastructure, building codes, improvements, comparable properties, and artistic integrity.*

The man who had made the motion to table the cookie issue stood again. "Get to the point, Troy. You're boring me to death."

Troy shot a dismissive look in his direction and continued pontificating.

"Mr. Dayton," Betsy said, sounding like an irritated school teacher. "Renovation of single family homes don't need council approval. Why are you here?"

Troy gripped the sides of the podium. "Right, well, the project is just a teeny weeny bit beyond the scope of a renovation."

"Teeny-weeny, did you really just say that?" Betsy rolled her eyes. "And beyond the scope of renovation? Exactly how big is the project?"

"Well, what the architect and builder have designed is a—"

"Stop." Betsy held up her palm. "Short and direct answers only or you'll be dismissed. What's the size of the current house?"

'Yes ma'am." Troy's chin dipped. "Current structure is fifteen hundred square feet."

"And after the *renovation?*"

"Just under six thousand."

Several people gasped.

"I wouldn't call that *teeny-weeny*, Mr. Dayton. Sounds like a new house. However, we need not belabor the point. What's the size of the lot?" Betsy asked.

"Over an acre."

"Fine. As the chair of building and housing, I declare, based on lot size, the project meets the parameters of a single family home renovation." Betsy pointed at the realtor. "But it better not go one inch over six thousand square feet."

"Excuse me." A frail voice came from the back of the room. "I'm terribly sorry, but I object."

Rebecca turned to see a tiny gray-haired woman dressed in her Sunday best, as if attending the council meeting were on par with going to church.

Troy closed his eyes and shook his head. "There's nothing to object to."

Patty whispered to Rebecca. "Oh, this is gonna be good."

"Is that Trudy Klein?" Rebecca asked. "I haven't seen her in ages."

"That's our Trudy, a Clearwater fixture," Mrs. Larson said. "She's lived in the same house her entire life. I heard she actually was born in the kitchen back in 1928."

Betsy walked toward the old woman. "So nice to see you, Trudy. Here, let me help you to the podium." She escorted her to where Troy stood.

"Why does she get to speak? No motion was made," he said.

"Sit down, Troy," said Betsy, an imposing figure with the voice of an orator. "For goodness sake, have some respect."

The realtor leaned in front of Betsy. "Mayor Kilpatrick, I strongly object to—"

"To what?" the mayor asked. "Somebody helping our dear Trudy to the podium so that she might voice an opinion? Let's be a bit flexible. This is a town council meeting, not a joint session of Congress. Now go take your seat."

Troy grumbled as he marched back to his chair.

A ripple of excitement filled Rebecca's chest. Mayor Kilpatrick was her new hero.

Betsy returned to the table at the front. "Trudy, you have some concerns about the project?"

"I do." The old lady spoke a little louder, her voice was high and tinny. "The property is right next door to mine. A big house like that could block my view of the lake. And the construction will be a terrible nuisance—all those trucks coming and going, the noise, the workers, the dumpsters, the—"

"Excuse me." Stephanie Carter raised her hand. "May I speak?"

The mayor gave her a half-hearted nod. "Go ahead."

Rebecca watched as Stephanie approached Trudy and draped a gentle arm over the old woman's shoulder.

"Hi Trudy, remember me? I designed your garden a few years ago."

Trudy looked at her with wide eyes. "You did?"

"Yes, and I promise you the project will not block your view or disrupt your lovely neighborhood."

"Oh," Trudy said in her soft voice. "In that case, okay."

"Good." Stephanie coaxed her away from podium. "Now let me help you back to your seat."

Patty grumbled. "Well, that was disappointing. Thought old Trudy would stand up for herself with a little more oomph."

"I did, too." Rebecca had seen both sides of the conniving landscaper and didn't buy her sweetness for one second.

Betsy, frowning, whispered something to the mayor and the other council member. The three of them engaged in private conversation for a moment.

Mrs. Larson jabbed Rebecca with her sharp elbow.

"Ouch. What?"

"Now's your chance."

"My chance for what?"

"To make a motion." Mrs. Larson squeezed her wrist. "You studied the book, didn't you?"

"Yes, but I—I thought I had to be on the agenda."

Mrs. Larson huffed. "Didn't you read the book? You don't have to be on the agenda if a related topic is discussed, and this project is the perfect opening for you to bring up the ordinance."

"You can do it," Patty said. "The worst that can happen is that you—well, let's not go there."

Rebecca broke out in a cold sweat. Her red blotches bloomed

on the surface of her skin. She wished Brad Redmond were there, but he was away on business. And all her other friends, including her mother, were occupied elsewhere. Her support system consisted of Patty who could barely stay awake and the nutty librarian.

"What do I say?"

"You know what to say." Mrs. Larson placed a hand on the middle of Rebecca's back and applied a bit of pressure. "This is your moment. Don't blow it."

CHAPTER 40

*R*ebecca tried to stand on liquid legs. She wobbled then righted herself. Her voice stuck in her throat, refusing to budge.

"Oh, hi, Rebecca," Mayor Kilpatrick said. "How's your mom? I haven't seen her in a while."

"Good." Rebecca squeaked out the one word, which broke the dam blocking her voice. "She's been super busy at the lodge. But I'll tell her you say hello, if you do, I mean, if you want me to."

"Please do. Tell her I'll give her call soon. I owe her a lunch date. Now back to business. Do you have something to present to the council?"

"Hold on." The third council member, the man on the Mayor's right, studied Rebecca. "I don't think I know you."

Betsy interjected. "Of course you do, Joel, that's Rebecca Sparks. She's everywhere around here."

Rebecca showed a tightlipped smile. *Everywhere, yep, that's me.*

"Alright then, state your name," Joel said.

"I just told you her name." Betsy snapped at him.

"It's okay." Rebecca stepped up to the podium. "I'm Rebecca Sparks."

"And what do you do, Rebecca?"

"Do?"

"Employment? Job? Work?"

Mayor Kilpatrick shook her head. "Why are you grilling her?"

"I just want to know who she is, but if she'd rather not—"

"I don't mind. I, um I'm a..." she glanced at the floor, recalling Troy Dayton's arrogant words. *You're just a dog walker...*

"I'm a—a small business owner." Her voice grew like a balloon on a helium tank. "And a concerned citizen of Clearwater. Very concerned."

The six eyebrows in front of her lifted simultaneously, as if pulled by the same string.

"Please, go on." Betsy cocked her head to the side.

Rebecca's heart thumped so loudly she could hear it. "The proposed project, the one near Trudy's house, it—it might exceed the allowable expansion clause in the town charter." She paused, expecting someone to ask a question, but nobody did.

Mrs. Larson stood halfway, her head near Rebecca's waist. "Motion," she whispered, "make a motion."

Rebecca cleared her throat. "And—and therefore I'd like to make a motion."

Mayor Kilpatrick tapped her pen on the table. "Proceed."

Rebecca took a deep breath and tried to remember the details of the ordinances Mr. B had been investigating. This might be her only opportunity to make a difference, to see the town charter brought back to life, to prevent massive over-development from destroying her friend's property. "I'm making a—I mean, I move that a petition be, or at least maybe a notification about the project on—"

"Are you making a motion or not?" somebody shouted at her.

"I'm trying to, but..." she got dizzy and lost focus, like an actor on stage who'd forgotten her lines. "What I mean to say is that the—the thing, um, the project on Shorewood Lane is one that could—"

"Objection!" Troy leapt out of his seat.

Rebecca clamped her mouth shut.

"You can't object while a motion's being made," Joel said.

The shouts continued, and Rebecca couldn't even tell where they were coming from.

"That's the most convoluted motion I've ever heard."

"It wasn't a motion, it was incoherent babble."

"The town charter's an archaic old document, been dead for decades!"

The chatter swelled to fever pitch. Mayor Kilpatrick pounded her gavel.

Rebecca sank back into her seat. Mrs. Larson rubbed her back. Patty squeezed her hand. Their sympathetic gestures made her feel even worse.

Joel said something to Mayor Kilpatrick then walked over to Rebecca. "Do you still wish to make a motion?" he asked, implying it would be best if she stopped before making it worse.

Rebecca pursed her lips and shook her head, horrified by her inability to speak and her failure to make a simple motion. If only she'd never attended the meeting. If only she could turn the clock back and undo the last month, quit the day Chris refused to take Mr. B's notes seriously.

Tiffany's ominous warning echoed—*just don't drown.*

Sweat dribbled down her back. By tomorrow, everyone in town would know about her failure and humiliation. Maybe that was why Troy Dayton had mentioned the meeting, so that she'd show up and make a fool of herself. Concerned citizen or not, Rebecca Sparks was no match for powerful, smarter, better educated people who wanted to change Clearwater and had the resources to do it.

Mr. B had told her she must find her strength, but now strength and fortitude eluded her.

You must search for reasons to not give up, querida.

"I've run out of reasons," she said to herself.

Joel took his seat. He whispered something to the mayor who tapped her gavel on the table.

"Next on the agenda," she said, "is the event for…"

Rebecca hunched her shoulders and slipped out of the library, hoping to leave unnoticed. But she was an army of one in retreat. She might as well have been waving a huge white flag.

The evening air was warm and fragrant. The pleasant summer night made the indignity even worse. Rebecca skirted across the street into the park in search of refuge. Her sandals squished into the grass. Cool droplets of water dotted the skin on her feet.

"Hey, Rebecca, hold up." Troy's voice slithered into her ears.

She whipped around. "What do you want? To gloat, to say I told you so, to remind me, yet again, that I'm in over my head?"

Troy tipped his shoulders side to side. "Should've taken my help when I offered it."

Rebecca thought she'd sunk as low as she could go, speaking like an idiot in front of everyone at the town council. But leave it Troy to push her even lower. Challenging him now would bury her.

"I suppose so," she replied, barely audible.

"But don't worry about it. You'll be the talk of the town for a week or two—gossip loves to linger. Then someone else will do something stupid, and everyone will forget all about your failed motion. And besides, now that you're a *small business owner*, you're much too busy to worry about what people say."

Rebecca's toes curled. Her body grew taut, immobile. She was afraid to speak for fear of cracking like a mirror struck by a hammer.

"Anyway, when I broker the deal for Benito Becerra's land to go to a developer, perhaps you'll try and go up against me again. Unless of course, you've learned your lesson. But you naïve millennials, you all think you're so smart, can't be taught anything."

"What did you say?" Rebecca asked.

He spoke loud and slow, as if she were a dunce. "I said you naïve milleni—"

"Not that part." Rebecca pulled air into her lungs. It was a leap, a risk, but she had to take it. She widened her green eyes and infused her voice with dramatic despair. "The part about Mr. B's property."

"Ah, yes, your friend's property with the to-die-for view of the lake. At least three developers are interested."

"Are you sure?"

"What do you mean?" Troy's pompous tone flattened. "Of course I'm sure."

"Well," Rebecca bent her head sideways. "I guess that's good news for the agent who has the listing."

"What agent?"

"The one Chris hired before he went back to Seattle." She was not a good liar, but this wasn't exactly a lie—more of a rearrangement of words.

Troy tried to cover his bewilderment, but his face went white, and his lower jaw dropped. A tiny thread of spit stretched between his lips.

"Eww." Rebecca motioned toward her own mouth. "You have a little bit of—"

Troy swiped his lips with the back of his hand. Success. She'd released her last arrow and shot it straight into the bullseye.

"You're bluffing," he said through gritted teeth.

"If you say so. Now if you'll excuse me, I have some dogs to walk."

CHAPTER 41

*J*essica trembled as she fought back tears and anger. "You don't mean it, I know you don't."

Chris sat on the edge of the sofa in her apartment surrounded by half-packed boxes. "I'm sorry, but I do."

Her arms flew into the air. "Look at this place. I'm ready to move out. And now you're telling me you want to break up? I've spent two and a half years on you, waiting for you to launch your business. And just when it's about to happen you throw all of it, including me, away? I was right—you really have lost your mind!"

Chris didn't respond. He let her scream and yell and throw accusations at him. She was entitled to have her tantrum.

"Say something," Jessica demanded.

"Come on, Jess, we both knew this was coming. In the last year, we've broken up three times."

"Two times." She pouted. "This makes three."

Three's the charm, Chris thought. This time it would stick. Once he'd confronted his father, it was like throwing off a heavy chain. Jessica was the last link left. He'd been back in Seattle almost two weeks, but they'd hardly seen each other since he returned. Thankfully, she'd been preoccupied with an event. Then he spent a few days in the mountains camping with a friend from college. It gave him time to reset and come to terms with his father's betrayal.

Chris had received numerous texts since the night of the confrontation—apologies, excuses, and appeals for forgiveness. In their last exchange, Chris merely responded with a request for time. Perhaps, in the future, he'd be able to move on and let go of the hurt. But for now, he needed to figure out the rest of his life, a life without his father and without Jessica.

He pushed himself off the couch and stepped forward. "Jessica, you have to admit we haven't been happy for a long time. We don't want the same things."

"I don't think that's true. Not really." Jessica wound her hair around one hand. "Besides, how can you throw away your business? That's insane!"

"It's the smartest thing I've ever done. I want nothing to do with it or with my father."

"You're making a huge mistake."

"I don't think so. Being in business with my dad would have destroyed me."

"And marrying me?" Her voice quivered. "That would've destroyed you, too?"

Honesty was one thing, cruelty another, and Chris was not cruel. "We wouldn't have lasted, Jess. You're a larger than life personality. You want to be known and celebrated. Look at how many people worship you, all those followers who wish they could be like you. You crave their adoration, their love." He stopped there. Reminding her that they were total strangers would be mean, and he'd already hurt her enough. "That kind of attention makes me, well, you know. I just don't want any part of it."

She covered her face with both hands. "I—I can't believe this is happening."

"I'm truly, truly sorry," he said, meaning it so sincerely it almost made him sick.

"You're sorry?" She kicked an empty cardboard box, and it skidded across the floor. "You've pretty much dropped a bomb on my life, ruined everything we planned together, and for what? So you can flounder around and try to discover yourself?"

She made a good point. Chris wasn't sure what he would do or where he'd go. But he'd been set free. His grandfather's letters had rescued him. Knowing the truth, as painful as it was, had changed everything. He was only thirty-two. It wasn't too late for him to choose a new path, go a different way, find new love.

"I don't know what I'm going to do. But I will leave Seattle." He had friends in other cities, new opportunities to explore. And he owned a small house with a lake front view in the town where his mother and grandparents were buried side by side. The town where an exuberant, determined, idealistic, relentless, sticky-bun-eating girl was everywhere.

He had choices.

Chris stood and headed to the door. "I'm sorry, Jessica," he said again, because what else was there to say? "I'm sorry I hurt you and wasted your time and made you think I was something I wasn't."

His words, meant to relieve her, only made her madder. She grabbed a vase and threw it against the wall. The glass shattered and sprayed the room. She released a guttural wail, like a trapped lion. "I hate you!"

"I know." The calmer he remained the crazier she became.

She screamed again. "Why couldn't you be more like your father? That's the kind of man you should've been."

"Thank God I'm not." For the rest of his life, he'd strive to be like his grandfather.

"I promise you, you'll regret this, Chris.

"I promise you, I won't." As he opened the door, a vision of his stepmother appeared—her sorrowful smile as she stood on the stairway, her wave goodbye. "You should give my dad a call. He'll probably be looking for new wife soon."

He shut the door just in time.

CHAPTER 42

*D*espite being knocked off his pedestal, the obnoxious realtor had been right about one thing. Gossip loved to linger. Six days had passed since the council meeting, and Rebecca's mortifying performance was still the hot topic around town. She tried to ignore it, and while nobody said anything to her face, she heard the incessant rumblings. It refused to go away.

Rebecca suspected Troy of keeping the gossip alive as retribution for embarrassing him after the meeting. So it continued to spread like a slow-burning fire that never ran out of fuel.

But then a real fire broke out in the kitchen of Gerardo's pizza restaurant. They had to close for repairs, and the fact that nobody could get a decent piece of pizza in all of Clearwater pushed Rebecca off the top spot for gossip.

REBECCA DROVE toward Mr. B's house on her way to pick up a new dog client. She'd avoided the road for three weeks, ever since the day she forced Mr. B's letters onto his grandson. It was a moment she wanted to forget—the way Chris had thrown the box into the house, his face dark with rage. And who knew what he had done with the letters after that? Probably tossed them into a dumpster on his way to the airport.

As the sting of her last encounter with Chris faded, Rebecca decided she couldn't circumnavigate Mr. B's house anymore. It was on her way to almost everywhere she had to go.

She was about to accelerate and fly past the driveway, but she slowed at the sight of a black sedan parked by the mailbox. A woman opened the trunk and pulled out a large sign.

Rebecca's heart dropped. This was it. The property was on the market. It wasn't like she didn't expect it, but expecting it and seeing it happen in front of her face were two different things. Another bitter reminder of how she had failed.

The woman, dressed in office attire, lugged the sign across the driveway. In her haste, she caught her heel in the gravel and tumbled over. The sign hit the ground, and the woman went down hard.

"Oh, no." Rebecca rushed to assist her. "Are you okay?"

The real estate agent rolled into a sitting position, her legs splayed in an awkward angle. "I think so. How stupid of me to wear high-heels out here in the country."

Rebecca had to agree with that. She reached for her arm. "Let me help you up."

"Thanks." The woman, in her forties with short dark hair, groaned as she stood. "We just got new signs, and they're much heavier than the old ones."

It pained Rebecca to see a 'for sale' sign go up, but at least it didn't have Troy Dayton's greasy smile on it. "I'll carry it for you." She turned the sign over. "Wait. This says 'For Rent.' Does that mean the property's not for sale?"

"It does."

"Oh wow, that's unexpected. I—I know the owner, and I

thought he was going to sell, but if he's not, it means, well, I'm not sure what it means."

"It means the house is for rent, at least for now. Hopefully he'll decide to sell soon though. In the meantime, we're offering a short term lease. Are you interested? I can show you inside."

"What, me? Oh, no, not at all. Geez, I could never afford it. Although, wow, wouldn't that be something, me living in Mr. B's house." Nervous, excited laughter erupted from her throat.

"Well, if you hear of anyone looking, feel free to share my information. I'm Tammy Walker." She handed Rebecca a card. Everything about her was opposite of Troy Dayton—not pushy, not obnoxious, not all full of herself.

"I will," said Rebecca. "Would you like me to help you put up the sign?"

"Aren't you kind, thank you." Her smile was warm and genuine.

Rebecca pushed the spike into the grass. Tammy handed her a plastic box to hang on the post.

"What are these?" she asked.

"Flyers with the all the pertinent information."

"May I take one?"

"Of course."

Rebecca pulled one out and read the details. "It says four acres of land. The property is way bigger than that." She remembered from Mr. B's notes how there were acres and acres in all directions.

"I know, but the owner made some changes." Tammy opened an overhead photo of Mr. B's house on her phone. "The only area for rent is this portion here." She drew a circle with her finger around the house. "The rental includes everything from the road down to the lake where the pier is. Plenty of space for a garden, pets, kids, maybe a horse or two. It's truly a rare find. And the house is about to be painted inside and out. The owner said he wanted to maintain the integrity of his family home. Apparently, he has a real attachment to it."

"Oh." Rebecca hiccupped as tears filled her eyes.

"You said you know him?" Tammy asked.

"We're, well, we were friends—briefly. More like acquaintances." Rebecca distanced herself. "Last I heard he was heading home to Seattle."

"Right." Tammy straightened the sign and walked toward her car. "I was lucky he found me online. We've never actually met in person."

"I'm glad he hired you," Rebecca said. "There was another realtor involved for a while, but he was a real—well, never mind."

Tammy smirked. "Say no more. I've known Troy Dayton for years. Definitely not everyone's cup of tea. He threw a fit when I told him about the subdivision."

"Subdivision?"

"Yep, a huge chunk right out of the middle is being donated to the conservancy."

"Are you serious?" Rebecca grabbed the sturdy sign for support.

"Yes, ma'am." Tammy showed her the photo again. "Right here to the south of where the house is. Not sure what it'll be used for, but it pretty much splits the property in half."

"So it—it," Rebecca said, struggling for words. "It's not good for a hotel or condos or any kind of big development anymore, right?"

"Not with this area preserved. It's just too much land smack bang out of the middle." Tammy touched Rebecca's elbow. "Hey, are you okay? You look a little out of it."

"I'm—I'm wonderful." Rebecca's mind whirled. She could hardly believe it. Mr. B's wishes had been honored. Chris remembered the notes scribbled on those dirty crumpled up pieces of paper. He cared what his grandfather had wanted for his home, his land, his town. The letters Rebecca had forced upon him had changed everything.

Tears of relief, gratitude, validation spilled onto her cheeks. She ran toward the house, her arms flailing in the air as she spun in circles.

I did it, Mr. B, I didn't fail you after all!

CHAPTER 43

*L*ate that afternoon, as Rebecca's shift at Mariano's was ending, Brad Redmond came in to pick up a case of wine.

"That's fabulous," he said when Rebecca shared the big news.

"I guess you were right about showing Mr. B's notes to Chris. They mattered to him after all." Rebecca didn't mention the letters. At this point they were irrelevant.

Her joy over Chris's decision waned as she wondered what it had cost him—not financially but emotionally. What impact it might've had on his relationship with his father.

"I'm really proud of you," Brad said.

"Thanks, but I didn't do anything all that special, just kept finding reasons to not give up." Her words were a jolt, because they weren't her words, they belonged to Mr. B. So much of him and his wisdom remained in her subconscious.

She felt a need to go home and be with Mila, the dog at the heart of everything. The dog who brought Mr. B into her world and created a makeshift family—a man, a girl, and a dog.

When Brad left, Rebecca hung her apron on the hook,

locked the door, and headed out the back to her car. She swiveled at the sound of footsteps behind her.

"Don't freak out," Adam said. "It's just me, your friendly neighborhood wine maker."

"That's a relief." Rebecca exhaled. "Last time somebody snuck up on me, it was Troy Dayton."

Adam gave her sideways hug. "Yeah, that's one of the reasons I'm glad to find you here. But first I want to thank you. What you did, convincing Chris not to sell the property, it actually helps me out a lot."

Rebecca stopped in her tracks. "I'm not sure what you're talking about. The realtor implied the house might go up for sale anytime."

"Not the house—the land on the other side of the part he donated to the conservancy. I've got about twenty acres of grapevines growing there, and Chris said he won't sell that part off. So, you might think you didn't do much, but I'm pretty sure if it hadn't been for you, most of this would have gone a different way."

Rebecca hadn't even thought about the parcel of land on the other side. If Chris intended to hold on to a piece of his inheritance then that meant—well, she had no idea what that meant.

Regardless, Adam knew more than she did, and she wanted to squeeze every bit of information out of him. "You spoke to him?"

"Yeah, a few days ago."

"And did he—did he sound okay?"

"He did to me. Mentioned something about taking a trip, asked me to check on the guys painting the house. They're supposed to start next week."

"I guess he's not wasting any time."

"Nor should he. The sooner it's rented, the sooner it starts bringing in money for him."

"Makes sense." Rebecca knew Chris's business needed

money—that's what Mr. Harrington had said. And Jessica, she loved those fancy vacations.

They reached her car. "See you soon," she said, anxious to get home to Mila.

"Oh, wait, one more thing," Adams said. "It's about Troy Dayton."

Rebecca grunted. "Ugh, I was hoping he'd be gone for good."

Adam shook his head. "Not even. He and his developer client haven't given up on Clearwater. They're interested in a huge property up in the hills, something about a golf course."

"Why are you telling me?"

"Because you're the designated expert on the town charter now. If those land use ordinances were meant to protect Clearwater from over-development and projects that drain resources, this is the one to prevent. Next council meeting is in less than three weeks. You'd better start preparing."

Mila nudged Rebecca's elbow with her nose and whimpered.

"Not now, girl. I'm busy."

The dog trotted to her window seat, turned in a few circles, and settled on the cushion. Sitting at the desk in the corner of the living room, Rebecca researched small town ordinances and land use restrictions in communities up and down the coast. The more she read, the more interesting it became.

After several hours of study, she yawned and stretched out the crick in her neck. It was after one in the morning.

She crawled into bed next to Mila and wrapped one arm around her dog. "You've sure gotten spoiled. I know Mr. B didn't let you sleep on the bed."

Mila's answer was to kiss her nose.

Rebecca closed her eyes, exhausted, but her mind wouldn't stop. Her conversation with Adam bounced around her brain—

not the part about preparing for the next council meeting but the part about Chris taking a trip. He and Jessica probably were down in Mexico, maybe a Caribbean cruise, perhaps a stay at some luxury hotel in New York. Her imagination ran wild—the stunning couple lounging by a pool with fancy cocktails and enjoying romantic candlelit dinners. Rebecca flipped her pillow and punched it, as if it contained her jealous streak, the ugly envy she detested.

She reached for her phone and opened Instagram. She'd fallen into the rabbit hole dreaming up scenarios, so why not make it worse and see Jessica in action? View all her posts and photos.

She scrolled her screen searching for evidence of Chris's girlfriend's perfect life.

Nothing, a complete blank across all social media.

Rebecca sat up straight. She typed in the hashtags she'd seen in Jessica's prior posts. Still nothing. It was as if she didn't exist.

Jessica had gone dark.

CHAPTER 44

*C*hris cast his line into the water, set the rod on the holder, and grabbed a sandwich from the ice chest. "You want one?" he asked.

"I gotta cool off first." Marty, his best friend from college, jumped in the river then climbed back onto his boat. He shook his head like a soaked dog, long hair flinging water in all directions.

They'd been camping for five days. Breaking up with Jessica had thrown Chris for a loop. Despite his relief at finally doing what he should have done months ago, the change was a drastic one. Now he needed to figure out how to dismantle his life and put it back together.

Chris unwrapped his sandwich and bit into the soft bread. "Our last day, huh?"

"Yup." Marty popped open a beer. He was an associate professor at UC Davis, a mathematical genius. "And you're no closer to figuring it out. Man, I thought fishing and camping could solve anything."

"I wish." Chris dipped his hat in the water and put it back on. His scalp tingled as the water trickled through his hair. He patted the ice chest that contained all the fish. "Been a good week for fishing but not decision making."

Marty puffed his lips and chuckled. "You sure let go of a great catch when you dumped Jessica. Of all the girlfriends you've had, she was by far the hottest."

"That helps a lot, thanks."

"Sorry, but what guy does that?"

"A guy who realizes he dodged a bullet." Chris still couldn't believe how close he'd come to marrying her. He'd even been looking at rings. But then his grandfather died, turning everything upside down. In a mystical way, his grandfather's death had given Chris a new life. If only he knew what to do with it.

"I still think you've gone off the deep end," Marty said.

"Because I broke up with a woman I'm not in love with?"

"Yeah, that, plus you inherited property worth millions and want to give a chunk of it away. That's insane. Then you dumped your share of a business you've been working on for years."

"I regret nothing," Chris said.

"And now you're pining after some wacky dog walker like a moonstruck teenager?"

"I am that." Chris had Rebecca on his mind day and night. It was giving him a headache. "But she'll probably never talk to me again."

"She can't be that mad at you."

"I don't know." Chris recalled the last words he'd said to Rebecca, words that weren't even directed at her. They were a reaction to the realization of having being betrayed. The moment he'd seen the envelopes, Chris knew exactly what his father had done.

Marty slapped Chris on the back. "Come on, if anyone can charm a girl, it's you. You're like a modern day Don Juan."

"That's not a compliment. If you'd studied literature instead of statistics, you'd know he was a narcissist."

"Oh, so more like your dad. Yeah I can see that."

"Exactly." Chris agreed with his friend's assessment. "It's the opposite of me. I'm a regular nice guy, even if I do overthink everything."

"Fine line between thinking and overthinking," Marty said. "What I can't wrap my brain around is you and this girl. It's not like you to be not in control. Every time I've seen you interested in a woman, you've had the upper hand."

"I know. This is unchartered ground for me." Chris groaned. "What if she hates me now?"

"Jesus, you sound like my little sister."

Chris dropped his head into his hands. "It's pathetic."

Marty tossed him a beer. "Listen, I'm no expert on women or relationships or family dysfunction, but I do know numbers."

"Numbers?" Chris burst out laughing. It was the best laugh he'd had in ages. "You think this has to do with numbers?"

"Numbers clarify everything."

"If you pull out a deck of Tarot cards, I'm jumping ship."

"I'm talking about probability. Statistically speaking, you and your dog walker should never have met. Two months ago, you didn't know she existed. And then the world randomly threw you together. You didn't want to attend the funeral, and everything you had to deal with you could've taken care of remotely."

His friend was right. Mr. Nash said Chris could sign all the paperwork with a notary in Seattle, and Troy Dayton was more than happy, obviously, to take care of every aspect of selling the property.

"I get it. There was no reason for me to go to Clearwater. The crazy thing is it was Jessica who talked me into going. Said I needed to check out the property before handing it over to some guy I'd never met."

Marty laughed. "Bet she regrets that now."

Chris scoffed. "Who knows?" He'd texted her a few days

after they broke up to see how she was doing. After all, he was still a nice guy. But it appeared she had blocked his number.

"Bottom line," said Marty, "is that the probability of you meeting this girl was pretty much nil. And yet, you did."

"You're saying it was meant to be?"

Marty hemmed. "I don't know, maybe it was. But what I do know is that if anyone in this world is destined to meet his soul-mate, it's you."

CHAPTER 45

*O*ver the next few weeks, Rebecca hardly came up for air. When she wasn't working or walking dogs, she was studying. She'd never been a good student, but no subject in school had ever interested her as much as the inner-workings of small towns and how to preserve them.

"Are you ever going to help me out around here again?" Alice lifted a slice of pizza out of the box and put it on Rebecca's plate. "I've never seen you so immersed. Even Mila's starting to feel ignored."

That got Rebecca's attention, and she looked away from her reading material. "Is that true, Mila?"

The dog whimpered.

"My poor girl." Rebecca sat on the floor and pulled Mila into her lap.

Alice sat at the table and pushed the screen on Rebecca's laptop down. "Now, let's at least eat dinner together."

Rebecca joined her mother. "Sorry I've been so busy. After the September town council meeting, everything will go back to normal."

Her mother flashed a suspicious eye. "You sure?"

"Yeah, totally." Rebecca wolfed down one piece of pizza and started on a second. "I just want to be super prepared to make this motion so that I don't sound like an idiot again."

"I'll tell you something, honey. You are far from an idiot. And the way you've managed everything these last couple months has really impressed me. It's like you've, I don't know, finally grown up."

"Finally?" Rebecca asked. "Not sure that's a compliment."

"Maybe finally isn't the right word, but you are almost twenty-eight."

"I guess I am." Rebecca couldn't believe she'd be twenty-eight soon. "And I still live with my mother. Do you think I'm pathetic?"

Alice squeezed her hands. "Do you think I am?"

"No." Her stomach knotted. She pushed away her half-eaten piece of pizza. "The thing is, I can't even imagine not living with you. But I can't live with you forever."

"Well, you can," her mother said with a wistful smile. "But I suspect sooner or later you'll be ready to leave to nest. The only unknown is how far you'll fly."

THE CEMETERY WAS DESERTED. Mila strained against her leash and led the way. She knew exactly where they were headed.

It was the two month anniversary of Mr. B's death. How could something that happened only two months ago feel like a lifetime?

Rebecca divided the daisies and put them in the holders with fresh water. The Becerra family, unknown to her five years ago, had become a driving force in her life. She'd internalized their pasts, their heartbreaks, their dreams—especially Josephina's. If only she'd had more years, time in which she could have raised her son, reconciled with her father, maybe even found herself a better husband.

The grass was cool and prickly against Rebecca's legs. Mila sniffed around for a minute then settled herself on top of Mr. B's grave. She crossed her front paws and rested her chin.

"You're the best dog ever," Rebecca said. "I don't know what I'd do without you." She pulled her knees into her chest, wrapped her arms around them, and tried to let her mind relax. Only eight days until the first Thursday in September. The more she prepared for the council meeting, the more resolute she became. Knowledge was power, preparation was power, and the willingness to challenge authority was power. Plus, being the underdog had its advantages. Expectations were low.

As Rebecca drove home, bright shafts of light shined through willowy branches and bounced off the windshield. She considered going out of her way to avoid driving by Mr. B's house since Mila was with her. But she was in a hurry to return to her studies, so she opted for the most direct route. At the stop sign, Mila stuck her nose out the window. She whimpered softly.

Without thinking, Rebecca pulled into Mr. B's driveway. The rental sign still stood there.

Curiosity got the better of her. She lifted her foot off the brake and rolled toward the house. From a distance, it looked unchanged. But as she got closer, Rebecca could see that work had been done. The entire house had been painted white, a new lawn had been planted, and the old front door had been replaced by a gray Dutch door with divided light.

She parked in front of the porch and slipped Mila's leash over her head. Together they got out of the car and walked up the steps. "I can't believe how nice it looks."

Rebecca glanced toward the road to make sure they were alone before circling the perimeter. Comfort and familiarity enveloped her like a hug as Mr. B's old rocking chairs came into view.

"Should we sit?" she asked Mila. "Watch one more sunset?"

Rebecca sat in her usual chair, the one on the left. Mila pushed her nose into the empty seat as if it held her master's scent. She paced back and forth a few times then settled down in front of Rebecca's feet. Leaves rustled in the breeze, insects chirped, a faraway windchime sang a tune, and children's laughter carried up from the lake. The water shimmered as if covered in diamonds.

Rebecca rested her hand on the arm of Mr. B's rocker, closed her eyes, and inhaled. A light touch fluttered against her upturned palm, and she opened her eyes to see a blue butterfly resting on her open hand. It remained for a long moment, its wings twitching, and then it flew away.

CHAPTER 46

"This is unbelievable," Mrs. Larson said. "Never has attendance been this high. I'm afraid we might exceed capacity."

People were dragging in chairs and benches from the other rooms and maneuvering to take seats.

"Why so many tonight?" Rebecca asked.

The librarian peered at her through lime green glasses. "Maybe to hear you. Last month's performance did generate some attention."

Rebecca cringed at the memory. Thankfully, this time she was prepared.

Mayor Kilpatrick pushed her way through the crowd followed by the other council members. Betsy stopped beside Rebecca.

"Hey, good luck tonight," she said. "And remember, do not get defensive. No matter what anyone says, stick to your facts and your message."

Rebecca's throat tightened. "Why would I get defensive? I'm just making a simple motion."

"You never know." Betsy waved a hand as if to dial back the

warning. "Sometimes things get heated. But, yeah, if your motion is a simple one, there shouldn't be any—any blowback."

"Blowback?" Rebecca didn't like the sound of that.

"Ack, you'll be fine." Betsy patted her shoulder and followed the mayor to the head table.

Mrs. Larson offered a pained smile. "She's right. You'll be fine. Either way, it'll all be over soon enough, kind of like having a tooth pulled."

"Great, thanks." Rebecca's confidence leeched out of her. She was as prepared as she could ever be, but there might be unknown forces looming. The agenda had been available to the public for a week, so anyone who looked at it ahead of time knew what Rebecca's topic would be—*Town Charter and Ordinances*. Totally vague, but not for those who were aware of her research.

Troy Dayton and Stephanie Carter entered the library like a couple of camp counselors, behind them an entourage of people Rebecca didn't know.

Rebecca's folder slipped from her hands, and her notes scattered across the floor. She couldn't quite catch her breath.

"Let me help you." It was Brad Redmond. He gathered the papers and stacked them up. "You seem nervous."

"I'm a total wreck. Did you see all those people who came in with Troy Dayton? I think he's packing the box, or whatever you call it. I don't know what's wrong with me, thinking I could go up against someone like him, them, people with money and power and influence."

"Now, Rebecca..." Brad sounded like a disappointed father.

"It's true." She started to hyperventilate. "Troy was right all along, I am just a dog walker."

A tap on her shoulder made her jump. "Tiffany? What are you doing here? Oh, wait, how's Curly?"

"He's very depressed. We've been through three dog walkers already. It's so hard to find good help these days." Tiffany, in gray slacks and a crisp white shirt, scanned Brad, her eyes sweeping over him. "Hello."

"Hello," Brad replied in a lawyerly voice.

"He's married," Rebecca said. "To one of my best friends."

"Oh, in that case, never mind." Tiffany's sultry look turned back to business. "I'm here because I have an interest in a particular issue on the agenda that is being brought up by one Rebecca Sparks."

"Are you trying to intimidate her?" Brad asked.

"On the contrary, I'm rather proud of her."

Rebecca edged in between them. "Tiffany encouraged me to do this, at least I think she did."

"I absolutely did." Tiffany straightened up. In her high-heels she was taller than Rebecca. "Remember what I said, and you'll be fine."

The information in her head was spinning around like glass inside a kaleidoscope. "Which part?"

"All of it. But mostly the part about making people mad, because you already have."

"You certainly don't mince words, do you?" Brad said.

"I certainly don't," Tiffany said.

Rebecca wished she had a fraction of Tiffany's confidence. Her stomach did a flip. "I think I'm going to be sick."

"Please, do not get sick," said Patty. "It would be so embarrassing."

Tessa pushed Patty out of the way as she, Cece, and Natalie joined them. "You're not going to be sick," said Tessa. "You're going to be fine."

"That's right," Cece said. "You've been studying for weeks."

"And we're all here to support you." Natalie placed an arm around her.

"Wow," Tiffany said. "You have quite the fan club, don't you?"

Rebecca tried not to cry. Gratitude overwhelmed her. "These are my friends," she said. "My wonderful friends. And my mom."

Nonna and Alice nudged their way in. The gaggle of women enveloped Rebecca in a huge hug. Nonna pulled Tiffany into the embrace.

"I don't think I'm part of—"

"Don't fight it," Rebecca said, squished in the middle and nose to nose with Tiffany. "Once you're caught in the net, you'll never get out."

The gavel pounded on the table.

"Okay, folks, let's get this party started," Mayor Kilpatrick said. "Take your seats."

Every chair and bench and stool were occupied. Some people had boosted themselves up onto Mrs. Larson's counter. Those who couldn't find seats leaned against the walls.

"Anybody see the fire chief?"

"I'm right here." The captain of the fire department waved from the back.

"Nice to see you, Chief Kilpatrick," said the mayor. "We may be a few over our limit tonight. You okay with that?"

"Yes, honey."

"Wait." Tiffany leaned toward Rebecca. "The mayor is married to the head of the fire department? Isn't that nepotism?"

Nonna patted Tiffany's knee. "No, dear. They were married long before she became mayor and he became the fire chief."

The gavel struck the table again, and the meeting was called to order. Rebecca, reviewing her notes, half listened to the continuing cookie controversy, the budget for refurbishing the gazebo in the park, and whether they should hire the clown balloon twister for the upcoming fall festival. Evidently, the last time they used him, he'd frightened most of the children and a good many adults.

Rebecca crossed off agenda items one by one. Her name inched upward. She rocked back and forth in her chair. All the advice and guidance and admonitions she'd received had muddled her mind. She needed to focus on one—one nugget of truth that resonated deep within. It needed to rise above the noise, speak to her, propel her forward.

She closed her eyes and summoned the voice she ached to hear.

We are all tested in this life, querida... but challenges are not for winning or losing. They are meant to push you toward becoming the person you are meant to be.

The gavel sounded like the crack of a whip.

"Next on the agenda," Mayor Kilpatrick said, her voice monotone, "is Rebecca Sparks. You ready, Rebecca?"

"I—I am." She stood, expecting her knees to buckle. They didn't. She stepped up to the podium with her folder containing her notes and put her mouth near the microphone. It released a high-pitched screech. "Sorry," she leaned back a couple inches. "I'd like to make a motion."

A hush fell over the room.

"Yes, it's on the agenda here," said the mayor. "Go ahead."

She opened her mouth, but the words were stuck. She closed her eyes, took a breath, and heard Mr. B's voice— *become the person you are meant to be.*

"I move—" she started slowly, but she didn't stumble or stutter. Her chest expanded, and confidence bubbled up like champagne poured into a flute. "I move that the ordinances in the town charter pertaining to land use, building permits, and development be reaffirmed so that citizens of Clearwater are notified in writing of all construction projects exceeding specific limitations."

Mayor Kilpatrick's eyebrows rose, Betsy showed her two thumbs up, and Joel, who served as recording secretary, typed furiously on his laptop.

"Do I hear a second?" ask the mayor.

Half the room shouted their support for the motion.

Patty jumped in the air. "Pick me! I was first."

"Fine," the mayor said. "Seconded by Patty Sullivan. Any discussion?"

The room broke into chaos. Rebecca stayed at the podium, stunned, as it unfolded. People yelling at one another, at the mayor, at her. A controversy had been unleashed, and Rebecca stood at the center of it. But instead of shrinking, she swelled with determination and conviction. She believed in her mission and was committed to it.

"Order! Sit down and raise your hand if you wish to speak. Mr. Dayton, do you have a comment?"

"I do!" he said, his face red with fury. "The ordinances to which Ms. Sparks is referring have not been applied to any project in over forty years. Therefore, a precedent has been set. The ordinances are no longer enforceable."

Rebecca's head snapped to the side as Brad stood and spoke. "That's why we're here, Mr. Dayton, and why the motion has to be made. Ms. Sparks is proposing an up or down vote to renew the ordinance. It's quite simple."

More rumbling ensued, the discussion continued.

"Can you explain," Stephanie Carter asked, "how this would be enforced if the ordinance were renewed? There's nobody in this room who was even alive when the town charter was written who can speak to the true intention of the law."

"I was here," Trudy said, struggling with her cane to stand. "And I remember the meeting. The ordinance was designed to maintain the tenets upon which our town was founded. Our early citizens and leaders envisioned a culture in which neighbors worked together, supported one another, and embraced honesty."

Rebecca wanted to hug the old lady. She leaned toward the microphone. "Trudy's right. There are many other ordinances in the charter that address community needs. This is only the tip of the iceberg."

Troy scoffed and laughed. "Looks like we're going to be here all night." He glanced around as if expecting support for his sarcastic remark, but nobody gave him so much as a pat on the back.

Rebecca marched into the stacks and retrieved the town charter. She set it on the podium with a loud thump. "This book is a guide, a bible. It contains everything we need in order to be true to our founding mothers and fathers." She held it up high and pointed to the cover. "Look. It says *history, laws, codes, ordinances, and rules for a Cohesive Community.* The town charter is like a mini-constitution. It cannot be dismissed or ignored because it's old and out of practice. I believe we need to review it and revive it and amend it when necessary. We need to honor it!"

Rebecca's statement was met with a groundswell of excitement and approval. Her ears filled with the sound of applause so loud it was as if a rock star had run on stage.

"Enough discussion, time to vote," Mayor Kilpatrick said.

The motion passed. In the scheme of things, it was a small victory. But for Rebecca, it signified a monumental shift.

Rebecca's friends, the people she loved and admired, the ones who were there when she was at her lowest, were by her side now in this moment of glory.

Tears burned her eyes, but they did not fall. In only two months' time, Rebecca had discovered her purpose and the path she would take toward becoming the woman she wanted to be.

The town council meeting was winding down, people chattered and helped themselves to cookies from Costco, a few gathered their things to leave.

"We're not adjourned yet," said the mayor. "Anyone have new business to present?"

"Yes, ma'am. I do." His voice, strong and deep, traveled from the back of the library and rose above the din of other voices. To Rebecca, it was like the startling blast of a trumpet.

CHAPTER 47

"*N*ame?" Joel looked up.

"Christopher Harrington."

The chatter faded. A man behind Rebecca whispered, "That's Benito's grandson."

"I understand you wish to bring new business before the town council," Mayor Kilpatrick said, "but I'm afraid only residents of Clearwater are permitted to do so without prior request. However, if you'd like to submit—"

"I am a resident. I just moved into my grandfather's house today." He hadn't looked at Rebecca yet. When his gaze landed on her, she almost lost her balance, swept up in the fairytale moment.

One corner of Chris's mouth flicked upward, just a hint of a smile, as if asking *are you happy to see me?* She replied with a smile so broad and unrestrained that her answer was evident.

"Well then," said Mayor Kilpatrick, "welcome to Clearwater, Chris. What new business would you like to present?"

"Thank you. I, uh, I'm Benito Becerra's grandson and the heir to his property over by the lake. It was brought to my attention shortly after he died that he'd wanted a portion of his land to be preserved. So I'm in the process of transferring a section to the conservancy."

Applause broke out along with high-pitched whistles and shouts of appreciation.

Rebecca turned to see Troy Dayton shoving his chair to the side. He threw a dismissive glare in Chris's direction before snatching his jacket and stomping out of the meeting. It gave her great satisfaction to see his highfalutin façade crack, especially in front of the entire town.

"I'm not sure what the process is," Chris continued, "but my request is that the council name the land in honor of my grandfather." His voice cracked.

Mayor Kilpatrick rose from her seat clapping and nodding with approval. "That's a wonderful idea. And as mayor I have within my authority the power to approve this request immediately. And upon completion of the transfer of the land to the conservancy, the council will host a dedication ceremony in which we will honor the generosity, foresight, and unyielding commitment of Benito Becerra."

REBECCA STOOD on the sidewalk in front of the library accepting praise and accolades. Her concise motion and suggestion that the town charter be reviewed and revived were met with enthusiasm. Although immersed in conversation, she kept an eye on Chris. He lingered as well, surrounded by those wishing to shake his hand and acknowledge his gracious donation.

They exchanged furtive glances every so often, which had Rebecca's heart pitter-pattering. Eventually, the crowd thinned.

"Hi." Chris approached with a shy tilt of the head.

"Hi." Rebecca sensed the change, a subtle shift in the way he looked at her, as if a barrier had come down. "I didn't think I'd ever see you again. Thank you for—"

"No." Chris moved closer. "I have to thank you."

The street lamps flickered to life.

"Would you take a walk with me?" He extended his hand, palm up.

Rebecca pictured her hand in his, but she wavered.

"She's not here." Chris had read her mind. "We broke up for good. And I'm out of the business with my dad, gave it all to him. Everything's changed."

Rebecca couldn't believe it. He had dismantled his entire life. "I'm kind of in shock."

"To tell you the truth, I am, too." He slipped his hand alongside hers and gently folded his fingers. "May I?"

"Yes." Her fingers relaxed and molded into his hand.

They crossed the street into town square park and walked the path toward the wooded area, a small forest where the trees formed a leafy canopy overhead.

"I have a lot to tell you," Chris said. "But not tonight, at least not all of it." His hand tightened around hers, as if to say there'd be plenty of time. "You're so quiet. It's making me a little nervous."

Rebecca found a few words. "Why would you be nervous?"

"Because I'm a guy who's falling for a girl, but I'm not sure if she feels the—"

"She does, oh my God, she totally does." Rebecca discovered her voice and the floodgates burst. "I can't believe you're back here, and you're not mad at me about the letters. And, and you don't have a girlfriend anymore. And I was really worried about you because…"

A smile spread over Chris's face as she rambled. "There's the Rebecca I know and love."

She gulped. Did he say 'love?'

"I'm gonna have to get used to how much you talk though."

Rebecca raised her shoulders. "I'll try to control it."

"No, don't change a thing."

"Well, if you ever want me to be quiet, like, you know, if you're busy or talking on the phone or need to leave or want some—"

"I'll just do this..." Chris pulled her in close, wrapped her his strong arms, and pressed his lips against hers. It was the kiss she'd waited for her entire life. It stirred within her the kind of emotion she'd only ever dreamed of, so intense and impassioned that her knees went weak and her neck went wobbly. Chris tightened his hold around her body and drew back, his eyes searching her face. "I hope it's okay that I kissed you."

"Are you kidding?" She threw her arms around his neck and answered his kiss with one of her own, the kind that would knit their hearts into one and link their souls like two puzzle pieces destined to fit only with each other.

CHAPTER 48

*T*he letters read like a journal. In one of them Mr. B even wrote: *I believe that I'm writing as much for myself as for you.*

Chris had given Rebecca all of them. "They belong to both of us," he said. "These letters changed my life, my world. They saved me, and so did you."

He left her alone on the back porch with the vibrant sunset and a glass of sweet, cool horchata.

As Rebecca consumed the letters, it haunted her how close Mr. B's words had come to being lost. She didn't understand why he'd never told her about them. Perhaps he underestimated how meaningful his letters to his grandson would be. But that was all in the past. The letters had been on a journey of their own. By luck or fate or divine intervention, they were discovered and became the seed from which a new love flourished.

It wasn't until Rebecca got to the last one that she fell apart.

MY DEAR CHRISTOPHER,
    It's been many months since I've written to you. I was caring for

your abuela throughout her long illness. She now has been laid to rest beside your mother, and I am at peace. While I have struggled with my faith, your abuela carried no such burden. Her trust in God was unwavering. In keeping with her steadfast conviction, I choose to believe that my two loves, my wife and daughter, are now together in heaven, angels watching over us. And that gives me great comfort. My life has been long and, for the most part, rewarding. The letters I've written to you over the years attest to that. My joys and sorrows have come and gone, as is the case with most ordinary lives. Recently, however, something unexpected and particularly joyful has occurred.

Whoever could imagine an old man such as I would be fortunate enough to make a new friend, a delightful girl with wild red hair, a contagious smile, quick wit, and a tendency to ramble. We met shortly after your grandmother's passing. I was visiting the animal shelter and stumbled upon this young lady inside a crate caring for a dog near death. Half-starved, the poor dog could barely stand. She appeared to have lost all hope. In need of a new purpose myself, I believed I was meant to save her, or, if unable to keep her alive, at least be sure that in the end she would know compassion and love. As it turns out, after weeks of uncertainty, the dog is thriving. She is a little miracle, and reminds me of Daisy, the dog we had when you were a boy.

REBECCA COVERED HER FACE. Mr. B's voice filled her head. *"... reminds me of a dog I used to have."* Daisy—daisies on the kitchen table, daisies at the graves. She choked on her tears. There were only a few lines left in this last letter, and Rebecca didn't want it to end. She wanted to cling to his words, his voice. The final sentences would be like the last bite of chocolate, something to be savored.

But she needed to finish and then let go. Although the story of Mr. B's life told through his letters was nearing the end, Rebecca and Chris's story lay ahead, as yet unwritten.

· · ·

IT WAS as if the dog and the girl were a single gift. They came to me together, and this past month has been a time of healing and happiness for me. They both have given me new purpose, laughter, and a reason to keep living. They have become my family—an old man, a dog, and a vivacious young girl overflowing with life and love.

As I finish this letter, I feel as if I've written a story that has reached its end. It is my prayer that one day you find yourself back in Clearwater, for it is here on our land and our lake where you will always have a home. Te amo, mi nieto.

REBECCA FOLDED the letter and held it to her heart as the sun slipped beneath the golden horizon and vanished.

AS SUMMER ROLLED into fall and the nights grew cold, Chris and Rebecca spent hours in the attic, which they didn't even know existed until Chris discovered a pulldown ladder in an upstairs closet. In the small, dusty space they searched trunks and boxes, uncovering a treasure trove of history, memories, photos.

Together they came to know his papa and her beloved Mr. B even better.

They found Josephina's scrap books and Antonia's wedding gown and a box of photographs documenting the one unforgettable year that Chris lived in Clearwater. The date, place, and occasion were written on the back of each one—a visit to the Monterey Aquarium, beach days at Bodega Bay, Chris's birthday trip to Disneyland, and dozens of pictures of him playing basketball, swimming in the lake, and roughhousing with Daisy.

Chris and Rebecca nurtured their love like a precious gift, because it was just that. An unlikely story that never would have been told if not for Rebecca's strength, persistence, and a few simple twists of fate that pushed her to take chances and face her fears.

Shortly before Christmas, they marked their three month anniversary with pizza served on Antonia's beautiful china, the dishes Rebecca had wrapped and stored to insure they wouldn't end up crushed by an earth mover. Now, she knew they'd be treasured as deserved, and not by some stranger who'd come across them in a second-hand store.

ON A CHILLY NIGHT IN MARCH, Chris built a fire in the fireplace while Rebecca sat at the desk finishing an email. As the new Administrative Assistant to the Town Council, she'd been tasked with researching ordinances in the town charter and making recommendations for revisions and applications. She'd only been at it a few months, but already she had found great purpose. It was as if the job had been created specifically for her. Because, in fact, it had.

Mila yawned and stretched out in front of the flames. The wood crackled and filled the room with the scent of pinecones and cinnamon.

The interior of the house had been painted a gentle shade of blue and the wood floors refinished. Chris had purchased a new slipcovered sofa, coffee table, and a flat screen TV. But the old recliner remained, and the warm, cozy atmosphere Rebecca noticed the very first time she walked into the house had been preserved.

Chris placed a mug of hot chocolate beside her elbow. "Are you done yet?"

"I'm done." Rebecca tapped 'send' and closed her laptop.

They snuggled up on the new sofa together with their drinks.

"Mmm, Kahlua." She licked whipped cream off her upper lip,

still in awe that her crazy life had landed her with a boyfriend like Christopher Harrington.

"I've been thinking about something," he said.

"Yeah? What?"

"Well, I was wondering what you'd think about Mila living with me full-time."

Rebecca pulled away. She and Mila had been together for nine months. "I guess, if you really want her to. Technically, she is your dog. But I feel like she's my dog, too. Then again I suppose if—"

Chris halted her rambling with a forceful kiss on her lips. He opened a drawer in the coffee table, removed a piece of paper, and unfolded it. It was his grandfather's last letter.

"Look what he wrote right here." He pointed and read aloud. "*It was as if the dog and the girl were a single gift. They came to me together...*"

Rebecca gasped as she realized what he was saying. "Wait. You want me to come, too?"

Chris nodded, his eyes wide with hope.

"Oh my God. I can't believe it!" Thoughts flew through her head like a flock of nervous birds. "I—I, well, I'd have to move out of my mom's place, which I can totally do. We've lived together forever, but she'll be fine, I'm sure, like as soon as I—"

Another firm kiss quieted her. "It's my turn to talk, okay? Try not to interrupt."

Rebecca clapped a hand over her mouth and nodded.

"Now," Chris said, holding back laughter, "Rebecca Sparks, I can't say you are the girl of my dreams, because I never dreamed I'd find someone like you. I've had my share of girlfriends, and not one has made me laugh the way you do. I love the way you talk too much, the way your skin turns pink when you're flustered, the way you say *totally* in every other sentence. I love how you're obsessed with dogs. I love that you love your mom. And more than anything, I love that you brought my grandfather so much happiness in his final years. You did what I was unable to do."

Chris took her face in his hands. He caressed her cheeks, wiping her tears with his thumbs, and kissed her with soft, parted lips. He tasted of chocolate and cream.

Rebecca sniffled. "Can I talk yet?"

"Not yet. I found something, and I think you'll like it." He reached into his pocket.

Rebecca held her breath. She glanced at Mila who was sitting right in front of their knees, as if she knew she was part of the deal.

Chris opened his hand. Resting on his palm was a thin gold band, a tiny diamond at the center with rubies on either side. "It belonged to my grandmother."

Rebecca burst into tears at the sight of Antonia's ring. "It won't fit me."

"I know." Chris slipped it onto her pinky. "We'll take it to the jeweler and have it sized. But only if you really like it."

"I love it. It's so beautiful." Rebecca wasn't sure exactly what the gift meant, not yet anyway.

"Good. Because I found this one, too." Again, Chris reached into his pocket and withdrew another ring. It was the man's version of the one he'd given Rebecca, a wider band without the gems He slipped it onto the fourth finger on his left hand. "What do you think?"

"You want us to wear matching rings?"

"I do. Because in my crazy world where nothing has made sense for as long as I can remember, you make sense."

"I make sense?"

"Totally." Chris picked up a curl and tucked it behind her ear. "You did from the moment we met, the day you chased Mila across the park and stood there trying to figure out who I was."

"I remember," Rebecca said. And she did, all of it. How his

hands caught her attention, how intimidated she was, and how she'd tried to hide the stain on her shirt. "It was awful."

"It was wonderful—a beautiful girl with long red hair running toward me like a scene in a movie." Chris entwined his fingers with hers. "I was drawn to you even then, and now I never want to be without you. Please say you'll marry me."

For once, Rebecca was at a loss for words. Her lips moved, but no sound came out.

"Say something. Don't leave me hanging, not after I just asked you to marry me."

Rebecca gulped in some air. "Yes," she said, releasing only the one word.

"Yes?"

"Yes." She fell against him. "Absolutely, totally, a hundred percent yes!"

Mila jumped onto the couch and pushed herself between them, kissing their faces and wagging her tail as if she knew something wonderful had happened.

FIVE MONTHS later

The wedding took place down by the lake where cool water lapped at the sandy shore, a spot where they both had memories of the man they had loved at different times in their lives.

Rebecca faced Chris, enchanted by him and the unlikely events that brought them together. The changes that had unfolded in only one year still astounded her, a year that began with unimaginable heartbreak but culminated in joy and gratitude.

A warm breeze tousled her red curls and ruffled the full skirt of her wedding dress, an ankle length gown made of satin and lace with thin straps and sweetheart neckline. Surrounded by those who loved them best, Chris and Rebecca became husband and wife.

Chris swept his bride into his arms, kissing her lips and twirling her in circles. Champagne was poured and toasts were made as a vibrant orange sun touched the water.

The newlyweds stole a moment away, kicking off their shoes and wandering along the edge of the lake. Mila ran ahead of them, prancing and leaping. She grabbed a stick, dropped it at Chris's feet, and barked at him until he tossed it high in the sky. The excited dog watched it sail, but just as she was about to catch it, something distracted her.

With her paws in the water, Mila stood straight and tall, staring at the horizon. Her tail swept side to side expectantly.

"What is it, girl?" Rebecca asked.

Mila tilted her head, whining softly. She looked up at Rebecca as if to say, *don't you see him?*

Rebecca caught her breath. She'd seen thousands of sunsets over the lake, but never one so magnificent. Ribbons of iridescent colors hovering above the horizon, painted by angels, a gift from heaven.

Mila and Rebecca remained motionless—and mesmerized—until the sun slipped beneath the surface. His voice traveled on the breeze. *Never tire of sunsets, mi querida...*

The trance broke. Mila barked, retrieved the stick, and ran with it back toward the gathering. Chris took Rebecca's hand in his. "You good?" he asked.

"I'm so good." She shivered slightly. Then the warmth of her husband's touch spread through her body.

They rejoined their guests, the festivities began, and Rebecca stepped forward to begin her new life. A life she stumbled into thanks to a man with a gentle, brilliant soul and a little lost dog who was, indeed, a miracle.

AFTERWORD

You're not done yet! The fifth novel in the series takes us full circle. In One Last Dance, Natalie gets her own story:

SHE DID EVERYTHING RIGHT, BUT GOT IT ALL WRONG

Natalie Lurensky is stuck. Stuck in the town where she was born, stuck with a job she never wanted, and stuck in a rut she can't escape.

At thirty-eight-years-old, Natalie is committed to saving her parents' legendary but financially strapped dance academy and preserving the legacy of her revered mother.

When a favorite former ballet student goes missing, her predictable life takes a sudden turn. In an effort to help find the teenager, she embarks upon an amateur investigation that lands her in front of one aloof and intriguing detective, Daniel Garrett. Natalie ignores the attraction, but as the search intensifies and their paths continue to cross, the chemistry is impossible to ignore. Finally, Natalie opens her heart to a new love.

But when a crisis at the dance studio threatens to ruin Natalie's livelihood, damage her most important friendship, and destroy her mother's legacy, she is forced to make a heart-breaking decision. And if she chooses wrong, she'll never be able to make it right.

One Last Dance, the fifth novel in the Clearwater Series, is a story about life-long friendship, dreams revived, and romance that pops up in the most unlikely places.

View One Last Dance on Amazon

Thank you for spending your reading time in Clearwater! There are so many books to choose from these days, and I'm truly delighted you selected one of mine. I hope you enjoyed Rebecca's story and will take a moment to post reviews on Amazon and Goodreads. Personal recommendations are the best way to share your love of reading and books!

Review on Amazon:
The Everywhere Girl - Amazon
Review on Goodreads:
The Everywhere Girl - Goodreads

If your book group reads one of my novels, let me know. I'd love to zoom into your meeting and chat with readers. Keep up to date by subscribing to my newsletter and joining my reader group on Facebook.

Links for E-readers:
Julie's Newsletter
Julie's Reader Group on FB
Julie's Website

ABOUT THE AUTHOR

Julie M. Brown is an author, playwright, and essayist. A California girl all her life, she now lives in Palos Verdes, a Los Angeles suburb, surrounded by trails, horses, and wild peacocks. Wife, mom, and dog-lover, Julie enjoys mentoring young writers and interacting with readers and bookclubs. She's an active member of Women's Fiction Writers Association.

When not writing, rescuing dogs, or baking banana bread, Julie can be found in a quiet corner somewhere with coffee and a laptop.

To view Julie's website, go to:
juliemayersonbrown.com

*While you're there, be sure to **subscribe** to my newsletter ~ it's a great way to get in touch and find out about my new books and projects.*

Let's connect on social media, too!

ALSO BY JULIE MAYERSON BROWN

THE CLEARWATER SERIES

Long Dance Home

Road to Somewhere

The Lonely Sommelier

The Everywhere Girl

One Last Dance

A Clearwater Christmas ~ a YA holiday novella

Welcome to Clearwater
A Box Set of the first three novels in the series

~

The Accidental Life of MF Ascher
Under the collaborative pen name, Ivy H. Booker

www.ingramcontent.com/pod-product-compliance
Lightning Source LLC
Chambersburg PA
CBHW052025240626
47153CB00006B/1953